THE WAY BACK TO
EDEN

THE WAY BACK TO
EDEN

BOOK 2 *of the* JAGUAR ORACLE SERIES

KURT MÄHLER

MEDIA.COM

The Way Back to Eden
Book 2 in the Jaguar Oracle Series
Copyright © 2025 by Kurt Frederick Mähler

www.kurtmahler.com

Published by
Illumify Media Global
www.IllumifyMedia.com
"Let's bring your book to life!"

Library of Congress Control Number: 2024915388

Paperback ISBN: 978-1-964251-46-2

Cover design by Debbie Lewis

Map by Cody Oakley

Printed in the United States of America

For my daughter Alyssa
The beautiful sign at your birth has come true.

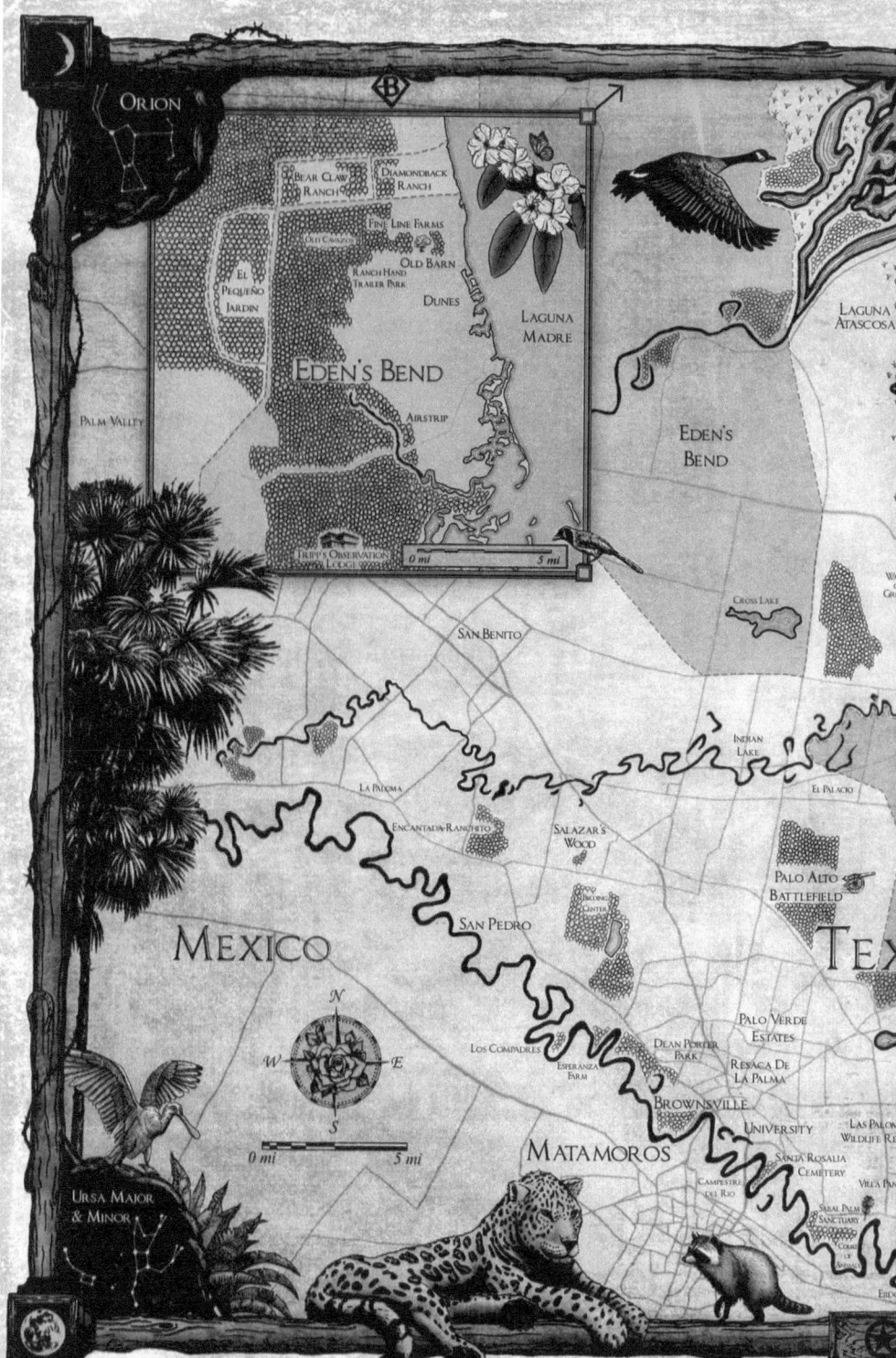

ORION

𝄪 B

BEAR CLAW RANCH DIAMONDBACK RANCH

PINE LINE FARMS

OLD CAMAZON

EL PEQUEÑO JARDIN RANCH HAND TRAILER PARK OLD BARN

DUNES

EDEN'S BEND LAGUNA MADRE

AIRSTRIP

PALM VALLEY LAGUNA ATASCOSA

EDEN'S BEND

0 mi 5 mi

TRIPP'S OBSERVATION LODGE

CROSS LAKE

SAN BENITO

INDIAN LAKE

LA PALOMA EL PALACIO

ENCANTADA RANCHITO SALAZAR'S WOOD

PALO ALTO BATTLEFIELD

MEXICO SAN PEDRO

TEX

N

W E

S PALO VERDE ESTATES

LOS COMPADRES DEAN PORTER PARK RESACA DE LA PALMA

ESPERANZA FARM BROWNSVILLE

UNIVERSITY LAS PALOM WILDLIFE RE

0 mi 5 mi SANTA ROSALIA CEMETERY

MATAMOROS CAMPESTRE DEL RIO VILLA PAN

URSA MAJOR & MINOR

VIRGO

GREEN ISLAND
(COLONY OF THE LOST)

LAGUNA
MADRE

EL REALITO

SOUTH PADRE
ISLAND

	RIVER/RESACA
	ROADS
	COASTLINE
	TREES/FOREST AREA
	MARSH
	RANCH BORDER
	EDEN'S BEND

SWOG'S
WALLOW

LAGUNA
VISTA

GASTON
RANCH

N'S
D

PORT ISABEL

GULF OF

MEXICO

LAUNCH PAD

BAHIA
GRANDE

SOUTH BAY

AS

BOCA
CHICA

PALMITO
HILL

LA BURRITA

RIVER'S
END

THE LADY RIVER (RIO GANDE)

EL
CONCHELA

OUTHMOST

GORGAS
OASIS

EL RANCHO
Y REFUGIO

LA ESPERANZA

RENO

OPHIUCHUS

Contents

We somehow know we were made for more than this. It's like we're born with a memory of something we've never seen. We yearn to return to a place we've never been. We mourn that loss and seek it every day, no matter what our religion, or none.

—Frederica Mathewes-Green
Two Views of the Cross

1

Dragon's Breath

Patch, Plod, Bog, and Paco labored through thornscrub in the heat of the day, far from the bands of molten earth now hardened, the roads of Man. Paco, whom the animals called Miracle, lolled atop Plod along with Bog, who hunkered in the dubious shade of the horse's mane. Patch trundled along beside the horse so as not to burden the old beast overmuch beneath the glowering August sun. They picked their way through a thicket of tenaza trees, whose shade provided some relief. Bark had flaked off the trees, as it often does with the tenaza, carpeting the path for the friends, and the spines of the trunks were few. But the branches, which normally bore creamy white flowers the shape of puffballs, had none.

Bog croaked. "It looks like these tenaza haven't bloomed since the Pink Moon of spring. A touch of rain or a trickle of river is all they need for their fragrant glory to burst forth, but neither rain nor stream have touched them."

Patch inspected the tenaza as he walked. "When do you think the next rain will come? I mean *real* rain, not just sprinkles. This is worse than the Double Moon Drought of '55. Mom and Dad used to tell the story that it was so bad the coyotes called a truce with the rabbits so they'd show them where the water was."

Plod flapped his lips. "It will rain when it will rain. Nothing to do but carry on until it comes. But when I was a foal, Father and Mother told me a tale that might give us a green blade of hope in these dry days. The purple sage— the one Man calls the cenizo or barometer bush—she has a special quality, they said. When the air changes to favor rain and fills its breath with the drops to come, the purple sage blooms first."

"Quite true," Bog said. "My family used to sing stanzas about it to comfort tadpoles trapped in puddles, for her blooms assured the tadpoles their puddles would become ponds once again. Thus, we honored the purple sage in song. If we ever see the cenizo bloom, then we will know the drought is done and rain has come. The clouds will be heavy with it, waiting for the first brave drop to fall to the ground as a sign of the countless drops behind him, that they too should descend and cover the earth."

The friends finished wading through the tenaza thicket and enjoyed clearer terrain beneath broad-branched mesquite. The shade was better beneath the mesquite, and the air calmer, if not cooler. Finally, they reached a prairie, and across it they saw Sabal Palm Sanctuary. The signature tree grew in abundance there, and the sight reminded Paco so much of home he blinked, for sabal palms flourish on the Yucatán Peninsula along with more numerous palms called Florida thatch and everglades.

Paco rubbed his eyes. "These are like the trees of Mérida!"

He felt for the Gatorade bottle he had shared with Plod. A red drop still rolled inside it. The boy rested the bottle upside down upon his upturned mouth while he squinted his eyes shut before the sun-filled sky. He waited. The warm drop turned into a thread, dangled on the rim, and fell upon his tongue. It remained there just long enough to send the boy's body a message that all would be well if he could hold on a little longer. Paco returned to watching the palms, which jostled in the wind.

"See how they wave *buenas tardes* to us. Time to go greet them back! Let's sit with them for a while."

Paco nudged Plod forward into the shade of sabal palms, cypress, and ebony trees. There, the boy slid off the horse and rested upon a bed of fallen fronds. Setting out his marbles, he lay on his side before them.

Bog remained on Plod and croaked a distress signal to any toad within earshot, asking for the way to the nearest pond where the travelers could drink. No one croaked back. Only the hum of patrolling dragonflies and summer-dazed katydids reached his ears.

Patch did not immediately follow into the sanctuary but remained in the prairie. He stood on hind legs amid bent and broken stalks of grasses that had succumbed to the drought. He surveyed the air, his nose twitching rapidly.

"I smell things moving back and forth. Something anxious is hiding in the quiet! Plod, we need to hide somewhere."

A shadow flitted overhead. Patch, Plod, and Bog glanced up to see the spoonbill from the Colony of the Lost. He circled and landed before them, bowing a greeting as his lanky feet skipped to a halt.

"Greetings, friends of the manchild Miracle!" the spoonbill said. "Thought I'd take a turn at keeping you company. Salt the owl told me trouble was afoot when I relieved him of the watch this morning. He was right! The coyotes aren't far behind you."

Patch scampered into the shade of the nearest sabal. "Oh no! What more can you tell us?"

The spoonbill drew near, wings folded, head lowered. "They picked up your trail when you went round the manrealm called Southmost. Range is their leader. He is on the hunt, for another coyote has challenged him in the days of his graying. He won't stop until he has shown his rule still has teeth in it."

Patch scanned the prairie. "We'd best go deeper in the sanctuary."

Plod gave a gentle snort. "Whether we're here or deeper in makes no difference to the coyotes. They don't abide by the law of refuge when on the hunt. Their law of pursuit allows them to step over the law of refuge."

"Well, what are we going to do?" asked Patch.

Plod considered the branches above them. "Have the boy climb a tree with you. Bog can hop up as well. I will graze, and when they come, I'll play a game of hoof-and-chase to lead them away."

"But the sabal palm is no friend to climbers with all its rough edges," Patch said as he tested the trunk of one; fibrous wreckage of dead fronds covered it and blocked the way up. He looked around. "What about that cypress?"

Patch climbed the cypress, whose height rose just above the surrounding canopy of green. Its slender leaves rustled with the weakness of a rainless summer as he ascended.

"I can't believe how strong these branches are when they haven't drunk a drop of rain in so long," Patch shouted to the friends below.

"It's the same strength that's defied a dozen droughts before the present affliction was even a rumor," Bog shouted back. "Such is the mystery of a tree that seems as if it should be dead but is more alive than the blades of grass coming and going beneath us—a mystery only the story of the roots can explain."

The raccoon reached the top as the spoonbill lifted his wings to return to the sky. The final branches rocked Patch back and forth. Cradled where he could no longer climb, he viewed Sabal Palm Sanctuary. Over five hundred acres of forest stretched away beneath him: trees of palm, ebony, and cypress like the one upholding him. Here and there he spied a clearing or the hint of a pond. Far off, the roof of a century-old Victorian home rose above the trees. Its cupola in Queen Anne style jutted up like a wizard's cap, and its chimney mimicked the parapets of a citadel.

Patch looked beyond the sanctuary, where the Lady River glinted back a greeting to the relentless sun, a salutation more gracious than his heat merited. Beyond her was another land, the manrealm Mexico, where roads, ranches, and smokestacks lay very still and half real behind the horizon's chalky haze. Patch followed the edge of the sanctuary with his eyes as it curved back toward him in obedience to the great bend of the Lady River. And as he followed the tree line east, then northeast, his eyes fell upon a strange sight: a lighthouse! Another lighthouse!

Or was it?

He looked closer. *Hmm. It's tall and white and looks like a tower, but there's no glass manplace on top of it and no beacon of light. Just a point like the end of a spear.*

He shouted down. "I see a manplace that looks like a lighthouse!"

"A lighthouse?" asked Bog. "But there is only one."

"I know, but it's tall like one and white like one. Come up here and see!"

Bog made a careful ascent. Reaching Patch, he climbed onto his fur, since Patch's body was easier to cling to than the slender, waving branches at the topmost of the cypress. He looked out upon the forest, slowly surveying it in every direction. Then he gasped and moaned, slumping upon the body upholding him.

Patch became as still as he could. *I'm not sure what Bog's moan means.*

There was silence for a time, and the raccoon could feel the toad cling more tightly to his fur as he quivered.

Bog wept.

Patch pondered what to say. *Bog's probably never climbed to the top of a tree before. He must be overcome by how high in the sky he is. Or maybe he's amazed at how big everything is. Or maybe he recognizes the second lighthouse from an old story he had forgotten. I'll try to find out.*

"Ahem. Well, Bog, I'll be! Aren't you amazed at this... this great forest? Enough to cheer anyone up, isn't it? Enough to even cheer a toad to tears, I guess. Um, you're crying for joy, right?"

"For *joy*?" replied Bog. "No, I weep for what is *lost*! Don't you *see*? This sanctuary is all that is left of the great and thick forest that once adorned the Lady River in a robe of emerald splendor from her lovely mouth at Boca Chica to miles upriver from here. No, Patch, my innocent friend, I weep for the felling of this forest! There was a time when this realm was one hundred times greater! A hundred and a half another hundred! Oh, the grand robe of the Lady is now a tattered shred! A ripped remnant! Oh me! Blessed are my ancestors who did not live to see this day! Blessed are they! And woe to me who has seen what has befallen the trees! Woe to me!"

And the Gulf Coast toad named Bog, the son of William Longlegs, the grandson of André the Log Wanderer, wept until his heart had broken. And as it broke, a song came out, one so sacredly personal that no one was permitted to remember it, and no one wanted to. It was revered with silent awe and a secret name: The Unsung Song of Bog. The dragonflies and katydids stopped their humming when they heard it. And the leaves of cypress, sabal, and ebony revived, for the rain of the tears in the song of the toad reached deeper into the trees than the rain of the clouds of the sky ever could, even if it had come in that hour. And if it had not been for a lonely cloud that happened to be wandering over the sanctuary at that moment, no one would have ever recorded the song. But clouds absorb all things, even songs, and when this cloud changed into a misty morning dew, she whispered to Bog's descendants the essence of his lament:

Oh Lady River, Lady Grand
What trouble from the human hand
Has stripped you of your royal train
And left you widowed to remain
A beggar in a field of dust
A tributary running just
Enough to keep your course alive
Enough that hope may yet survive

But see! The stories disappear
As tree by tree and year by year
The memories of wooded lands
Are felled and fallen, leaving strands
Of broken tales once green and rich
Now buried under tar and pitch
Forgotten by Man's hasty plan
To tame the wild and muddy land

If only Man had asked of you
A token of your riches through
Exchange of tree for sapling young
The stories would have ever run
And you, the Lady River, could
Be laughing through a verdant wood!

Patch closed his eyes and curled himself into a ball, trying as best he could be become a nest of comfort for his mournful friend.

In time, Bog looked at the horizon where Patch had said the second lighthouse was, and there, through the blurry veil of tears, Bog saw the strange tower.

"Yes," he said with a sigh, "that is new. It is not in the tales of the toads nor in the maps we croak to one another. But, as you say, it has no manplace on top nor any light to talk to ships."

"Maybe Man is building a new lighthouse," Patch said. "Maybe he hasn't built the light-place on top yet."

"Perhaps, Patch. No way to tell except by going there ourselves."

Paco reached the top, stopping one boy-length below his friends at a place where the cypress could still support him. He saw the tower too.

"A lighthouse!" he shouted, then at once he, too, hesitated. "But there is no light on top and no glass house to hold it. Still, maybe Mamá and Papá went there because they did not find me. I shall go and see."

He hastily climbed down. Patch followed, carrying Bog. The raccoon, skilled as he was in tight turnarounds, descended headfirst, and his descent was as graceful and rapid as the climb. At the bottom, Patch announced the find to Plod.

"But there is only one lighthouse in the Valley," Plod insisted.

"I know," Patch replied, "but it's tall like the other one. Maybe Man is building another."

Plod neighed softly. "Perhaps, but it's been quite a while since Man built lighthouses. These days he builds towers for guiding ships in the air, not ships on the water. Those airship towers look a tad different than the watership kind, say the seagulls who circle both."

Patch tapped his fingery paw on an ebony root. "Still, maybe Miracle's parents mistook it for the watership kind. We should go and see, and maybe we'll find Miracle's parents! Then we can deliver the boy to them and return to the sanctuary to wait for the new thing to come! Yes, yes, that's it! That's what we should do! What a kind tree this cypress has been to help us find that second tower! Now, let's see what Miracle—"

Before Patch could finish his words, the sound of breaking underbrush reached the friends from the shadows of the sabal palms, a sound accompanied by the obedient moan of a manmachine.

The boy climbed onto Plod with the help of a stump. Plod lowered his head as Bog hopped into his mane. The toad sent another message to his kin of the forest for directions on which way to go, but still, no one croaked back.

Patch tensed his body for action. "Run, hide, or fight? What do you say, Bog?"

"I say the silence of my tribe tells me something comes to us that is as bad as the pit bulls we ran into—or worse."

Plod raised his head. "Miracle is sitting very still on my back. Let us follow his lead and do the same."

They waited. The sound grew, and if it did not bring Patch any hope, at least it pushed away the memory of his fright with the pit bulls.

"Here they come," Bog said, tongue too dry to say more. He met the danger with eyes wide open.

It was not what the friends had expected. A Man appeared in a Gator, a small camo-patterned all-terrain vehicle. His hair was white and somewhat long, gracefully swept back with oil, and his mustache, which was just as white as his hair, was so large it was hard to tell if the Man was grinning, or grouchy, or neither. But his eyes had a spark in them—a flame of resolution. The Man stopped his Gator.

"¡Buenas tardes, muchacho! Another traveler hiding in Sabal Palm Sanctuary, I see! Who are you?"

"I am Paco, and these are my friends."

"Ah, friends," the Man said, looking them over with a pondering frown. "Good to have friends in times like these— if true friends can be found. But if not…Tell me, son, what are you doing here?"

"I went to *El Faro,* the lighthouse, to find Mamá and Papá, but they were not there. Then this tree made me tall, and I saw another tall place. It is far away. It looks like a lighthouse, but it has no light on top. I know they are waiting for me. Maybe Mamá and Papá are waiting for me there even though there is no light."

"Maybe," the stranger replied. "I know the place. It is behind a barrier three fences deep. And you are right; there is no light on top. It is not a lighthouse, my boy. It is a tower very different from that—a tower that lifts off the ground with fire and goes far up into the sky, farther than any cloud or bird can go. And if Papá Eli could do it, he would climb into that flying tower and go up there, too, and never come down."

"Who is Papá Eli?"

"That is me, son. They call me Papá because I have lived much longer than people normally do in my profession. And that is why I am here. I am trying to *retire*, you see, but that is a word too big for you just now. I live in a pleasant home with plenty of palms, but I come here whenever I have—shall we say, special guests at my gate."

The boy's face brightened. "Can you take me to the flying tower?"

Papá Eli nodded. "My ranch neighbors the flying tower. When my guests leave, I can certainly arrange for that."

"My friends are coming with me."

Papá Eli considered the horse and the raccoon beside him. The two animals stood watchful, silent, and still. Bog, in the horse's mane, was not visible to the Man. He wiped his face with a silk handkerchief patterned in orange and forest green.

"The horse can come, but the raccoon, no. He cannot."

"But the raccoon *must* come. He knows how to rescue marbles. He knows their secrets. He knows the story of the one I rescued from the water when Mamá and Papá went away."

The old man froze, the handkerchief in mid-stroke across his forehead. "Your mamá and papá disappeared in the water?"

"Yes, the sea. That is the last place I saw them. Like I said, I went to *El Faro* and searched for them. They were not there. Now, take me to the flying tower."

Papá Eli shook himself as if awakening from an unintended nap. "Wait! You came here from the *sea*? How long ago?"

The boy puzzled over memories. "I do not know. I have not counted. All I know is that the moon helps me. At first, she showed just more than half her face as she moved ahead of me to show where I should go. Now she is as round as a marble. And she told me last night the good cat was going to be okay."

Papá Eli craned his neck forward and stared at the boy. Astonishment fell over his face.

"You...you...Paco, who captained your boat? Tell me."

"Tío Sergio. That was his name. He wore sunglasses all the time, even in the night. How could he work in the night with sunglasses on? I did not understand. My papá—he worked in the day with goggles and the starry fire before him, sticking metal to metal. But Sergio had no spark before him like Papá did. He did not make metal to be friends with metal like Papá. No, he ran the metal of our boat onto something metal sleeping in the water beneath us. The metal of the one did not like the metal of the other. Our boat split open like a fish splits after Papá catches it and pulls the knife to prepare it for supper. Only after that did I see tío's eyes. Only after he and I were floating in the sea. And they were white, for he was afraid. I was afraid too. And Mamá and Papá were gone."

Papá Eli's jaw dropped. Then his shoulders sagged as he stared at the ground. The katydids filled the silence. A dragonfly hovered nearby.

Suddenly, Papá Eli became very interested in his handkerchief, folding it with the delicate motions of a horticulturist caring for a tender plant. When he looked up, he flashed a pleasant smile.

"Paco, my son, come with me to see the aquarium at my ranch, El Pequeño Jardín. Once we are there, I would be honored to help you."

"Help me find my parents?"

"Help you find out." He looked away from the lad. "Then I will take you to the place of the flying tower, a ranch called Eden's Bend. I have two good friends who work there, friends I trust more than anyone who works for me. Or used to."

Papá Eli led Plod to the back of his Gator and tied the rope lead to a bar there. Paco looked back at Patch.

"I will not go without my friend," the boy said. He slid off the horse and dropped to the ground, his bare feet meeting a mat of dead leaves with a thump. He went to the raccoon beside the cypress tree. Turning, he stood with stern lips, bowed-out chest, and fists on his hips.

Papá Eli climbed into the driver's seat with a nonchalant air. He lit a cigar. For a moment, the old man's face was hidden within a bluish cloud of tobacco smoke, the aroma of which was so strong the boy's eyes stung and watered. But when the smoke cleared, there was no water in Papá Eli's eyes. He blew a ring of smoke resembling a tractor tire and motioned toward the thicket of the palms.

"Well, son, it seems to me you have to make a choice. Either stay here with your raccoon friend in this unfriendly forest where strangers appear from behind trees, or come with me for clues about your parents."

He began to slowly drive away. Plod followed, constrained by the rope.

Bog called to the raccoon. "Wait here with Miracle, Patch! Wait for the new thing you told us is coming! Yes, be faithful to the end! Farewell, my friend! Farewell! Give the new thing our greetings! And remember my last words: *to the end!*"

Patch jumped forward a step. "I...but you...we will follow you!"

Plod slightly turned his tethered head. "Nay, neighbor. The Man takes us. It is the way things are with our kind. Stay with Miracle. Wait for the new thing. Happy trails, friend." And he tossed his tail in farewell.

Paco had one hand on the back of his friend the raccoon and one hand stretched out to the back of the departing stranger. The manmachine grew smaller as Papá Eli guided it into the shadows beneath the palms. Plod, following on the lead behind, passed through a small cloud of cigar smoke.

"You cannot go!" the boy shouted. "You break my friends apart and you take the clue to where my parents are!"

He ran after Papá Eli. Reaching the Gator, he climbed in and seized the steering wheel. The old man and the child wrestled over it as the vehicle slowed down, wobbled, and stopped. As it did, Patch scrambled to the first branch of the cypress and poised as if to leap.

"No!" shouted Paco. "You will not leave my friend!"

"Stop it, boy!" Papá Eli shouted back. "There is great danger here! We've got to go!"

The sound of pounding hoofbeats caused the two to look up; a man on horseback dashed toward them from among the trees. Behind him was another horse with an empty saddle, which the rider led by a line to the halter.

Papá Eli let go of the wheel. "Ubi, what are you doing here?"

"They're coming for you, señor! I'm just ahead of them! Get on!"

Papá Eli acted as one alone. He hurried out of the Gator and mounted the spare horse. But as he took the reins, he turned to the boy with an angry urgency.

"Come here!" he barked. "Trouble is coming—trouble that will never let you go!"

Paco stared at Papá Eli and Ubi. He glanced back at Plod, who stood stoic and docile, submitted to the way things are with his kind, swishing his tail at the flies.

Tears filled Paco's eyes. "But my friends!"

"Your friends are fine! They will not hurt them! They only hurt people! But if you do not come with us, you will never find your parents, hear me? Never! These men coming are wolves! Flee with me, and I will help you!"

Paco's eyes burned. He climbed out of the Gator and came to Papá Eli, hand stretched upward to him, head turned back toward Plod, Bog, and the cypress, where Patch sat, perplexed, upon its lowest branch.

"I will not forget you!" the boy shouted. "Thank you for helping me! I will tell Mamá and Papá!"

Papá Eli grabbed Paco by the upper arm and threw him on his saddle at the horn. Ubi slapped the back of his horse, and together both horses galloped into the shadows of the sabal palms.

The air was silent but full, as when one stands at the edge of a diving board, unable to dive but too ashamed to turn back. The dragonfly landed on a yucca spine, and the katydid signaled one short note. Flies clouded around the empty ATV as Plod stomped a hoof to warn them off. Another span of silence followed. Then two manmachines came crashing through the brush. Out jumped four Men with firearms.

There's a strange cloud around these men, Patch thought. I *can't see it, but I can feel it in my gut.*

The Men searched the Gator and the space about it. They scanned the face of the forest 360 degrees.

A Man lowered his weapon. "Got away again, Izzi."

"But we were close. And we've got his Gator. It won't be long."

Izzi inspected the vehicle. Beside it, he found a cigar. He picked it up and glared.

"It's still warm. Yes, this time we were very close."

"Close is not enough for El Dragón," a Man replied. "He will be angry with us."

Izzi gave Plod a look of disdain.

"Why would Papá Eli weigh himself down with such a useless beast? Does he think showing kindness to an animal will make us believe he has repented? No one flees and does good once they've done what we've done. No one turns over a new leaf in winter. We must cut the tree down. But you, old thing, you have no part in this story. No guilt. No mouth that would betray us like the old man's."

Izzi untied Plod from the back of the Gator.

"Now go!" He slapped the horse.

Plod startled, backed up, and trotted toward the cypress where Patch was. He hesitated, turning toward the direction where Papá Eli and the boy had fled; the Men of El Dragón stood in the way. Izzi lifted his weapon above his head and fired a single round. The burst filled the air with fear. Patch dropped onto Plod's back, and the three friends fled in another direction, mourning for Miracle as they did.

2

THE THIRD GATE

The fright of Izzi's gunshot strengthened Plod to canter beyond what his old bones thought possible. The horse fled for almost an hour, and the weight of Patch and Bog did not slow him but, on the contrary, spurred him on to save them. When Plod finally ceased cantering to walk, they were in a forest of Rio Grande ash and mountain laurel trees running along the edge of cornfields as dry as paper, where vacant concrete pipes, airways to the aqueducts below, stood upright like sentinels above the barren harvest. For the rest of the day, they meandered through the forest, foraging for food, wondering what to do, and only sure of one thing: avoiding the mescal beans of the laurel tree, whose bright red seeds appealed to the eye but poisoned the body.

On the second day, they found a space in the great barrier Man had built and walked the bank of the Lady River. They greeted her, but her reply was a faint whisper to them, as faint as the current passing through her, and even as she spoke, she fell asleep.

"For my mouth will one day close," she said. "The land will bridge my banks, and I shall pass into the world beneath my riverbed until I rise again. I slumber now to save my strength."

Bog hopped from Plod's mane into the shallows near the bank.

17

"Wait, my Lady!" he croaked. "Don't drift off just yet! Do you have news of a manchild named Miracle or of his friend the new thing our comrade Patch speaks of?"

The river rippled sluggishly. "I have no word of a miracle, save for the new thing who mingled in my waters as he crossed: the lord of the Valley."

And with a sigh, she ceased to speak, and the waters moved no more.

Plod and Bog stood amazed.

"'Lord of the Valley'?" Bog asked. "I know that epithet. It is reserved for the great feline frog eaters full of cunning and speed. Their teeth are the theme of many a last stanza of the songs of my ancestors. No lord of the Valley has ruled the animal kingdom here since the time when my late uncle Roland took on the House of One Hundred House Cats in Port Isabel. Oh, the fur that flew! Have I ever told you about it?"

"You sang that ballad often in the Great Freeze when we couldn't leave the stable," Plod said. "Let's save it for Patch until we have another roof to rest under."

The raccoon hopped down and faced his two friends, paws up on outstretched limbs. "Now, don't be alarmed! Calm down, everybody. *This* lord of the Valley prefers *fish*. Yes, I admit he's got teeth and he's got speed, but he's not like the other fur-covered hunters you know. He remembers a time before teeth and speed. He remembers the Days of First Things."

Plod raised an eyebrow. "The Days of First Things? Before the law of prey and predator?"

"Yes, before the law of pursuit, before the law of the kill, before all the laws governing this side of the story we animals have to bear with. He remembers what Adam spoke to the first of our kinds. You will see, Plod. Yes, when you meet him, you will see!"

Plod swung his heavy head down to look Patch straight in the face. "Partner, you talked me into serving you and this 'something new' at the stable with the help of some sweetwater. Then at the first lighthouse, I decided I needed to help the manchild, sweetwater or no. But the Lady River makes it clear this 'something new' is harder to tame than badgers and bobcats."

"You're right, Plod, you're right. I can't deny what you're saying any more than I can hide the rings on my tail. No use calling a porcupine a pillow. But at the right time, I'm sure you'll meet him, and it will be the sort of 'something new' you'll be glad you risked hoof and hide for. The path to him is a thorny one, but there's clover in the middle of it for you, Plod, I promise. Better than sweetwater, though maybe harder to swallow at first."

Bog hopped back into Plod's mane. "Patch, either you're full of foolishness or full of the best news the animals of the Valley have ever heard. When we meet this new 'lord of the Valley,' as the Lady River calls him, we'll find out which one!"

On the third day, finding the roads hosted too much traffic to cross even with the reconnaissance of the spoonbill, they turned toward Sabal Palm Sanctuary again, keeping just within its leafy borders as they traced a path under the cover of the branches. Late in the afternoon, they reached a clearing. Sabal, mesquite, and yucca were gathered around a dying pond, broad but ankle deep, whose banks bore the body-gouges of alligators who had evacuated the night before in search of better pools.

Here the friends rested. Bog plopped into the pond, whose remnant of water still welcomed him. Plod took a sip, but its brackish liquor kicked back at him and kept him from drinking more. He tried to graze, but noxious weeds called buffelgrass and guineagrass had choked out the native growth.

He nibbled reluctantly. Patch foraged in the branches of a persimmon tree, also called *chapote* in the mantongue. The shadier branches offered the raccoon tart and withered fruit, dark purple in color, and he ate them without complaining.

Evening came. Exhaustion overtook them with sleep. Far above, the constellation Little Fox slunk by with a goose in his mouth while other celestial birds looked on.

In the third watch of the night, the sound of fluttering wings awoke the friends. The whip-poor-will of the Colony of the Lost had come to relieve the spoonbill. She alighted upon a mesquite's tallest branch, which reeled under the momentum of the bird's haste.

"Range of the Hidden Path has come!" she warned in notes of urgent cadence. "Range and his pack! Range and his pack! They hunt for anything afraid! Anything afraid! Fly, now, fly! Hear how near! Fly, now, fly! Hear how near!"

A sound of four-footed fierceness reached their ears. The night air awoke with a yip and a yap and the patter of approaching paws.

Patch rose on his hind legs and smelled it all instantly. "Range! Run!"

Deeper into the sanctuary they fled, but the rapid thud of canine feet grew louder. The sound of panting reached them like smoke before fire. Without time to think, they dove into the nearest thicket, a stand of whitebrush and lantana screening them from sight. A stench stung their senses, a smell shooting fear through them. But the urge to hide drove them to the deepest spot in the thicket, where they stumbled upon the source of the stench: the decaying carcass of a cow. All eyes watered, not just from the loathsome displeasure of the odor but from the ghastly testimony thereof that they, too, were destined for dust. A cloud of flies awoke and settled on the friends, their nimble legs covering each of them with the urge to swat. But they froze, for the fear of death was stronger, and they let the flies crawl over them as the keen-nosed coyotes arrived. They stood just beyond the veil of leaves, inspecting the air with rapid-fire sniffings.

A coyote gagged. "Wretched, rotting bovine!"

"A smell stronger than ironthorn!" growled another. "Go round! Go round!"

A bolder voice howled toward the moon. The pack crooned their clashing melodies in reply to the bold one while two pups yapped in excitement. The sound of movement gathered in one place, then stopped.

"Comrades, hear me!" the bold voice barked. "Listen, oh brave ones who gather about their rightful chief tonight! Rally with me to preserve our pack! The honor of our tribe is at stake, for the traitor Thud has hoodwinked the young males. 'Fight for me!' this deceiver says. 'We will share a common kill! No more will you wait while your chief eats first. We are equal! Equal!' With wicked words like these, he would lead the young astray and overturn our ancient ways. He would depose our pack and set himself up as king! His lair is not far from here; I am sure we will find it. And when we do, who will fight for me? I swear by the Paw of Canis himself, whoever slays one of these rebels will have a whole kill as his spoil, booty enough for him and all who warm his den!"

The pack met the speech with howling approval. Coyotes yipped, and the pattering of their feet grew louder, then softer, then louder again as each one ran a slalom of palms in his restlessness.

A pup barked with a shrill whine. "Father, let us search too!"

"No," ordered the bold voice, "you are too young. Thud's thugs will kill you."

"But we are fast!" another pup declared.

"And you are foolish," pronounced his father. "Remain with your mother!" A sharp cry and whimpers followed. Small paws shuffled away.

The bold one lifted up his voice. "Disperse now, my scouts! Search until your eyes awaken the dawn!"

The friends heard paws jogging away in long arcs while noses sniffed the ground. For a time, the sound of a single canine remained, panting and investigating the outer shrubs of their hiding place with a persistent snuffle. Twice the whitebrush stirred as the coyote tested the acrid cloud of the dead cow. Then he, too, departed.

The friends remained as still as stones, looking at one another's silhouettes inside the shadow of death. Even the flies grew still.

At last, Patch whispered. "That was close! I thought for sure we were goners, but this poor lost Bessie helped us! She must have eaten the lantana. It's poisonous like those mescal beans we saw the other day."

"Yes," Bog said, "her tragic tale made us invisible to them and worked for good, though she did not live to see her noble deed. Oh, bless Bessie's soul in that bovine realm of endless green! Bless her in yon Elysian Field, where tender shoots caress her placid maw! Bless her for her last-ditch defense! Her decay saved our hides! Her final act was her finest!"

Plod flapped his lips in anxious thought. "We'd best leave the sanctuary again. Both Men and coyotes are on the hunt here. Soon trackers will come for both. This forest will get as crowded as a barn in winter."

Patch shooed the flies from his nose. "You're right, Plod. Let's make again for 'the lighthouse with no light' we saw from the cypress. Maybe the manchild found it somehow. I'm hoping everyone's been in such a hurry that no one will go back the way they came, and we'll have a quiet path till sunrise."

"Worth a try," said Plod.

"Let us face what comes our way," said Bog, "just as my ancestor George of the Muddy Trail did. In the time of the cattle drives under the Lone Star, George journeyed south on the empty trail after the dust of the north-marching vaqueros had cleared. But he met the wagon wheel of a straggler, for he hadn't reckoned on the chuck wagon, heavy and slow with all its kettles and pots. Nor had he reckoned on the swift tongs of the cook. Have I ever told you the tale of George and the Last Stand at Iron Rim Stew?"

Patch climbed Plod's tail and feigned a smile toward the toad. "Um, that'll be a good way to pass the time once we find the lightless lighthouse, but for now—let's not share the glory of your uncle with any left-behind coyotes!"

And Bog begrudgingly consented.

The whip-poor-will joined them, flying bush to bush a furlong ahead, singing songs of deliverance from harm as she guided them to the quiet places where all but the ferns were still. In the heavens, the moon, stone-shaped and waxing, drove off the constellation of the fox, chasing him down to the western horizon.

The sun broke upon the fourth watch of the night with liquid gold, and the heat of that aerial molten metal fanned into flame the dawn clouds. The forest still slept, but the top of the lightless lighthouse caught the first sunbeam shooting across the sky. The whip-poor-will told them so from her perch on a utility pole.

"I can see it, I can see! I can see it, I can see! Not far now! Follow me! Not far now! Follow me!" And on ahead she flew.

The friends came upon a break in the underbrush. An unpaved road tunneled through it, a road so fresh the white dust of its gravel still powdered the poison ivy on either side, which grew in bright green sprays from shorn clumps and shattered stumps where machines had torn back the wilderness with swift chains of steel. The friends scanned the road. At one end it disappeared in a soft curve meeting trees covered in thorny vines. At the other end, renegade cedars asserted themselves above fiddlewood shrubs. A gate stood open.

"It's anyone's guess why Man didn't shut that gate behind him." Plod said. "Could mean he was in too much of a hurry or it could mean he'll show back up in a minute and throw a lasso over our journey. What do you reckon?"

Patch hopped down and sniffed the gravel. "I don't know, but this is a new road to a new manplace, I bet. Man's busy here. See the dust? It's what my tribe calls 'busy dust.' Different from the 'sleepy dust' that settles when Man gives up on something and lets it lie there. But gosh does he smell busy on this road!"

"Follow it, follow it," sang the whip-poor-will from a cedar. "Goes to his place, goes to his place."

"'His place'?" Bog frowned in puzzlement. "Whose place?"

But the whip-poor-will took wing. "Morning has come, I fly! Morning has come, I fly!" Her voice faded beyond the branchy canopy.

"Why only riddles from that whip-poor-will?" grumbled Bog. "A better scout than the spoonbill, but still a poor guide for our quest, I say! She speaks a clue we can't crack. A place is around the bend, but we don't know who's there."

Plod gave a stoic snort. "Let's hit the road and find out. No way to know but to go—though without a doubt, Man will find *us* when we find *out*. That's how it is with our kind."

The friends passed through the gate and moved east-north-east as the sun rose. They reached a clearing. A barren pond lay at roadside's edge, a thin plate of water and clay ringed by withered grass. The faint remains of fish lay imprinted on what had once been the pond bottom before the drought had uncovered it. At the center, where the water had gathered to make its last stand before the conquest of the sun, a host of bird footprints revealed who had been there to bid the oasis farewell. And in the Gulf Coast wind blowing in ever-warmer gusts, here is the whisper the friends heard:

Kite and kestrel
Bonaparte gull
Sanderling, heron
Watch in the lull

Northern harrier
Big little blue
Impudent starling
Flitting right through

Here in the silence
We bid farewell
Here in the reverence
Promise to tell

Once there was water
Mirroring blue
Speak, Son of Adam
Make all things new

The whisper stirred in Plod the aroma of old stories he remembered but had ceased to speak of. He groaned under the weight of them. Patch, standing beside him, heard and touched him with his shoulder as if to help with the burden. Unconsciously, he breathed a sigh that bathed Plod's fetlock, lingered about the hoof and ankle, and found a doorway up the cannon bone of the old horse's leg. The breath flowed into his arteries and veins, milling about the body of the weary beast until it found a home among the four chambers of his heart. There, within those chambers, the breath became a song. And Plod gave the song a voice:

Dapple, down, roan, and black as jet we run
In ranks and rows rolling over toppled
Barricades and last-stand clusters gathered
To go down with bayonets thrusting wild
At our unrelenting chests whose heartbeat
Scorns the point of death and splits with high hoof
The clattered crumbling of the falling foe
And on we go

Cantering down the steep bank now sliding
Hurling full weight into unplumbed rivers
Crossing fears hidden 'neath the surface where
Solid ground is not below but on
Our unburdened backs burdened only by
The joy of riders come back from the dust
With laughter fiercer than the booted feet
Who trampled them

We gallop on the wind till stirrup lifts
And riding crop forgotten for the wings
That take its place with bare feet pressing on
Our frames in haste to lift our masters
After lead steed bearing the Unbeaten
Beaten Body: feet bare, too, bruised like his
Hands holding seven stars in living scars
Now glorified

We reach level ground of never-ending
Plain where every hoofprint births a spring of
Pools and afterward a rain that washes
Every tear of pain till all cascades through
Cataracts of wild, undaunted joy where
Neither bit, nor bridle, nor callous hand
Can separate us from our masters grand
Soon returning

I brood upon the pasture past the falls
I stir before the promise of a child
I call to wild ancestors in the dust
"Red day's fading! The green you sought has come!"
Children lead the cavalcade proceeding
From amnesia to ambrosia waking
Never again to muddy Eden's springs
Resurrecting

The friends honored the song with silence. It was as if a supply train of treasure-laden wagons for kings had passed through, though the air was still and nothing in the trees had moved. And yet it was clear to the friends that something, or someone, had indeed passed through. Even Plod, from whose mouth the song had come, knew the words were not his own—or rather, that the song had passed through him and had taken on who he was. So, all honored the song by remaining in reverence for a time.

—ᴍ—

They continued on the chalk-dust road and turned eastward, Plod carrying Patch and Bog. For a long time, the only sound was the steady crunch of hooves and the distant cry of a green jay. Winged insects passed by on errands of their own, though curiosity often caused them to redirect their paths to get a closer look at the travelers, their faint buzz fading in and out of the ears of the friends. Bog let them remain at their leisure with the exception of one fly who had the misfortune of landing on his nose.

The toad and the raccoon watched every branch they passed under. Only an occasional sparrow appeared, but they were always too shy to speak. After a nervous glance and a flitting between branches, the sparrows would disappear with a chirp. But the unseen green jay called out in regular cadence, modulating between two vibrating tones and giving generous space for silence between each call.

Then a crunching rumble grew from behind them, signaling the sudden coming of a manmachine. The friends dove behind a tangle of pampas and vines just before a white pickup truck roared by. After it disappeared, the friends returned to the road, walking through the lingering cloud of "busy dust" the manmachine had kicked up. In time they came upon an open gate where the truck had rushed through. A tall chain-link fence crowned with barbed wire framed the opening. On both sides, the fence panels held aloft spotless red-and-white signs like coats of arms heralding a new domain:

DANGER!
LAUNCH ZONE
I.T. MENEFEE PERSONNEL ONLY
EDEN'S BEND

"We've crossed someone's line," Plod warned. "The grass smells different here."

"Yes," Bog said, "but without a doubt we are near the tower Miracle saw."

Patch scanned the road in both directions. "The Men will come back and shut this gate and the one we found open at the poison ivy. We need to cross while we can."

And so, they passed through. The gulf breeze ceased and the air held its breath. The sound of Plod's hooves filled the space, and scores of insects called to one another from unseen realms.

They came to a third fence, this one taller than the two before it. But the gate—a row of steel bars on a rail embedded in the ground—was closed. Bending toward the friends on a post was a green box bearing a numeric keypad.

Patch leaned forward for a closer look. "I've seen these before. Man touches them with jumping fingers, and the gate opens. Pull up to it, Plod. Let me hang on to your mane and give it a try. Bog, you mind switching places with me?" And Bog hopped to Plod's back while Patch found a thick bunch of horsehair to grasp.

The raccoon went to work. He called on the secrets in the rings of his tail, memories from the sacred ceremonies of his youth. Scenes from the Rite of the First Ring returned to him, a ritual dance instructing through mime how to open lids, gates, and doors, the skills inspiring the Powhatan mantribe to name him He Who Scratches With His Hands. And these memories, in turn, were baptized into a deeper memory from the Days of First Things: the moment Adam had named the first of his kind—the memory Oracle had given him when he had breathed on him at Garfight Pond. And Patch remembered Eden, a garden whose gates had living doors standing open and innocent to a whole wild world.

He touched the keypad.

3

THE PRINCE OF EDEN'S BEND

Chasing Eagle enjoyed her breakfast view. A vast ranch stretched beneath her airplane window, while the owner of that ranch—Travis Menefee III—stretched in the seat facing her. A dawning amber rose doused the tops of the trees with fire, casting the contours of their branches into living relief. Beneath her glided the sagging stable of Plod and Bog, who, along with Patch, meandered at that moment far to the south in a long arc back to Sabal Palm Sanctuary. Chasing Eagle saw new stables thrusting their sterling panels into the sky. Farther on, triple helix wind turbines, white like gulls, spun joyfully as power flowed down their stainless-steel stems to a complex of buildings whose copper roofs gleamed like burnished shields in salute to their master above. In the distance a gravel airstrip cut through the brush.

The Beechcraft King Air banked, and the rising sun kissed the man's face as he finished his stretch: boots out, back arched, elbows up, fists behind his head, eyes shut tight to the blinding light. When he opened them, he followed the limits of his kingdom below.

The woman considered his eyes. The irises were sorrel brown, crowned at the rim with a bold black line. His face bore a faint hint of the Comanche chief's daughter hidden in his bloodline, and the natural half squint of a gaze, peering as if behind a rifle sight, still spoke of the Texian rebel who had

31

founded his dynasty upon the broken arrows of that same Comanche chief. Unkempt hair crashed like a wave over his forehead. He wore western work boots, jeans, and a denim jacket over a white cotton dress shirt.

The trees filling Chasing Eagle's window were of many kinds. Honey mesquite were ubiquitous, but she also identified live oak, cedar elm, and Rio Grande ash. Without conscious thought, she played with the silver locket on her necklace as she considered the trees. The locket was round, engraved with a series of circles and bead-like patterns, and was about the size of an American nickel. A lapis lazuli stone adorned the center. And under it, inside the locket, rested a tiny scroll.

"So, all that I'm looking at is yours, Tripp?"

"Yeah, Chase, we've broken past 260,000 acres with the acquisition of Diamondback Ranch. Bought it for more than it's worth. The owner claimed the ranch has a secret spring, but he hasn't worked that land for a coon's age. Lives in Colorado. He's some kinda cousin to Oso Kennedy at Bear Claw next door. But we have a timetable to keep, so we bit the bullet and paid him. At least he *sold* it. Some owners just won't budge. Right now, a couple of stubborn snowbirds are blocking us from a beautiful slice of coastal access. They're holding on to their beach houses for more than those matchstick shacks are worth. 'Sentimental value' is what they call their price gouging. But they'll cave in time, or their kids will when they're gone."

Chasing Eagle stared at him coldly. Tripp cleared his throat.

"Sorry, Chase, sometimes I get a little too goal oriented. We can bypass them—they're just a couple half-acre lots. No harm letting folks live out their golden years the way they want."

Chase set her coffee down. "Tripp, you're adding land faster than my impact studies can keep up. I'll either need to resign as zoo director for a full-time role, or you'll have to hire me a staff. I can't give you the eco-data you need in time."

Tripp downed an orange juice in a single gulp and planted the cup on the table between them with a saloon-style gasp of satisfaction. "Yeah, Chase, you'll have to hit the ground running to catch up. I need you to give me the best picture possible of how to distribute natural resources between wild places and workspaces. Balance, Chase, balance. That's what we're aiming for: that sweet spot between nature and nickels."

"Those are hard ones to reconcile."

"That's why I asked you to drop everything and come down here today. I'm about to hit the J curve and really need your insight on how to do things right. Eden's Bend brings together a lot of moving parts. A lot of investors too. You've got what I need for the animal side. When my deep pockets ask about it today, I need your voice and your stats."

"Who you got coming?"

"Everybody I've been working on, even Mr. Barrow. If everything times out right tonight, I'll be giving the funding pitch while a Texas sunset lights up the sky behind me. Should be good. Real good, I hope."

Edwin, Tripp's personal assistant, came from the mini galley to serve each a Danish with long steel tongs.

"I've already buttered these for you, one patty each. Less mess that way. Enjoy! And Tripp, FYI, the executive chef of The Charging Ox arrived from Houston yesterday and got right to work. Three courses, just like you ordered. The emu steaks won't see a freezer between the butcher and the table. I will make absolutely sure of that."

"Thanks, Eddie, I knew I could count on you."

The attaché smiled with self-satisfaction and turned his attention to tidying the galley.

Chase gave Tripp a skeptical look. "The Charging Ox? Seriously?"

Tripp shrugged, fanning out his hands. "That chef cost me one heck of a silver dollar, Chase, but it's what I gotta do to impress our potential investors with real Texas flavor. Rated better than any steakhouse in Manhattan, ya know."

She smirked in doubt. "Well, okay. That side of things is your wheelhouse, not mine. You must be putting them up in the new guest center. You're dropping prefabs about as fast as you are buying out your neighbors."

"I know, Chase, but the more land I'm able to pull in, the more margin we've got for working out both sides of the equation."

"Nature and nickels."

"You got it. We're picking up a nice chunk of the original San Juan de Carricitos land grant—a name from 1792 that shows up on just about every property abstract in our neck of the woods. The king of Spain sure set the playing field for us, didn't he!"

Chase turned away to view the land below. "The king of Spain just saw it on vellum when he signed off on the deal. I doubt he dreamed about it like you do."

Tripp chuckled. "Yeah, you could say I've obsessed on South Texas a bit more than most. But that's how it is when you're acquiring so much of it! We're pushing down from Port Mansfield with a dogleg around Laguna Atascosa National Wildlife Refuge. We've got chunks on both ship channels, the Harlingen one for wildlife and the Brownsville one for the high-tech stuff. Now it's just a matter of connecting everything one piece at a time. Like Old Cavazos, where my dad spent time as a kid, and Oso's place—Ha! Never met a rancher who cares for his fish as much as his prize bull! The refuge people are buying up land, too, but mostly toward Bahia Grande and Boca Chica as they try to complete a corridor to the border, so we usually don't find ourselves competitors for the same real estate."

Chase tapped the table. "Yes, but the refuge people are procuring land for the wildlife, not for high-risk projects that will turn into time-shares if they fail."

Tripp gave Chase a flustered look. "Yeah, I know: we're 'building an airplane in midair,' as you've told me countless times. I hear you. Not a lot of cushion if a wing falls off! I know the risks, Chase, but think about the *vision*!"

"Oh, I think about it. That's why I'm here. We've got oryx, impalas, and kudu strolling about free of the fear of poachers—"

"—and ready for a fair hunt with bows and front loaders."

"Yeah, that too."

"Takes the rewilding movement to a new level, wouldn't you say?"

"I guess so. But the verdict's still out whether you're adding to the rewilding movement or building a monumental resort."

"Look it, Chase, high-end hunters expect glamping not camping, and my A-listers who post a selfie a day need Wi-Fi in their bungalows like a fish needs water. It hasn't been cheap. But I'm betting on it to pioneer how things are done. Same with Fine Line Farms. Ostrich and emu are the new cattle. They flopped in the '90s, but with emu oil, it's a whole new ball game. People might be slow to eat the bird, but they're sure eager to try anything that softens their skin and saves their hair! I've got my marketing wizards working on it. Now, wizards work best when they've got a village to gather in, so I build what I gotta build to keep them happy and productive."

Chase leaned forward, jutting open palms toward Tripp. "But your new construction is leaving quite a footprint. And the *launchpad,* Tripp." She flopped back in her seat as she rolled her eyes and slapped her knee. "Your engineers rerouted an *entire creek* with those runoff pipes from the pad coolers!"

Tripp squirmed like a sophomore in the principal's office. "Um, well, yes, they went too far; I'm with you on that. My bad. The EPA and a dozen other agencies won't like it either. And by the way, the water's not mainly for cooling the pad. It's for absorbing the sound. Those thrusters can turn peanuts into peanut butter!"

"Really?"

"I don't know if '*really.*' Guess I'll have to put a bag of goobers in the payload to find out! I'm just making a point. I want to do things right as much as you do, but if I can't generate enough income from the ranch and the rocket, the whole dream will dry up. I'll have to subdivide, and neither of us wants that. It's all about cash flow, Chase. Cash flow and venture capital. Money can go a long way in getting us back to Eden. True, it also takes your expertise in conservation to reach that goal. That's why I'm flying you down here. But if I might be candid with you, Chase: I brought you on board to be my copilot, not my air traffic control."

Chase narrowed her eyes. "I'm doing just that! I *am* being your copilot. Look at your 'instruments' and not the clouds! We're on empty, Tripp! There's not enough water as it is, and your six 'cutting-edge' projects are going to wreak havoc on Eden's Bend, animals included. We're on the same team, Tripp, but you've got binoculars stuck to your eyes. You're seeing so far ahead that you're blind to what's in front of you."

Tripp dove into his phone, but the silent stare of the Cheyenne chief's daughter proved stronger than the items beneath the glass of his device. He put it away and popped his knuckles.

"Let's end on a high note before we land. What's the latest on our hidden treasure in the heart of Texas?"

Chase obliged. "The jaguar is doing well. We have him in a new area that gives him the seclusion he needs. Visitors view him through a glass barrier, which gets them close enough to behold his beauty but keeps them at a dignified distance. At night he watches the moon. Honestly, I haven't ever seen a cat who contemplates the moon like this one."

"Fascinating."

"I think just as fascinating is the fact that a jaguar appeared here at all. Imagine, Tripp: After decades of extinction, the lead animal of the ecosystem came back to the Rio Grande Valley. What a dangerous journey it must have been for him!"

"Boy, I'll bet! But he's safe with you in the zoo, Chase, until you and I can figure out the eco side and the PR side of having him back down here. Before we caught him, I think he had eaten an old horse I acquired with some of the Old Cavazos property when we bought it. At least that's what I figure. The horse went missing about the time we discovered the jaguar. Good thing we got him out of South Texas. You know how Sheriff Bud Gibson and his deputies would have reacted if they had gotten involved—Oh, hey, look down there. No, there: It's the new wildlife observation lodge. That's where we'll all be tonight."

Chase spotted Tripp's lodge, a two-story home reminiscent of a Frank Loyd Wright design of cedar, pine, and glass. The roof spoke back to the sun through a phalanx of solar panels. Wildebeests grazed nearby. A bulldozer pushed back brush to afford the perfect panoramic view the prince of Eden's Bend required in every direction—a circle of tamed earth subduing the scrub.

Chase turned to comment on it to Tripp, but she noticed he was looking at the empty chair across the aisle.

"I guess Felicity couldn't make it?"

Tripp's face soured. "No, she couldn't. Never will. We're done, Chase."

"Oh. I'm sorry."

"Not sorrier than me! That girl turned out to be as sharp as a bow hunter. Made off with all my passwords. My dignity too. Dad even broke his silence and actually *texted* me. He saw it coming seven days ahead of the meltdown. 'Don't fall for her looks! It's only dust and water.' I thought he was just bitter from his own failures, but, boy, was he right! I think falling off a cliff would have been a nicer experience. You won't ever see Felicity again."

"I thought you'd already bought the ring."

"It's at the bottom of a stock tank. Can we change the subject, please?"

Chase found her thoughts flowing in an unintended direction, as when rainwater finds a dry creek bed. She rerouted the creek. "Sure…I've got the latest on the rhino quarantine."

"Thanks. What's the status report?"

"Ten days with a clean bill of health and the port will release him to us."

"Ten days? What a headache! The rhino already passed his thirty-day quarantine at the Port of Houston when it entered the US. Who do these South Texas port people think they are to add ten more? That makes a total of forty days in a seaside hoosegow, like they're managing Noah's Ark or something!"

And they laughed.

"Anyway, all things considered, it's going to be one for the books by the time we're done: the most future-minded ranch in Texas. I'm going to pop the cork and give them a front-row seat to the testing of the rocket engines. I'm betting on the roar of those babies to sink into their bones and leave them craving for more. It's the Big Ask, Chase. If I get the buy-in, I'll have what I need—and you'll have what you need to keep Nature happy. Maybe a staff too. I'm hoping all of them throw their hats in the ring by the time I send them back to their empires. If I can secure all that, the funding pipeline will be in place for some time to come."

Edwin approached with a pot of coffee. "Try this Columbian light roast. It's from our partners in the Huila region at Finca Monteblanco. They ferment the beans in passion fruit and an indigenous fruit called the cholupa."

Chase lifted her cup; the steam of it carried the vapor of distant soils through her as she breathed it in.

Soils of a land where jaguars still roam.

She glanced at Tripp above the rim, but he had returned to his phone. She looked out the window. The land sank away into the sky as the pilots turned the King Air into its final approach for the airstrip of Eden's Bend.

4

THE PHOTO

W elcome to Eden's Bend Lodge!" Tripp's outstretched arms touched the cedar columns framing him before his guests. Behind him, a full-length window revealed the glory of the Texas landscape.

As Tripp delivered his keynote, Chasing Eagle stood to one side, note cards at the ready. Her hair lay in a sideswept ponytail on her linen blouse. The cuffs and mandarin collar carried the patterns of her heritage, embroidered geometrics with the symbol of the morning star, a diamond-angled square from which radiated four lines, one on each side. Two tiny conch shells adorned the ends of her collar. Lapis lazuli ear studs matched the same deep blue stone on her silver locket.

Tripp brought the speech home, prepped his listeners with the extensive credentials of the zoologist about to speak, and gave Chase the floor. She presented a slide-enhanced overview of Eden's Bend and the fresh opportunity it offered living things to flourish. She spoke of the challenge of the drought. The challenge of balancing the ranch's work life with its wildlife. And the need for funding. But she concluded with a music video of the recent release of Serengeti gazelle. The investors were still applauding when she gave the mic to Tripp. He swung his gaze across the gathering of guests as a beacon sweeps across the air at a Hollywood premiere.

"The executive chef of The Charging Ox outdid himself this time. You'll be hard-pressed to find a more tender cut in Texas. I made it challenging for him and his chef de cuisine, I tell ya. They're working in a kitchen that's a far cry from their Houston one. I see them with their staff lining up at the back to bring you the main course. You'll want to finish up those gulf oysters to make room for what's coming. One more round of champagne while they're setting them out, Edwin. Bon appétit, everybody."

At the back of the room, behind the white round tables, Chase stood looking out a wall-sized window beside a bookcase. Her champagne remained untouched, its contents aglow with the same sunset flooding the savannah outside. Beyond the long shadow of the lodge, gazelle grazed amid bobwhite quail, whose speckled camouflage mimicked the field so well they only became visible when they moved. The one closest to Chase had a fair brown face, attentive eyes, and a brindle crest. Her body bore a tricolor pattern almost houndstooth in design, causing it to blend with the blades of grass and ground cover.

Farther off, Chase noticed a lone Canada goose walking among them as if keeping watch in a motherly pose. Chase leaned closer to the window.

Why would the goose abide here out of season? The flocks migrated north in March, and this dry savannah is no place for the food she prefers. Whatever the reason for her visit, it's not for a meal.

The sound of tapped crystal turned her attention to the center of the room. Tripp spoke from the head table.

"InfoTech Menefee is as much your dream as it is mine. I may be the founder and CEO, but you are the ones who bring the dream into reality. We've come a long way since we launched our first app. Our office used to be a garage apartment.

Now we're stacked taller than Austin's capitol building. And soon we'll grow even taller—a launch of the literal kind. Our first private-ops payload into space. Tomorrow you'll see a test fire of the engines."

Chase watched the goose as the pitch continued. When the bird departed, she browsed the bookcase, whose varnish still boasted the odor of being new. There were rows of Clancy, L'Amour, and Grisham. Many looked uncracked.

Most everything is audiobook for Tripp. He's always listening to something. When he does, the look on his face is like a tracker searching for the freshest trail.

Chase's eyes followed the book spines of more Westerns, spy-tech novels, and a spate of annuals from his University of Texas alma mater. She came upon a group of books more worn than their neighbors. The dust jackets were tattered, the bindings frayed.

Now here's an exception. He's opened these a lot.

Chase read the titles.

The Tree Where Man Was Born: Tales from the Heart of Africa
Field Guide to Sub-Saharan Birds
A Parting Glimpse of Eden: One Hunter's Pioneer Account
The African Bestiary
King Bekele's Lament
Squandered Eden
Animal Tracks and Signs
Eden's Last Days: A Station Chief's Memoir

After those titles, Chase saw a number of black leather-bound books: diaries, scriptures, and sacred songs seven generations old. Intricate embossments covered some of the spines. Chase touched one, and a wordless energy flowed from it. She pulled out the book and opened it to stanzas on yellowed leaves in a foreign language. She lifted the book close to her face and closed her eyes.

These pages smell like the oak trunk in the ship that transported them. When was it that someone last knew them? That time is a sea and a world away. A time no one in living memory knows.

—⁓—

The Big Ask was flawless. Afterward, informal chats meandered into the late hours until all retired for the night, chauffeured to the guest center under Edwin's care.

In the morning, they returned. Edwin filled the dining room with music from a playlist matching the guests' demographically predicted preferences. The voice of Nat King Cole crooning "Unforgettable" faded into Bobby Darin singing "Beyond the Sea." A personal pour-over of Edwin-approved coffee awaited each one, steaming and ready at their tables. Ruby Red grapefruit slices burst on their tongues, for Edwin had preserved the sweetest of the May harvest in the ranch's walk-in freezer, and there was no lack of this and other bounty of the Valley to enjoy while the executive chef and chef de cuisine of The Charging Ox prepared each omelet to order. Toward the end of breakfast, Tripp showed them artist concepts of the plans for Eden's Bend, each frame gliding over the other in smoothly projected images.

As the last image faded, Edwin struck an empty water glass. "Ladies and gentlemen, if you would kindly board the shuttle bus, we will depart for Mission Control. Tripp is eager to show you how close we are to claiming our portion of the space-travel market. It is a cutting-edge innovation guaranteed to make us a viable competitor."

They drove in an open-air shuttle bus across the Savannah Sector, where wildebeests appeared as if on cue, causing the guests to fumble for their phones to capture the moment. Pulling up to Mission Control, they saw Chase standing at the glass double-door entrance. Edwin stepped off the bus first.

His smile was bright, but his eyes were dark with frustration. "Chase, you look like you're greeting people coming to a family funeral. Perk up, please."

"I will, Edwin. When our guests are close enough to look into my eyes, I will cover those windows and offer a lamp. They will each receive a freely offered handshake."

Edwin dropped his smile just long enough to show exasperation. "You sound like a queen."

"I am. But a gracious one. These men are forgiven. They're only doing what they know to do. Or what they think they know. But their 'cutting edge' cuts both ways."

Edwin smothered his response. By the time he had turned to the bus, his fluster had become a cheery face again. He summoned the guests. True to her word, Chase welcomed them graciously.

Tripp stood in the foyer, backdropped by a wall-sized mural of an imaginary colony on Mars. At the top of the painting, the planet's red-pink horizon curved below a sun two-thirds the size of Earth's. In the foreground, underneath a vast crystalline bubble lined with floodlights, inhabitants cultivated rows of crops in six shades of green. White domed homes on delicate legs sat between each field, creating an alternating pattern of garden and dwelling. From a fountain welling up in the middle of the colony, waters flowed north, south, east, and west until they reached the rim where the bubble met the Martian terrain outside. There each river disappeared into a subterranean watercourse recycling back to the center in an ever-replenishing stream.

Tripp led his guests to a mezzanine where they viewed below them two rows of personnel bent over consoles. Three wall screens dominated the room, the center one of which featured a great white column on a platform. From its base, a faint wisp of steam wafted up, as when a kettle is ready to boil. The Mission Control director quietly motioned Edwin to his side while Tripp turned a shining face toward his guests.

"A few connections in Austin helped speed up the permits for today's performance. I am a *Menefee*, after all. My namesake signed the Texas Declaration of Independence. I wasn't around back then to fight for a new way of doing things, but I'm fighting for it now. A new way to make space travel sustainable, accessible, and most of all *profitable*. Today you'll see a test of the engines we'll use on the first launch. That event will be historic as we add our own contribution to the Texas space industry and the global market. I assure you the champagne will flow as freely on that day as it did last night for those who invest early."

Personnel leaned to one another in intense whispers. A few guests did too. Tripp did not notice.

"We have three camera angles for you to enjoy on the big screens, including a pan from a drone." He raised his finger to make a point, but Edwin hastened to interrupt him.

"Sir, I'm afraid we've run into a bit of a glitch."

Tripp turned to the screen showing the rocket. A horse stood beside it, placidly grazing grass at the spillway for water absorbing the roar of the engines. A raccoon sat near his hindquarters, inspecting the launchpad with his nose.

Tripp looked closely. "What? Zoom in on that. What on God's green earth is my horse doing out there?"

The potential investors laughed. Each pulled out their phone and took a picture of it.

"These will go viral in minutes," said one, whose bass voice prevailed among the others.

Edwin spoke as he smiled ear-to-ear. "You're right, Mr. Barrow!" Then Edwin leaned close to Tripp's ear. "Time to improvise, sir."

Tripp activated a gleaming smile and awkward laugh. "What a relief to know my lost horse is safe and sound. At least now we know the *jaguar* didn't eat him!"

Chase raised her voice slightly from the back of the mezzanine. "Perhaps he recognizes your handiwork in the rocket you are launching. You are his new owner, after all."

"Jaguar?" Mr. Barrow's voice rang out.

"Yes—yes, he was a real surprise for us," Tripp replied. "Quite a PR find—an asset worth playing up when the time is right, wouldn't you say? But this horse—gentlemen, my apologies. He went missing about the time we caught the jaguar. We thought the horse had become his dinner. We took the cat offline so as not to get government folks involved too quickly and slow down our enterprises. He's on the endangered list, as you can well imagine, extinct in all but Arizona if I remember right, or maybe New Mexico. My people shipped him off to the zoo we sponsor under Ms. Chasing Eagle's leadership. It's a stopgap until we can figure out a long-term solution. Ms. Chasing Eagle is taking real good care of him, I assure you. She's a personal friend of mine and, as you know from her stellar presentation, she's in charge of making sure everything here is living in perfect balance. In the meantime, this horse is back out of nowhere. Chase, whether he knows my 'handiwork' or not, he's pushed back our whole testing sequence."

Edwin's tenor voice took up where Tripp left off. "That just gives you one more chance to run through prelaunch." His face invited agreement from the guests.

"Yes, he's helping you, Tripp," Mr. Barrow said. "Every wise horse knows you can't be too careful. He even brought a ring-tailed techie with him. Have your launch team do another dry run while you and I go fetch your horse. And on the way out, be sure to snag a few apples from the snack table in the lobby. They'll sweeten the deal for the fella when we grab his lead."

Tripp's face flushed. "Thank you, sir, much obliged for how you're framing this. I'll tell the hands to prep the saddles. Mr. Barrow, may I have the honor of your company on this rescue mission? Eddie, come with me and Instagram this into something positive. Let's spin this thing right."

"This grass will make me a spring colt if I eat enough of it," Plod said. "Haven't found such rich blades since I was that young." He tore up turf in the shade of the launchpad, where drainpipes had nurtured a lush lawn with the water dripping from them. "We didn't find clues at the foot of this tower like you had hoped for, Patch, but we did find something good for the journey."

Bog's throat bloated like a balloon as he sounded off. "Good for *your* journey, that is. The flies are afraid of this place. I don't know why, but they keep far from it. The last flies I found were at the final fence line. They know something we don't know. Mark my words, I smell a trap. It reminds me of the doom of my late uncle Leopold at the Tomb of the Unknown Turtle. Have I ever told you about it?"

"Yes, back near Southmost Road, thank you kindly," Plod said. "No need to repeat it."

Patch rose on his hind legs, searching. "The empty air puzzles me too. Nothing's moving in it, but this tower's full of motion under its steel skin. Can you hear it?"

"Yep," Plod said. "Machines are pumping a blood of some sort. It's flowing up and down inside the tower like a thoroughbred ready to run. There's fire in its bones."

Patch returned to all fours. "Sorry about leading you and Bog all the way here for nothing. It looked like a second lighthouse to me from far away. I thought maybe the lighthouse Miracle was looking for might be this one, just no light built on top for some reason. But now that we're here, I see there's no one around, not even a fly. And what giant feet this tower's got! They're like stork legs with fish fins, each as big as a cloud. What a strange manplace! Anyway, no sign of Miracle here, and no sign of his parents either. All I can think to do is go back to the thicket where the Men took Miracle. I know we're zigzagging worse than a sparrow, but maybe we can find a better clue to follow if we go back to where this mess started."

Plod lifted his head toward the sound of hooves. Patch and Bog turned toward what he saw. A Woman and three Men approached on horseback.

Patch sniffed the air. "I'm not sure what they want, but I can see they aren't nearly as anxious as the Men in the sanctuary were."

"Could be for better, could be for worse," Plod said. "At times Men come to adore us as if we're a gift from heaven, and at other times they come to beat us as if we're the cause of all the misery in the world. Only time will tell. Nothing to do but wait and see. That's the way things are with our kind. Now, let me get one more good tuft of this sweet grass for whatever's ahead." And he pulled up a plug of luscious green.

Tripp and his three companions halted before the friends. Edwin and Mr. Barrow took pictures. The horses beneath them browsed the blades of grass, resigned to the way things are with their kind.

Chase whispered to the others. "We should let silence speak first. If we do so, we might speak something our tongues cannot."

The riders obliged, and in so doing, an air of calm safely corralled the animals standing at the foot of the rocket. Yet Tripp's gaze upon them spoke.

"Those eyes rule here," Patch said. "They warn us as much as they woo us."

Chase spoke in a still, small voice to the friends.

"Peace, brothers. Time to rest from your journey."

"Did you feel that?" Patch said. "The words passed over us like a cloud on a hot day."

"We can't outrun those words," Plod said.

"Can't outleap them either," Bog said.

Tripp offered an apple to the horse and placed a gentle hand on his neck. Plod eyed it while he carefully completed his mouthful of grass. A lasso was in the Man's hand.

Patch saw it. "Just like you predicted, Plod! This time I won't hide under a haystack like I did at Gaston Ranch." He climbed atop Plod by way of the tail. Tripp startled and reached for his riding crop.

Mr. Barrow laughed with an authoritative roar. "Leave the critter there. It's plain to see he's riding shotgun with his traveling buddy. He ain't unwelcome. There's a story here. If these critters could tell us, they would. Now, let Eddie get a good photo of 'em to post for you, Mr. Menefee, and it will help your reputation a bit."

Tripp led the weary beast to a new stable, where Patch also found a place to lie down. Bog, holding on inside the mane of his friend, arrived at the new stable too. He sang odes to his ancestors Roland, George, and Leopold long into the night, until the sounds and rhythms of the words caused the friends to sink into sleep.

—⟋⟋⟍—

Neighbors as far away as Port Isabel heard the test fire. It rattled potted plants and woke many a house cat from her slumber, bonding the feline with the house dog in their common fear of fireworks. But aside from such small dramas, the test was a success. So was the fresh-catch lunch of redfish and speckled trout afterward. The afternoon was relaxed for everyone but the host, who met back-to-back with each deep pocket and wrapped up the chat with a pitch, an appeal, and a parting gift his vaqueros had saturated with sweet-and-salty marinade: emu jerky from Fine Line Farms.

"It's low in fat, high in protein, and tastes like beef!" he gushed. He knew at least two of the three statements had data to back him up.

As Tripp's guests boarded the limo van for flights back to their empires, Tripp observed that everyone was warmly engaged in the small talk of the inner circle. He let them continue until a natural lull, then bid them farewell on the cabin microphone.

"Those of you who have a longer wait at the airport will be pleased with the VIP lounge. Edwin here even had them steam-clean the carpet! He'll be following up with each of you from our time together."

Tripp stepped off the limo van and blessed it with a tap and a smile. He did not mind the dust the parting van replied with. He paced the covered porch framing his lodge as he sent a barrage of farewell messages to his recent guests. At sunset, Tripp ceased fire. He put his phone away, breathed deeply, and went inside, where he paced the perimeter of the room, glass walls on one side, empty chairs on the other. He heard the limo van crunching to a halt in the gravel parking lot, followed by the voices of Edwin and the chauffeur.

Scanning the vista, Tripp could just make out a bobcat at the tree line who watched him with a cautious eye. He took up his binoculars, which hung from a hook near a sliding glass door. The bobcat was carrying.

"Huh, a second litter," Tripp whispered. "That's a good sign."

The bobcat lingered there, smelling the air, surveying Tripp's manplace.

Edwin approached Tripp. "Looks like almost everyone has weighed in at the level you had hoped. Only Mr. Barrow is noncommittal."

"He's my late adopter," Tripp replied, still watching the bobcat through the binoculars. "Always has been. But that way he keeps his reputation for coming through to save a deal. 'Mr. Eleventh Hour' is what the folks in River Oaks call him."

Edwin affirmed Tripp's smirk with a chuckle as they turned. The attaché squared away the meeting area as Tripp flopped on a couch and threw his feet onto the coffee table. He noticed a large book.

"It's an extra copy of the parting gift I gave them," Edwin said. "Thought you'd like one."

Tripp read the title: *El Valle: The Rio Grande Delta*. He opened it, and the world of the wood-columned lodge faded as he beheld photos of the Rio Grande Valley, where tropical forest, salt-soil wilderness, and beach sands met. Animals both common and rare looked at him from generous color close-ups. Plants displayed their blooming beauty.

"This is a good land. What's left of it."

Edwin came into view above the book. "Tripp, I don't want to break the bubble on your hard-earned moment of solitude, but we have a lot of planning to do between now and the opening of our new roasting facility. With your permission, I'd like to contact the San Antonio team. They have a Zoom call with the Columbia growers tomorrow."

"Sure, Eddie. Use the conference room." Tripp flopped on a couch before the window.

Edwin scanned his phone notes. "Chase lands in Waco in half an hour. She sent you a memo from her meeting with Pike Sorensen of Parks and Wildlife. It went well."

"That's good. Chase sent me a quick text about it along with a pic. I remember that guy from when we released the zebras. He warned me those animals had an attitude, and did they ever! No love lost between the camera crew and those characters."

"Yeah, I know. Also, Pike and Chase wrote up a report for how you can mitigate the impact of your new structures."

"I noticed that. Thanks. And, speaking of Chase, I've gotta look into the creek damage she's worried about. Get the engineers on it, Eddie. Permit people too. I'm sure there's a long lecture in their report about that creek."

"Will do. Tripp, are you free later to check the quarterlies before they go public?"

He rubbed his eyes and did not speak for a time. "No, Eddie. It's all good. You go ahead. I need a breather. Just cross-check with the exec team and send it to press."

"All right. Tripp, are you okay?"

He sighed. "Kind of—I mean, yes, of course. Just…just tired, that's all. No sweat left to pour from my brow after charming my guests with emus served like filet mignon. Great-tasting stuff, wouldn't you say?"

"Yes, that balsamic drizzle made all the difference."

"Who would have thought that olive oil and brown sugar could be persuasive enough to ensure funding for a 260,000-acre business venture!"

Tripp threw his hand toward Edwin in a lazy high-five from the couch.

"Good night, Eddie."

"Good night."

Edwin left. Tripp stared at the wall of windows. It was night now, and the glass panels were black and blank because of interior lighting. Beyond the windows, in his mind's eye, he saw the mother bobcat staring at him from the tree line.

"We're both wild at heart, but I'm behind glass like some app."

He poured himself whiskey on ice and returned to the couch. His body deflated with a sigh, his lips flapping the last of the air like a work-worn horse. The open book lay before him on the table. He put the glass down and picked it up, browsing the pictures, cradling the large volume in his lap. Then, in the midst of the colorful pages, a black-and-white image came before his eyes, an old photo upon which the photographer, a Mr. Wright from San Benito, had scribbled these words:

TIGER CAT. 7½ FOOT LONG.
WEIGHT 200 POUNDS, CAUGHT JAN. 30, 1946

It was the last jaguar of the Rio Grande Valley. The cutline beside the photo said so. There he was, strung dead on a rope, surrounded by men and boys of uncertain conclusions about what they had done.

Tripp looked long at the jaguar.

"The last one. The last jaguar of the Valley. Extinct now... Extinct...except for Chase's guest."

And the thought of that last jaguar, combined with the news of the new one, settled like a sliver of whittled wood upon the many other thoughts piled beneath the table of his ever-working mind. A thought that was aflame.

Tripp fell asleep.
There, in Eden's Bend, he dreamed.

He was standing in an ITM board meeting. Leather-bound presentation portfolios lay open before each board member. Water bottles stood like guards at their right hands, bottles so cold that sweat rolled down their sides and formed pools at their bases. The conference room had no visible light fixtures, but the members of his board were each lit from above by a single glaring beam, casting angled shadows down their faces. At the head of the table was a huge, dormant flatscreen. Tripp searched the screen for action, but no picture broke onto it.

He scanned the ceiling, invisible in the darkness. Rows of ITM apps cruised in formation like a convoy of ships while he watched them like a hunted submarine. Tripp reached up to grasp the apps and place them before his board members in their folders, but his hand struck an invisible pane of glass.

Let me open 'em, then. He tapped the glass. None responded. The apps kept sailing until they disappeared into the oblivion at the edge of the ceiling. He beat the glass. The apps cruised on. He prepared to give a defense to the board members.

Then, on the flatscreen, a jaguar appeared, wrestling an alligator in a marsh. The reptile's tail swung about and splashed water out of the screen and onto Tripp and the boardroom table. A murky stream began flowing from the puddles on the table, lifting the portfolios and tipping the bottles.

"I can explain! Be patient, please!"

But the board members scowled. The chairman rose.

Tripp lifted his hands to calm the board. "Give me time to find the words!"

But no words came.

The chairman opened his mouth, drawing in a deep breath as if to pronounce an official decree committed to memory well before the board meeting had begun.

But the chairman never spoke, for at that moment the jaguar in the flatscreen rose up, pulling the reptile onto his hind legs. Both beasts fell out of the screen and slammed onto the flooded table, locked in combat. Lifting his dread paw, the jaguar struck the alligator with such force that he reeled back and slithered off the table. Victorious, the jungle cat turned and faced Tripp at eye level, staring into him with a zealous flame from beryl-green eyes. The jaguar roared.

Tripp awoke and sat up, blinking hard. A hint of morning touched the glass, a gray color holding hues of pallid yellow and bashful pink. In the stillness, one arm's length outside the window, a bobwhite quail stood still, pausing from foraging, perceiving the movement of the prince behind the glass. Unseen bobwhites piped the call of their kind, and the one before him responded.

Tripp slid a hand down his face from forehead to chin. He noticed the glass of whiskey. It was still full. The ice had melted. The picture book still lay in his lap, the photo before him.

"That was no black-and-white memory."

5

RETURN OF THE SPIRIT

As Tripp dreamed, Oracle was awake. Far to the north, in the Waco zoo, the lord of the Valley paced within view of a tribe of spider monkeys. The cat of the Yucatán sensed them gathering on the uppermost cable of their trapeze, which, like the crow's nest of a ship, overlooked not only the jaguar's home but much of the zoo. Oracle kept watch, pacing, turning, and pacing again, following a trail of earth the shape of his dwelling, a path made by the nameless pacer who had dwelled there before him. Sabal palm saplings, newly planted by Man, bobbed drowsily as he brushed past them. A hibiscus bush slept, and a young mahogany tree, newly transplanted like the flowers and palms, slumbered in the shock of the change.

The moon, waning gibbous, rose at midnight in the east to impart her strength to the lord of the Valley. Her faint kiss touched the pane of glass through which Man watched him during daylight hours. Oracle could just make out the smudges of a child's hands on the glass where he had lain sideways across the stone supporting the window. Oracle had greeted the boy in parallel form, lying on his side across the same stone, the clear barrier in between, touching the glass with his paws where the child's hands were. The onlookers had smiled, the boy too, and all hearts warmed. But here in the dead of night, the glass was as silent as a sheet of Arctic ice

56

flung far from its polar home. Oracle saw the moon's reflection in it and turned his face up toward her.

"Greetings, you who see the friends of my long journey," he whispered. "Greet them for me, from the monarch in her Sian Ka'an hibiscus home, to the Fair Bandit who borrows, to the manchild the birds have named Miracle."

"I will," the moon said. Her arc across the heavens was low; as she rose, she journeyed southward and entered the shadows of the cottonwood trees, where a flock of grackles slumbered. Beyond the trees flowed the Brazos River in a long, meandering arm.

Oracle sighed. "Oh moon, if I could reach the river, it would carry me all the way to the Gulf of Mexico and the long bar of sand reaching even as far as the place where Miracle washed ashore. The black crowned night herons speak the map to one another."

"Yes, it is so," the moon whispered. "You could reach the beach and travel it back to the place where Miracle came to shore. From there you could find him again. From there you could find the friends. But I depart now behind the leafy veil of the trees. Another will have to tell you all I know. Until I rise above them and return to bless you, lift your eyes to the stars."

Oracle did so. The constellation Pegasus rose above the cottonwoods hiding the moon. The winged horse whinnied for joy, bejeweled by the double star Enif at his nose while the quadrant stars Alpheratz, Scheat, Markab, and Algenib adorned his body. Oracle searched both in and around the Great Square these four guardians made, and as he did, new wonders whispered in their midst: spiraling galaxies. Spinning planets. Swirling quasars. Gatherings of stars whose brilliance struck into one another like the flames of a thousand candles touching at the wicks. Enough awe in one spot in the sky to be soul-armor for a seer below if he could take in that much perspective.

I will take this in.

And yet, even as the cat drank in the joy of the sight, from the rim of his vision, he saw spasms of hand motions as the spider monkeys ordered one another to be absolutely still. The cat of the House of Panthera Onca turned his eyes upon the chief spider monkey, who seemed suddenly unaware of Oracle as she shivered and threw an angry stare at her kin. She spoke in a harsh whisper to her tribe.

"Who brought the cold air up here, you rat-tailed squealers?"

"How can we bring cold air up here, impertinent queen?" retorted a monkey. "Who can catch it? Who can tell it what to do?"

"Silence, you ignorant ingrate," the chieftainess replied. "You mightn't have brought it, but you certainly *called* it. I can feel it coming and going."

"It's that *spirit!*" a mother monkey said as she clutched her suckling infant close.

Oracle considered the spider monkeys. *Although they are huddled close together, each one behaves as if utterly alone.* He watched each one search the dark with horror.

"I'll throw a fig at it!" a youth shouted. "Maybe it will do more to that spirit than it does to that jaguar. He doesn't get mad no matter how many figs I pelt him with!"

Oracle smiled. *Nor will I ever be angry over your figs. Their debris attracts the birds and the possums, and I impart to them the Breath of Remembrance. Then, little by little, the air of this whole mangarden changes for the better. The effect of your figs is more fruitful than you know and goes further than you can throw!*

Oracle's thoughts returned to the drama above, for another spider monkey, one who appeared to be the oldest, spoke.

"Hush! You know nothing at all. That spirit is *wind*, you see, and *breath*. A whole basket of figs would do nothing to stop it—not even a whole fig tree, leaves and all! There is nothing you can do against what it throws at *you*..."

"What does it throw?" the young one said.

Oracle watched the old spider monkey stare into a patch of starless sky, eyes wide as saucers.

"*Fear...*"

And with that, a blast of howling cold swept over the cat and the line of spider monkeys. The lord of the Valley remained unmoved, though the fur of his coat rippled like a field of grass before a gale. But the primates curled over until all that showed were quaking backs on a quivering cable.

The spirit hovered midway between the place of the jaguar and the spider monkeys. It glared at the cat. Oracle looked upon it but did not let his gaze linger there. Instead, he chose to look *through* it, spirit that it was, and focused on the stars in the sky beyond, just as the moon had encouraged him to do.

The spirit growled. "Stare on, oh cat. Stare into the black hole of space until your eyes grow dim. You did not listen to *me*, and so here you *are*. My curse prevailed over your silly dreams."

Oracle continued to look at the stars. He traced a path among them to the south. "What you say is what you see, but there is more than one way to tell this story."

The spirit scoffed. "Oh, a witty cat you are. A witty kitty! Use your smart head, your very wise head. Use your 'logic,' as the sages of Man would say. Did I not curse you to your face when you defied the way things are in your unfenced Sian Ka'an where you roamed wild and free? Did I not pronounce your doom when you refused the law of hospitality between my kind and yours? Behold what has befallen. You have lost the path. You are trapped in a place you did not want to go.

'Lord of the Valley' you call yourself? See, now you are lord of the *Pit*. That is who you are."

"Say no more," Oracle growled.

The spider monkeys whooped in nervous response—and in glee at seeing a new drama more important than all their domestic squabbles put together.

"Lord of the Pit," they twittered. "Lord of the Pit. That's who he is. Lord of the Pit! Lord of the Pit!" And they forgot their fear as they scorned the cat below.

"Ah, yes, yes, that is who he is," jested the spirit. "But the lord of the Pit makes a decree to 'say no more.' And such a proper decree from this sovereign. It is prudent to 'say no more' before the *truth* would be told. What more is there to say *but* the truth? You made a fatal error refusing to let me in, oh Cat of the No-Name Valley. A *grave* mistake. For the folly of honoring Kahoo the Grave, you have dug your *own*." And the spirit shrieked in laughter as it juggled its pun before the captive king.

"I am of a different spirit," Oracle declared. "No sorrow of soul will replace that center. I refuse to live in the story you tell. I choose the story I remember. The story of the Beginning, when the Namer named all living things."

"Do not bore me with that talk. It is rotten food and poison drink to hear it, and you know it. You know in your heart it has passed away. The darkness says so."

"I know in my heart who speaks in the dark. His light says so. He is the Lion of Eden. I remember his breath. I remember *him*."

And Oracle roared the call of the jaguar, the call of a king declaring the land within the sound of his voice to be his own.

The spirit shrieked and disappeared. A sound rushed through the night air, and then all was swallowed into a silence as dark as the inside of a coffin door. No one breathed. No one moved.

From the shadows of the cottonwood trees, a commotion erupted. The roost of sleeping grackles quaked in the throes of a collective nightmare, flapping and squawking as they awoke. They cursed and pecked one another in terror at what they had just seen. Then a grackle twice as large and loud as the rest appeared in their midst and thrust himself into the air above them. He dove at the cat. The grackles saw and followed, sweeping down upon Oracle in a swarm of thrashing claws and beaks.

"Go for his eyes, his eyes!" the lead grackle commanded. "Take away his vision. It is the same as taking his life!"

At first, Oracle attempted to swat every bird coming at him, and for a time, he succeeded, batting and bruising each one with the swiftness of a great lord from the deep jungle of Sian Ka'an. The birds were not accustomed to such fierceness, preferring as they did the parking lot prey of discarded fast food and half-dead vermin. But the cries of their injured brethren doubled their zeal to avenge the fallen. Soon they were clouding around Oracle so closely he could not counter all of them. He closed his eyes and flailed blindly at the flock.

The lead grackle spread his wings unnaturally broad over the battle. "We are winning, winning! The spoil of the eyes is ours!" And the spider monkeys shrieked at the spectacle.

At that moment Oracle made a choice. *I will let them do what they will, but I will open my eyes and protect their grace to see. I will defend my field of vision.*

And Oracle did so. No matter how many grackles plucked and tore at his coat, no matter how many welts and wounds began to seep through his fur of ruddy gold, Oracle fixed his mind on one thing: the protection of his vision. And with the arena of combat limited to this one place, the cat fought his foes one at a time. Some of those grackles never flew again, and the ones who did live to see the light of day warned their offspring to never mock a cat with rosette spots.

The lead bird fell and disappeared in the confusion. The black-feathered cloud lifted and scattered. Silence once again descended upon the zoo, where all the animals pondered in wide-awake stillness what they had just heard under a torn-open sky.

6

THE GRIN OF THE HERON

Later in the evening, as the moon rose above the trees and Pegasus cantered along the zenith, the broad wings of a great blue heron sailed by. Oracle watched the bird's gentle shadow cross the stars. The heron circled, dipped his neck to spy out a spot below, and landed beneath the young mahogany beside the cat of rosette spots.

"Hail, Lord of the Valley," the heron said. "The Colony of the Lost sends you salutations."

Oracle bowed. "Greetings, Father. Welcome to my green captivity. How did you find me?"

"You can thank the black-crowned night herons. They saw your arrival from their treetop roosts and sent word to kin on the coast, where I patrolled looking for any clue to where you might have gone. I heard their scuttlebutt at the mouth of the ole muddy river neighboring this place. 'That's a sure clue,' I told the night herons.

"But they added a word of their own to the rumor. It seemed the quail, with their mysterious songs in the night, had amazed my cousins with a tale of how they had helped you find the lost tree of Kahoo, the 'Lonely Tree,' they called it, and also the 'Lovely Tree'—seems you gave it a new name. I had heard about the Lonely Tree when the falcon of my flock mentioned it. He called you 'the Cat Who Remembers.' It seems he himself has remembered some marvelous things since he met you! But, being an aplomado and all, he's not chatty about the details.

"Anyway, when the night crowners told me all they had heard, I said, 'Much obliged. You've given me twigs from the nest I seek.' And I turned my wings upriver and followed the rumors from heron to heron till I found you. There was just enough strength left in these aching, hollow bones for the search. I'm grateful I found you before they gave out!" And he slowly stretched his wings before folding them again.

Oracle's eyes brightened. "How are my friends?"

"They're well, I reckon, but not without troubles. Good news first: The manchild Miracle is on the mend, and Patch found new friends to help him with the errand you had given him—a barn-sour horse named Plod and an ode-singing toad named Bog. The horse carried the child, and the toad sussed out the roads less traveled. That pair is from a manrealm called Eden's Bend."

Oracle curled and uncurled his tail. "Eden's Bend…The name rings true in my heart. I was there. I saw the tracks of Fair Bandit and Miracle; both entered a stable in that place, but coming out of it were the tracks of a horse followed by the raccoon. Yes, just prior to discovering the Lonely Tree, that is what I had found."

The blue heron bobbed his head. "Well then, your way weaves tighter with your friends than you reckoned. It's like when my egret neighbors fish with me in the fog. We share the same pool but not the same view."

Oracle marveled at the homespun sage. "Your bird's eye view helps me see what I cannot see, and your beak speaks what I need to hear. A welcome consolation."

"Well, thank you for the kind word, but there's more to tell that ain't exactly a plume of feathers. Your friends hit quite a headwind. They plodded their way to the lighthouse, but no one was home—only left-behind things that couldn't tell their story. So, Patch advised they all meet you in the Sanctuary of Sabal Palms, for he knew you had set out to go there. Among the palms they stumbled upon a Man fleeing Men like a spooked deer. He took the manchild Miracle to his refuge, next to Eden's Bend, but he left Patch and his helpers alone. They searched for a sign of where the manchild's parents might be, and of all the places they could have gone, they found one right back where the horse and toad were from, Eden's Bend! But clear on the other end of it, about as far from their stable as you could go and still be in that manrealm. A sign way down south.

"And what a sign it was! The raccoon and his friends found a tower strong enough to kick back at the ground with flames telling it goodbye. Men found them at that tower and took them to a new barn they had built. Now your friend Patch and your friend Miracle dwell side by side in two manrealms joined by ironthorn."

Oracle rose and paced the perimeter of his exhibit. He turned to the heron. "The news is both good and troubling. It is good to know where they are. It is troubling I cannot meet them."

"Well, as my kind are fond of saying, 'A missed meeting is a new greeting.' Something will work out, I reckon. There's always a minnow in the shallows if you wait long enough for it." Though his beak was long and straight, the heron was grinning. Oracle could tell.

"Your words are good for feathers, but they take time to sink through fur. I will carry your words until they make a den in me. Thank you."

The heron cocked his head and craned it forward, throwing his wings out as he did.

"Why, you're hurt! Couldn't see it in the dark before. My lands, you've been cut up by some ornery critters! And…well, I'll be! What's this? There's a few of them slain under the palmettos!"

"Yes, Father. An enemy came and robbed me of rest, first with the fraud of words and then with the force of a violent beak leading others in blind rage. A spirit."

The heron raised a wing toward Oracle. "Put a paw to its mouth, and it will be the end of both beak and talk."

Oracle shook his head. "I cannot shut its mouth with my paw any more than it can direct my thoughts with its words. It is free to speak, but I am free to choose. I choose to send its words into captivity, away from the helm of my heart."

Oracle slowed, then stopped. "Nevertheless, its accusations pierce me like fangs, for when I lean on the memory of what has happened since I found the Lonely Tree, what the spirit says seems true. It pronounced an undoing of my path, and behold, I am here in a world bound by the walls Man has placed around me. I put my paw forward to fulfill the prayer of the last jaguar as best I could, but now I am far from the Valley and everything familiar to me. It appears the spirit's curse has prevailed."

Silence descended on the cat and the heron. A breeze rustled the cottonwood trees, now empty of grackles. The leaves murmured, then seemed to applaud as the wind picked up for a moment before dying away. One cottonwood creaked in response to the breeze, a tree so ancient he still knew the story of healing springs that had bled heavenly water onto the river's soft banks before the Days of the Bow had been broken. The tree sighed as he drowsed in the drought-dry soil.

"But there is the dream," Oracle said.

"The dream?" the heron asked. "Did you see the dream this night?"

"No, I saw it many moons ago in the Yucatán. The dream is a place the spirit cannot go, nor can its words touch it, for it took place in my heart of hearts, where no one but the Maker can enter."

"Tell me what you saw."

"As I walked through the wetlands of Sian Ka'an, I came upon a great and noble cat. From his head flowed a mane taking in the flames of the sun, but he rested so quietly upon the earth he filled the air with the smell of fresh water. 'This is the lion our fathers have told us about,' I said to myself. 'It is the Lion of Eden.'

> *There is no sound and yet he roars*
> *There are no wings and yet he soars*
> *The air is clear yet full of rain*
> *And crowns the lion's love with pain*

"I could not prevent my eyes from gazing upon him, for he was lovelier than all the colors of feather, stone, and sky. I knew that to look away was to depart from life itself—though in the looking at him, something in me died. But after that death, I was free to explore where the two of us were. I saw beside the lion a lively creek speaking with a voice of laughter. It washed a million tiny gems gleaming with the colors of the rainbow and deeper hues besides, colors so deep I have no names to describe them. Behind the lion grew a tall banana tree.

"I bowed before the lion. He rose and greeted me. Then he spoke to me in the secret tongue of my fathers.

"'What will you give for this banana tree?' he asked.

"'One paw for the sake of the green,' I told him. 'The black and the yellow belong to the air and the sun.'

"'What if the sun will not have the yellow?' he asked me.

67

"'For them I give two,' I replied. 'If the heat comes, I will cover them.'

"'What if the air will not have the black?' he asked.

"'For them I give three,' I said. 'If they drop, I will gather them.'

"'And the root?'

"'For the root I give everything—heart, head, and paws.'

"Then the lion sang to me. I found the song itself singing in me too. The river rose as we sang until everything was inside the flood, and the flood, too, was singing. We were all together inside the singing river—the lion, the banana tree, the jungle, and I. No wave moved us, nor did any current sweep us away. The air was fresh beneath the waters.

"And before I realized it—truly I do not recall even blinking—I found the lion was no longer there, but in his place stood many animals, some familiar, some strange, but all confident in the call of their kinds. And as I listened to the sound of their calls, I found I stood on the shore of the sea, and the sun was setting where the animals had been."

The heron mused upon the vision. The crickets sang their nocturnes to one another, and the cicadas hummed their litanies. A breeze, warm and weary but carrying the fragrance of the honeysuckle, caressed the mahogany, who swayed dreamily.

The heron startled as if a firefly had just flashed past his eye. He grinned. Then he lifted a foot and pointed at the Cat Who Remembers. "If, in the dream, a river swallowed you, but you didn't drown, I take it as a good sign. You're alive, are you not? More alive than that spirit, I dare say. It's just a cold wind blowing hot air, but *you* are warm-blooded and full-bodied! That spirit can tell you what went wrong, but it can't tell you where you're going."

Oracle smiled. "Thank you. In this bitter hour, your words are as the hummingbird to the hibiscus. Fitting and sweet." And he bowed to the heron.

The bird returned the honor with outspread wings of blue-feathered blessing:

> *Do what you will, do what you must*
> *Keep your coat and shake the dust*
> *Find the path and set the pace*
> *Cross the creek that floods with grace*

Oracle received the blessing.

The heron strode to the glass observation panel, and, with a single, feather-aided stride, perched on the faux stones above it. "I depart now for the long flight home. What word would you have me bring your friends?"

"Deliver these words to Patch—and to his friends Bog and Plod, who are now my friends, too. Send these words to fill the gap marking our paths and fill that space with strength:

> *Oh distant friends beyond the rim*
> *Beyond the wall of what I see*
> *The surface of the tale is grim*
> *And vaulted into mystery*
>
> *No one can make unbent the grass*
> *Or circumvent the spider lines*
> *For through them everyone must pass*
> *Or trip on hidden, tangled vines*

Yet this I vow till sands have slipped
And filled up Waiting's bitter urn
I will endure the sharp-edged tip
Of separation out of turn

Until the open path is shown
And brings a springtime to this song
Until I fish with friends at home
And walk the realm where I belong

"But to Fair Bandit himself, deliver this command:

Carry the knot you can't untie
Carry the knot before you
For every seed of hope that dies
Seedlings will sprout behind you

Council I'll hold when I return
Council for those in hiding
Meanwhile be brave with friend and foe
Courage in heart abiding!

The heron received the words, rolling them like oak barrels into the storehouse of his memory. He drew his frame together, neck bent as if on the brim of a secret, gathering his power for the burst needed to break from the law of the ground to the way of the air. Then he leaped aloft, and, with no need to search or speak with anyone, returned to the Valley in half the time it had taken him to arrive. And the only burden he carried was one that put strength in his bones, the message of a king from a distant land to the realm where he was lord.

7

THE OATH OF THE CORAL SNAKE

The jaguar is wounded, Chase! He's got marks all over him except for his eyes."

Chase looked at the ceiling from her pillow and pictured the cat there. It was 4:12 a.m., and the night's lead for the zoo management team had called until he had broken through her phone's sleep mode. She sat up.

"What do you think happened?"

The lead hesitated before he answered. "It's crazy to say it, but it looks like he got into a fight with some grackles. There are several of them dead in his exhibit and a couple limping around the zoo, making an awful noise. Feathers everywhere. That fight must have been a sight to see."

"Thanks for calling me right away. Prepare a place for him at the infirmary. I'll get there as soon as I can."

Chase drove to work on autopilot, her eyes guiding both body and vehicle to the zoo as her mind moved through a library of possibilities, referencing what she knew and comparing it to the news of the battle between the jaguar and the grackles. She slowed to a stop at a carless traffic signal. Gently swaying from her rearview mirror was her father's dream catcher, a Cheyenne work truer to the tradition than the store-bought kind. Her parking spot was the first and closest to the zoo staff entrance and labeled accordingly: Reserved for Director.

71

Guiding her team, Chase put the injured animal to sleep and transported him to the infirmary. There they cleaned his wounds. Chase examined them closely.

"These are beak marks. Beak and bird claw. They went after him, or else he somehow provoked them to attack."

"But grackles don't behave that way, Chase," a teammate said, "and jaguars don't pick fights with birds. How on earth could this be?"

"I don't know how. I only know it happened. The marks make that clear."

Chase placed her right hand on the side of the sleeping jaguar. As the cat breathed, she felt his warm aliveness rising and falling beneath her hand.

Feels like the lapping edge of a great ocean.

She stepped back and took the whole animal in.

"Let's leave him to rest. I'm taking an hour off to call my father."

After she left, the novice of the team turned to the others.

"What's up with her? What's her dad got to do with this?"

"It's all good," said the team lead. "You'll see. When she's got a question, she calls her dad. He's on the ruling council of the Cheyenne Nation, something called an 'Old Chief,' I think. You know, the kind of person everyone listens to 'cause they know what they're talking about. Chase listens too. Not your average father-daughter relationship."

"They problem solve offline a lot around here," a team-mate explained. "You won't find Chase thinking out loud. She's about as opposite of a verbal processor as you could find. But the silence isn't a mood for Chase. It's how she handles life. When she finally speaks, it's only after she's done a whole lot of listening."

"And the longer the period of silence, the weightier the words when she finally breaks it," the team lead said.

The novice thought aloud. "So, she's searching for an answer to the mystery of the marks of the grackles by thinking it over and talking to her dad."

"You got it," replied the lead. "It's that simple. But just wait and see. She'll nail it. Does every time. More than any talker I've ever worked for, at least. More than the kind of boss who blows her own horn."

—⁂—

Oracle awoke. Above him a bank of fluorescent lights stood guard. A lone fly crept along one of the illuminated tubes, unafraid of the energy throbbing beneath her feet. She cocked her head and cleaned her forelegs. Curiosity kept her looking at the cat.

The aroma of another animal reached Oracle. He raised his head. Across the room, through the bars of a pen, a broad, striped face appeared, stark in bold colors of orange, black, and white. But the nose was dry and leathery, worn from a lifetime of breathing captive air. And the eyes, though glinting with pride, gazed at him through fatigued frames, as if the boldness of the stripes had outpaced the strength of their wearer.

"Welcome, my many-spotted cousin!" the tiger said. "A good deal of trouble you went through to get here! The hedgehogs who tunnel under us tell me Man caught you in the south and brought you in with secret fanfare. They say your lair is opposite mine, across the great manstone pond that is drying out in these rainless days."

"Thank you, my many-striped cousin. Yes, Man brought me here not long after I had entered a manrealm to the south. He hunted me down with the darts of sleep, not death, and he welcomed me here in this walled garden as a friend, not a foe. But last night a foe did find me, one not in the body of a Man. And the wounds of that war brought me into your company. Now, tell me about this realm we live in, for I see that you precede me."

The tiger turned his body in a slow twist, stretching out on his side and grunting as he did. "You are in the plushest prison you could dream of. All your needs are provided for—except one. A wooded park surrounds this mangarden we dwell in. On one side is a great ridge of tree-covered limestone, and on another side a river. But you will never climb the ridge, nor will you ever swim the river. You will only smell the waters of what might have been." And the tiger's eyes set themselves on a thought known only to him.

"A river to smell but never to touch," Oracle mused. "That is the way of the manrealms: the good is close enough to smell but never under the paw of the one who smells it."

The tiger growled a low moan. "I am weary of smelling it but never swimming it."

Oracle looked deeper into the tiger. "Tell me what you know, for I see in your eyes you do not only gaze at the sunset of what might have been but the dawn of what could be."

"Listen, cousin! The hedgehogs have told me of a way of escape. One day I will take it! I will break out and run for the river. I will swim—or die trying. I have lived half alive too long."

"How long have you lived here?"

The tiger sighed with a mix of gratitude and disgruntlement. "Long enough to become ill and well and ill again. Man is at work to take away the ache in my bones. That is why I am here and not in my bamboo garden. Man pierces me with steel stems, but they smart only a little, and what they contain helps my body rest for a time. Today they will return me to my walled estate by the manstone pond."

The hum of an air conditioner filled the silence. The fly leaped into a pattern of crazed aerobatics before landing on the same fluorescent tube in the exact same spot. Below her, Oracle watched the escape vision fade before the tiger's eyes, and, in its place, many memories paraded in a great circle. Oracle leaned gently forward.

"Tell me your story."

And so, the tiger did, though he told the story into the air, never looking at Oracle, as if the tiger were making a solemn oration before the senate of creation.

"I am the tiger Crash. In my cub days, I was the mascot of a company of players, a circus called the Wildwood Wanderers. They kept me like a house cat and trusted me as much until the day I tore into their food box and ate all the flesh I could find. Then they knew it was time to reward my growing up with a rhinestone collar and a chain. I became the symbol of their enterprise, beautiful and behind bars for all to see but none to touch. In time they trained me to perform before crowds whose mouths gaped half empty in awe and half full with the feed of their red-striped boxes. I jumped and roared my way through show after show.

"But in the end, like all beasts, I grew old and could no longer lead Man to wonder. Instead, I drew pity. So, my masters retired me to the sideshow, where I sat and licked my paws while children gawked. Then they brought me here.

"That is my story. It is a far cry from the tales of my ancestors, yes, a far cry from those who challenged princes and met glorious ends as trophies both alive and dead for the thrones of empires. Alas, the unleapable canyon between what was and what is!

"But whatever faded glory I may have inherited I have pounced upon, and I have played my part. A flame still flickers within me. I will pounce one last time."

Oracle considered the flame within his cousin.

There is beauty in it, but also vanity. There is boldness, but also recklessness. We are like-hearted, but not like-minded. To be sure, two are better than one when both desire to escape, but to escape with him is to yoke myself to his ways. That is a great risk. But, oh, how the river beckons me! How it calls my name! Perhaps the risk is worth it. Perhaps we were meant to risk together for a time.

Oracle spoke. "Your heart to pounce once more must begin where you are, so tell me about the bamboo garden where Man has retired you."

Crash groaned. "It is small—oh, how ashamed I would be if my forefathers saw what I rule! Yet it is good in its smallness. Its plants and soil, even its very stones, are from the great continent where my ancestors placed their paws. Begrudgingly, I admit it better than the bars of the Wildwood Wanderers, but for all its pleasantness, it is bound by walls and wires and the great manstone pond. It is not free, and I am not free. It is a hollow paradise. I would rather face the dangers of the realm of sturdy timbers north of here toward a place called the Red River, where deer prance in abundance—so the mockingbirds tell me."

"You want to escape, then?"

"I want to be a *tiger* and roam until I find my territory."

"But you are a ruling animal, too wild and too free for Man. He may only permit you a few days' freedom before he finds you and returns you here or else strikes you with the flying lead and sends you to the place of your ancestors."

"True, oh cousin, but in my eyes, it is better to run free for a moment than to be bound for a lifetime. I have waited too long. The leaves of my tree grow thin. I am in my autumn days. Better to run and fall than to never run at all!"

Oracle considered the words. *They smell of something gloriously old, yet intermingled in them is the scent of something off, like the sting of an overripe papaya fallen and fermenting in the path.*

He spoke. "Crash, I, too, desire to roam my territory. I, too, desire an open door to go there, however bound my time may be by Man's Three Choices:

To set me free and leave me be
To set a snare and pledge to care
Or send me back into the dust
My spirit to the Maker trust

"Where is your territory?" Crash said.

"It is the Valley, the place of the Great River far to the south, what Man calls the Rio Grande and the *Río Bravo* in the other mantongue of that realm. I am the new lord of the animal kingdom there. Like you, I must do what I must do, be that season short or long."

"New lord of the Valley, eh? The Valley is your home? Were you born there or did you win it in battle?"

"I was led there."

"Who leads us, oh cousin? We are the chieftains of the animal kingdom."

Oracle looked into the eyes of the tiger. "A story bigger than ourselves leads us if we will but listen to it. Open ears led me to my home, and it is home indeed, for I have made friends there. But my birthplace is Sian Ka'an of the Yucatán, a realm of deep forests and sacred dreams. I chose to seek the Valley when I learned from a monarch butterfly that no jaguar had ruled there for seventy springs. For ten moons I journeyed until I found the Lady River, who borders the Valley. With her help I crossed and found the Lonely Tree, where Kahoo the Grave had prayed for a successor before he died. I came, the Lonely Tree bloomed, and all looked as if it would become lovely. But Man took me before I could do more."

Crash stirred his aching frame. "What more is there to do?"

"To call a Council of the Cats and a Court of the Animals, beginning with the bobcat and ocelot, the stewards of the Valley, who rule a fallen feline realm. The cougars have exiled themselves to track the ghosts of Man, and there was another cat, a member of the council, called the jaguarundi. He has vanished, I am told. I must call the remaining stewards and their tribes together. I must speak to them. I must breathe on them what I remember from the Days of First Things, when the Namer named us."

Crash rose on all fours. "'The Days of First Things?' I have not heard those words since I was a cub leaning on the bosom of my mother. You speak of something from dreams I have long forgotten like a path swept away by a mudslide. And this 'Council of the Cats' you speak of: What good is it in these remnant days of ironthorn and circuses?"

Oracle also rose, his tail lithe and swaying. "It is good the feline remnant rule as they did before, as living things and not survivors only. Should the flower not bloom even if it spans only a day? Yes, I say, it should bloom, for otherwise, no one will behold it and the message the Maker has hidden there."

Crash lowered his head as if searching the floor for something, then lifted it again. "I see. It is a lofty thing you aspire to."

"It is a *loving* thing I aspire to. If others call it lofty, that is their choice, and it may be true. But as for me, love requires I impart my power to those who can go further than I ever will. The stewards should rule as *rulers* and not as caretakers of an endless interim, even if one of the stewards is missing. My time as their lord may be short or long, but either way, it will taper to an end like the branch of a tree. I would that

that end be fruitful, a branch ripe with others who remember their names."

"You speak as if legacy and love were the same thing."

"They are, oh cousin, for the one who lives it so."

Crash lowered his body to a sphinxlike pose, his tail moving in slow curves. "And what is this 'Court of the Animals' you speak of? I have heard of gatherings of a single tribe or even a tribe of tribes, like the Parliament of Fowls generations ago, when the birds debated the ways of love and marriage. But for all tribes of land and air to assemble in one gathering? I have not heard of such a thing since the days of the Long Sleep in the House of the Fallen Trees, when Father Noah ruled us."

Oracle growled in hope. "All the more reason creation should assemble. If the animals gathered during the Long Sleep, how much more should they gather awake and watchful, for then they could live their days fully alive, be those days short or long. And of a truth, as my father told me in my youth, such courts of the animals *have* taken place since the days of Noah, though tradition forbids the keeping of the record of those gatherings save only in the heart of the Maker, who sees all things."

The tiger turned onto his side in response to bodily pain. "Your words awaken something in me I did not know was asleep. But I cannot grasp it with my ears at first hearing, for my life has been confined to one closed circle of honor and shame. So go on. Tell me of your aspired quest, should you break free of this barred garden."

Oracle's whiskers brushed the bars of his pen as he spoke to the tiger. "Though the jaguarundi is no more, if the ruling bobcat and ocelot are willing, I will summon the animals in assembly, which they have not done since Kahoo the Grave held court in the days of their ancestors. I must speak to the Court of the Animals words that will be seeds of life for the

79

time when I am no longer lord of the Valley. For I, like you, am too wild, too free to remain long in the land before Man sets a boundary line on me, be that the realm of death or be that the realm of earth with pits and fences like the ones greeting our eyes each morning. We shall see. For now, I am indeed planted in a boundaried dwelling place along with you and a hundred other creatures in the captive garden Man has built for us. But this captivity must give way to activity, be that tomorrow or many moons from now. Yes, somehow it must."

Crash stirred the words into his heart with a long, slow growl.

"Then let us go together, you and I. Let us leave this manmade maze however we can—I to roam free among the scampering deer, and you to return to the Valley, where the Court and the Council await your rule. Yes! Let us do this noble deed! And if we do not reach the places we have set our paws toward, it will still be a glorious ending, one worthy of a song."

"I cannot foretell whether a song will be sung or not," Oracle said. "My paw is set on beginning, not on ending. I will let the end come as it may, for I cannot command the end any more than I can command the clouds to cover or discover the moon. Yet if my end and yours are worthy of a song that jaguars sing in the night to their newborns or tiger cubs hear from their tender mothers, so be it. Our lives are songs, our memories are blessed echoes, and all together they are whispers of the Singer who thought of us before the Beginning."

Crash closed his eyes. "Your words travel a river too deep for me to cross. I am sure they swim a stream that's full of good fish, but I find no footing for my paw there, no ground for contemplation. All I know is *action*. That is *my* depth, cousin. I will leave the deeper thoughts to you."

—〰—

The light hummed. The air conditioner poured cool air into the quiet that followed their conversation. The fly took off for another round of whirling circles, this time more slowly, her course curving to the flow of air from the air conditioner's louvered mouth. It shut off, having brought the room to the commanded temperature, leaving only the sound of the buzzing fly until she ceased her dance.

Crash righted himself and leaned forward. "The jaguarundis have not vanished, cousin."

"What? Truly? But the animals of the Valley have told me so, as have the trees."

"The coral snake knows a secret, and so does the turtle."

"How do *you* know?"

The tiger moved his tail from side to side on the floor of his pen. "In the winter, while I lay here for another illness, Man brought in a jaguarundi. Though her form feigned an otter, I realized she was a cousin, a cat native to the land. They doctored her from the wounds of the road, and she hung on for six days. In the end, her wounds won, but before she died, we had the nights to tell our stories to one another, and she told me that relatives of hers live in hiding, siblings far to the south in a place she called the Valley—*your* Valley, I suppose. She said they were the only family of jaguarundis there, and they had made the coral snake swear an oath to keep the location of their lair a secret. For a mother coral snake had found their home by accident while she sought a place to lay her eggs, and the jaguarundis had laid unsheathed paws upon her in warning, chanting:

Red and yellow kill a fellow
But we have the upper paw
Each of us now owns a stripe
And binds it to a solemn law

Lay your eggs, oh caring mother
Raise your brood in secret here
But you may not tell another
Of our hiding place so dear

Bind we now your tongue to silence
Bind we head and stripe and tail
To the sharing of this knowledge
To the showing of the trail

Just the turtle knows this secret
Only he our dwelling place
Had discovered ere you came here
Only with him is there grace

To discuss this darkened knowledge
To disclose the hidden lair
Only with the turtle present
Can your secret see the air

"The coral snake submitted, and the jaguarundis spared her life. She laid her eggs, and each season since then, her offspring return to birth their broods in the jaguarundis' home. The clan of corals who descend from that first mother have spread far and wide. They know one another through a riddle they speak, a riddle about the jaguarundi, whom they call the *shadow cat*. This is the secret name the corals gave the jaguarundi so their serpent tongues never slip with the knowledge of that tribe and its hidden lair. Yes, as with many things in the long history of Man and beast that the corals keep, they speak of the jaguarundi in ciphers and codes."

Oracle rocked back and forth with possibilities as he ruminated upon the revelation. "What else did our suffering cousin tell you before her body failed her in this house of healing where we lie?"

Crash whispered intensely. "She passed on a secret behind the secret, a hidden trail. On the day she knew she would draw breath no more, she confided in me that if a stranger seeks the riddle and answers wrongly, the coral snake will bite, and her poison will kill the stranger member by member—first paw, then leg, then heart—until Death covers the animal and brings him back to the dust from which he came without ever knowing the home of the shadow cat.

"But if the stranger can answer the riddle, the coral snake will give him a password. It is not the name of the *place* of the shadow cats, for the coral snake is bound by oath to never tell. It is a word to be delivered to the turtles, for the turtles are not under oath. The shadow cats did not think it necessary to bind them to an oath, for turtles speak so seldom and slowly that few among those who walk or fly have the patience to wait for them to speak their knowledge. The turtles pass their days in silent meditation before the sun, and they disappear beneath the water the moment movement makes a ripple in the air. But the password produces a peace stronger than the safety of the pond. It gives the turtles just enough trust in the stranger to no longer call him a stranger but a *seeker*. They answer his request. Yes, oh cousin, they, the turtles, will tell you where the shadow cats live."

Oracle savored the secret. "Oh, how helpful the grackles have been to send me here! What good news their rage has led me to! If I ever see the Valley again and hold a Council of the Cats, I will honor you at it. For now there is a way for the Cats of the Three Tribes to become complete again! The ocelot and the bobcat may find their missing third, the shadow cat, and the lord of the Valley can be at rest even if he himself returns to the shadows. I am grateful."

The tiger sighed and chuffed a sound of pleasure. "I am grateful too. We have redeemed the fatal wound of our fellow feline."

Oracle took in a deep breath. "Now, tell me, Crash, what is this way of escape you boast of? What have the hedgehogs told you?"

Crash had just opened his mouth to answer when the infirmary door opened. A Woman with the bearing of nobility entered with her team, which moved the tiger from his pen to a rolling crate as he groaned a loud lament for what might have been. The fly followed him and the team out, but the leading Woman lingered.

In the space of stillness serving the two living things remaining in the room, Oracle studied the Woman. Her face, with its high forehead and well-defined cheekbones, spoke of her Northern Cheyenne heritage. An invisible mantle crowned her dark hair and descended over the shoulders, a legacy from a time when the mantle was not only visible, but wielded great power. As they looked at one another, Oracle saw the deep brown of her eyes fill with a knowing. She opened her mouth, pausing as if letting the words form into a substance of her spirit and not her soul only:

"I am named Chasing Eagle. My father tells me you are a chief who has chosen the longest trail of your tribe, the trail called Surrender. The moon sees where you began, and the moon sees where you are destined to go. The grackles gave you gifts of wisdom, one for each injury, for a chief becomes chief indeed when he passes through pain. Then he is ready for the rest of the trail, for the wisdom that comes from being wounded will remain a sign like moss on the face of a tree, guiding him. Such a chief will not depart that longest trail; he will not lose his way. He will reach home."

8

INSIDE THE LITTLE GARDEN

While Patch, Plod, and Bog fled before the Men of El Dragón, Papá Eli and Ubi took Paco to El Pequeño Jardín. The way was fraught with gadflies feasting on horse-flesh and manflesh. Paco clung to the saddle horn as Papá Eli urged the horse onward. Ahead of them Ubi rode with one hand on the reins and a raised pistol in the other. All three jolted up and down, the sweat of their foreheads stinging their eyes. Each stab of a horsefly and jarring of the body length-ened time, strengthened the power of the heat, and weakened the hope of escape.

But in the rugged heart of the forest, full of fallen trunks where ATVs could not easily follow, Ubi and Papá Eli turned their horses in a slowly bending way through the trees, which, over the course of the afternoon and evening, placed them back on a path toward Papá Eli's ranch.

At twilight they reached it. A narrow path wound through thick and thorny guajillo trees. The guajillo gave way to bris-tling yucca, whose spiky leaves prodded the travelers into a single-file line.

Then at a turn in the trail, the wilderness disappeared before a carefully manicured lawn. Though the blades of grass were as even as a golf course, the ground was not, for all the trees had been cut down, and the roots remained as subtle mounds. Soaker hoses crept through the grass like snakes, dripping their precious commodity, and in the center of the lawn stood a huddled mass of trees.

Paco forgot his fatigue. *The grass is the sea, and the trees are an island. I hope Mamá and Papá found an island. One without volcanoes!*

Papá Eli's island grew larger before Paco. Brazilian creeper vines covered eight-foot walls. Above them, the shaggy heads of unpruned sabal, acacia, and bougainvillea protruded in a tangle of branches no landscape architect would have tolerated. Taller still were a score of Washingtonia palms dusting the sky with fronds waving to the rhythm of the Gulf Coast breeze.

Now that the illusion of the island was dispelled, it looked to Paco like nothing more than a great untamed thicket. But the fading light caught a copper roof among the trees, the straight edge and sloping angle hinting at a grand house. The flutter and snap of a pennant on the pinnacle of a grain silo drew the boy's eye. When he looked forward again, they were before a gate, faded rose in color, partially hidden by the surrounding vines.

The shadow of a sentry appeared in front of the gate. "They have left, señores."

Ubi, Papá Eli, and Paco passed through groaning gates and dismounted inside the compound. The front door bore a small viewing portal, a hatch behind wrought iron bars with a carven stone frame. A servant peered through the portal then opened the door. The three entered the foyer of the mansion, a room paved with flagstones of fired earthenware and Spanish Colonial-era walls.

A servant brought them ice water. The three fugitives did not speak but drank and wondered. The old man asked for a hand towel and bowl. He wiped the dirt-crusted sweat from the boy's face, then did the same for his own.

Papá Eli set his hands on his hips and breathed a sigh of relief. "Come, son. Let us go to my office. It is the inner room. There we will talk while my staff sponges down the horses and prepares your room. I smell the cook warming up Lupita's world-famous tamales. It is my housekeeper's secret recipe, you know. She refuses to even tell *me* what she puts in it, but it is clear she has special connections in Oaxaca. I tell you, if it weren't for her tamales, I'd have to wait in line like everyone else at Delia's in McAllen!" And he winked at the boy.

Once inside the office, the first thing Paco noticed was the aquarium. It was big enough for him to swim in, stretching from floor to ceiling and filling the center of the room as an immense, translucent-blue column. Inside at its center was a reef-like arrangement of stones hosting tunnels, corals, and sea anemones.

Before the aquarium were two leather-bound chairs, and behind the aquarium, a mahogany executive desk. Paco sat in one of the chairs while Papá Eli went to his desk. As Paco watched him through the aquarium, the shape of the old man stretched wide and vaporous, and a wreath of fish crowned his head.

The child pondered the slow ballet of sea creatures moving between him and his host. A mandarin fish bedecked in orange and cyan robes waved his fabric-like pectoral fins in arabesque motions at a passing blue tang. The eyes of the vivid oval creature warily monitored a bright-yellow butterfly fish proudly parading in the opposite direction. Flame angels and pink basslets played tag with one another. A school of neon gobies choreographed a starburst away from a blood-red hawkfish. And their dance revealed a song in the sea to the boy:

Beneath the waves, beyond the tide
Above the crab-clawed creature's shell
Where southern stingrays slowly glide
With horse-eyed jacks in carousel

Grouper, snapper, redfish, drum
Greet damsel and tang unicorn
Who joust with tarpon on the run
In gin-clear waters every morn

Sharks with fins tipped chimney-soot
Patrolling reefs and caverns dark
Where no airbreather's placed his foot
Since ages before Noah's Ark:

The box with all of Eden bound
That overshadowed silent deep
And from which came a hopeful sound
That woke us from our darkened sleep

"Son."

The word brought the boy back above the waves. It was Papá Eli. He was sitting down across from the boy.

"Tell me about your parents."

Paco sat up. "My father gave me a special name, and my mother gave me a special gift."

"Tell me about them—the name and the gift."

The child's eyes now looked upon something only he could see, and he gave words to what he saw. "One day I was in the plaza with Papá and Mamá—the place the towers ring and sing. There were many pigeons in the plaza, many pigeons and doves. They were white, black, and gray. The sun found purply-pink-and-blue colors on them too, colors like

89

the skimmers on Papá's morning coffee. There were so many birds they looked like a cloud creeping along the ground—a cloud that cooed!"

The boy leaned forward, eyes aglow in delight. "People were feeding the cloud on the ground, but I wanted to see the cloud fly in the air, for that is where a flock of birds makes its best cloud. So, I ran into the middle of the birds. Yes, I ran very fast! And the birds burst up in a storm. They filled the air. They flew around the towers. They circled and they spun, and the bells began to ring! Their song flew with every wing! Then the birds carried the song to every corner of the city. Every corner of Mérida. I sent the song because I ran.

"When I came back to Papá and Mamá, I looked at them and smiled. They smiled too. Papá said, 'You are not only Paco. You have another name: *Potrillo*. Little Colt!' And from that day on, Papá called me *Potrillo* whenever I ran."

Papá Eli placed his elbows on his knees, fingers pressed one to the other while the index fingers pushed into his mustache.

"Are your eyes hurting?" Paco asked.

"No, why?"

"Because you keep blinking hard."

"No, no, it's just that I can see the birds you describe. I can see them take flight. I can see their wings. Yes, those beautiful wings. You are a good storyteller."

He cleared his throat and straightened himself. "Potrillo: So, that is the special name Papá gave you. And Mamá? What was her gift? You said she gave you a special one."

A joyous wonder fell over Paco's face. He pulled a marble out of his pocket, one of the precious treasures Patch had given him. He slowly rotated it before his eyes, beholding the colored swirls within the little orb, peering as deeply as he could into the wavy tricolor bands. He pulled out another, and another, and still more, including the one he had rescued from the sea.

Then, from the bottom of his pocket, he lifted the thick threads of the old woolen saddle blanket Patch had given him for comfort's sake at the stable of Plod and Bog. The yarn-like, rough-hewn strands carried the colors of indigo, persimmon, and wine, among others dusty white and dark gray.

Placing the threads beside him in the chair, he lifted the seven marbles in the palm of his hand until they filled the place before his face.

Papá Eli drew near and beheld them too, each one displaying the still-life elegance of a flame, or leaf, or river, or cloud: each one a world within a world. Each one a story in need of a voice. Paco spoke.

"One morning when my eyes opened, I looked down where the bed met the wall. The dust was awake there. It looked like a baby rabbit. She had a gift sitting in her paws. 'Here you are!' the bunny said. I reached down and found what she was holding out to me: a marble! A blue-and-green marble! I fished it out. The sunlight played catch with the dust. Then I looked inside the marble."

He picked the marble from the sea and held it up. He peered into it so deeply Papá Eli was drawn into the marble too, where bubbles suspended inside the glass echoed in still life the bubbles streaming up the aquarium glass behind it as the boy continued.

"Mamá asked me, 'Where did you find that?'

"'Behind the bed,' I said. 'I saw it when I woke up.' I showed her where.

"'Then you are blessed today,' she said. I went outside to hold up the marble to the sky, for there was blue in it, and I knew the blue of the marble liked the blue of the sky.

"But the bully of the block found me. He and his gang, they found me. They saw me from the end of the street holding up the marble.

"'Look!' the bully shouted. 'His papá calls him *Potrillo*, but his real name is *Patillo*—Little Duck! He deserves it! For he does not walk like we walk! He is not like us!' And they blocked me when I tried to go away. Then the bully saw my hand.

"'Whatcha got there?' he said.

"I stood as tall as I could. I looked him in the eye. 'I found it in my house,' I said. 'I found it in my room. It is mine.'

"'Ha!' he said. 'You forget. The *block* is mine! The *marble's* mine!' He threw me down. The boys he bossed held me to the ground. 'The Stealer of the Marble has broken the law!' the bully shouted. 'He is a thief! He is a robber! Take from him what's mine! Mine!' And they beat me like they beat their dogs. But I held the marble tight. The more they hurt me, the more I held on. My head got hot, but the marble was cool like rain. I could feel it, and it made me strong. But they stomped my arm with their shoes until my hand would not obey me anymore. They took the marble I found. They took the treasure that spoke to me.

"'Punish the thief!' they shouted. 'Let us prepare Little Duck for dinner! Yank his feathers off!' They laughed at me. 'Pluck the duck! Pluck the duck!' And they did…They did."

The boy returned the marbles to his pocket, and his hands dropped. One hand touched the strands of the saddle blanket. Paco pushed them into the crevice of the chair between the arm and the seat cushion. He sat motionless.

Papá Eli clasped his chin as if he were an author trying hard to change the plot of a book he had already written and could find no way to unwrite. He sat up and gave a moment of silence for Paco to breathe while the fish swam slowly behind him. The old man felt for the rosary in his pocket, a gift his mother had given him. He formed an *L* with his arms, the rosaried hand touching his lips while the other hand supported the arm at the elbow. He pushed a single bead forward with his thumb. The boy continued.

"But for Christmas, Mamá gave me a gift, a gift that made me forget the bruises of the bully. It was a jar of marbles! Marbles of every kind! Red and yellow and the color of the old car we played in, the one with no wheels! One was green like an apple! One was pink like a gumball! One looked like the glass from Grandma's bottle, the one she always had in her purse. There were marbles from a box of Chinese checkers. They looked like the colors of everything sweet! Aguas frescas and jiggly flan! Key lime pie and ice-cold paletas!

"And do you know, Papá Eli, do you know the marbles never tell the same story twice? Each time I play with them, yes, each time I send one of them flying into the rest, their story never turns out like the one before—except that I laugh every time!"

The old man grinned. "It's been a long time since I played marbles. A long time since I've laughed with them. How pleasant to remember those days... That's quite a jar of marbles your mamá gave you!"

"Yes, even the jar itself was a gift. For do you know, Papá Eli, do you know what is special about the home of the marbles? The jar smells like *recado rojo*: cumin, oregano, garlic, and cloves! If you smell it, Papá Eli, if you smell it and close your eyes, do you know where the marbles take you? To the spice stalls of the *mercado*! To the place where people move like a river. To the place where they say 'Hello' and 'How much?' And it takes you to the table where Mamá gives Papá food—and many others too, so many that sometimes they do not eat: family and friends and neighbors and guests!

Yes, if you ever smell the jar of the marbles, that is where it takes you."

Papá Eli gazed at the boy. "You describe a world within a world. A home where no one hurts anyone, and where no story ever turns out the same as the one before. It's been a long time since I've known such a place." The old man closed his eyes and looked away, dismissing a sniffle with a quick brush of his hand. "Where is the jar now, son? Is it lost?"

"No, Grandfather, I left the jar with the bakers. Mamá told me I had to because we were going a long way north and could not take many things.

"'One day you can come back to get it,' she told me, 'one day when you are tall and strong. Your marbles will be here when you return, for the bakers are faithful. They always remain, for people always need bread. And your marbles will remain with the bakers. Your jar will keep company with the sacks of flour. Your jar will take their dust, but the flour will take none of your marbles. Your treasures will sleep long, but they will not forget who they belong to. The bakers will not forget either. When you return, your marbles will know it. They will wake up, and you can have them all. But, for now, choose ten. They will keep you company on the journey.'

"And they did. They laughed inside my pocket. They reminded me they were there when the sun came up and when the sun went down. That is when I took them out. They were always loud when the sun was low! And in the dark, long rides in the rooms with no windows, they whispered to me."

Papá Eli wiped a finger across each eye. "It was good of your parents to let you bring some of your marbles."

"Yes, it was. Out of all we left behind, we each brought something. Papá brought his goggles—dark, round eyes he used to put on in the place where he worked, the place where he wrote with fire. He took iron from rusty things and made new things out of it. I remember one day he was angry with me because I watched him work.

"'Do not look!' he shouted. 'It will make you blind!'

"'But Papá,' I said, 'how can I see what you do unless I look?'

"'You have to become blind first,' he said. I did not understand. Then he placed goggles over my eyes, and I lost my sight even though it was day. All was blank. I could not move. Then, out of the darkness, I saw the spark of Papá's tool. A star came from it. The star wrote its name on one face of metal, then another, until the two faces were lifelong friends. The star stopped shining. All went dark again. I sat still. Then Papá lifted the goggles from my eyes, and I saw he had goggles on his forehead too. He smiled at me.

"'You see?' he said. 'That is how it works. If you say, "I can see by myself," your eyes will soon fail you here. But if you place your father's eyes on, then you will see, and it will do you no harm. And not only will you see what I am doing, but you will learn and grow and build like me.'"

Papá Eli fingered his rosary, beholding the child as if before a church icon which, though at first seems flat and simple, becomes deeper the longer you look at it. He sniffled and swallowed.

"You father is wise. Your mother too. And your mother? What special thing did she bring?"

Paco continued with an air of both sorrow and wonder. "The night before we left Mérida, Papá gave Mamá a moonstone for the journey. 'This will sing to you when the moon is missing,' he said, and he kissed her hair.

"The next morning Mamá woke me so early my marbles were still sleeping. She bent down and kissed me on the forehead. She smelled like roses.

"'Time to go,' she said.

"'Will we fly on an airplane? I see them fly so high! I want to fly high too!'

"'No, Potrillo, we will travel on the roads and rails. You will see. But you will have to learn to sit still for a long time.'

"'How long?'" I asked.

"'Until we reach San Antonio,' she said. That must be an important place, because it takes longer to say *San-An-ton-i-o* than it does to say *Mér-i-da*.

"So, I did learn to sit still for a long time—a very long time. So long I knew that Mérida must be on one end of the world and San Antonio on the other.

"The days lost their names. The night stopped saying hello to the morning. The evening stopped saying goodbye to the sun. I never knew which one would be there when I woke up. I learned to hide under Mamá's poncho. I placed my head in her scarf. It was safe and smelled like home. It did not change. The places outside changed, places outside the big metal box we sat in. That is why I stayed with Mamá's scarf. And I learned the name of the thing we sat in. I learned the name of the train. They called her *La Bestia*."

Papá Eli shut his eyes at the word.

"What's wrong?" Paco asked. "I think something hurts."

"Nothing, child, it's, it's called a migraine. Certain sounds set it off. But continue. Tell me your story."

"All right. One day, my father said, 'Tonight you will not sleep, for we are going on a boat.'

"'What will the boat be like?' I asked him. 'Will it have flags?'

"'I do not think so,' Papá said. 'Rags, perhaps, but not flags.'

"'Will the boat have green and red lights?'

"'I do not think so,' Papá said. 'Green and red are too bright.'

"'Will the captain have a gold anchor on his hat?'
"'Gold teeth, perhaps, but no gold anchor.'"
Color flushed through Papá Eli's face, making his mustache look whiter than before. "That would be Sergio."

—ɯ—

Two taps in the center of the office door broke into the story without warning: two taps, a pause, and a third tap in the upper left corner.

Paco watched Papá Eli, on whom the sound of the knocking dawned like the voice of an old friend. "Come in, Ubi."

He entered and shook both of Papá Eli's outstretched hands while the rosary dangled. "You gave the old code."

"Yes," Ubi replied. "For old time's sake. Thought it might cheer you after what we just escaped. It is a blessing you are well. That ambush was much too close."

Papá Eli stroked his chin with a pistol-shaped hand. "Yes, it was, but the news of the fall of our friends in Matamoros waters down the blessing."

"A tragic loss," Ubi said with a sullen brow. "*Mis condolencias, señor.*"

"They were good men, those two," Papá Eli murmured, looking downward. "Like sons." He pressed his fingers until the blood drained from their tips. Then he stared with a searchlight glare into the eyes of his operative.

"Any word on the goods? Their truck was fully loaded."

Ubi shook his head. "No word, señor. But without a doubt, El Dragón has moved them to another town by now."

Papá Eli's nostrils flared. Breathing out a long sigh, he rose. He turned to Paco, pointing to a place before the aquarium.

"Stand over there, son, and watch the perfect world behind the glass while I think about what to do with you."

Paco did as he was told, but he could still see his host behind him, seated and stroking his mustache, for the glass reflected it where the faux reef within the aquarium provided a darker hue.

"Did the truck have people in it?" Paco asked the reflection. "Mamá and Papá and I were in a truck too. Before *La Bestia*. It was loud. It was full of people."

"No, son, the truck we are talking about was not full of people. It was full of what people crave. But it is gone now." Papá Eli pinched his brow. "My arm grows shorter and my shadow grows longer."

A spotted moray eel caught Paco's eye as it emerged from the crevice of a rock.

Ubi spoke. "If only your brother were still here, El Dragón would respect our truce."

"He is no more, God keep his soul," replied Papá Eli. "The Federales have their trophy."

Paco followed the gaze of the eel upward. A servant, a young man from Chiapas state in southernmost Mexico, opened the trapdoor above the tank, which came down from the room on the floor above. He poured out a plastic bucketful of live minnows and brine shrimp, which, for the more aggressive members of the aquarium community, was an essential routine to keep them from devouring their more delicate co-inhabitants who fed on smaller, spineless things. The dusty pink cloud of freshly dumped shrimp did not remain long; the fish inhaled most of them before they could scatter like the minnows had.

"Loyalty to our friends in the capital is costly," said Papá Eli. "Still, I am glad we have remained true to them. To be faithful to the sons of our godfathers is to keep a clear conscience."

"But at what a cost!" Ubi said as he brought a hand down on the back of his boss's chair. "We are reduced to vassals who fend off El Dragón while he lays siege to us! All we have left is our connection in Nuevo Progreso!"

Paco watched a minnow disappear into the eel's mouth.

Papá Eli acknowledged Ubi's comment with a nod. "We shall see who prevails by Christmas. Either we will keep that route open with gifts, or El Dragón will take it with bullets. *Plata o plomo*, as they say."

"They are traitors who broke away!" Ubi vented. "I trained them myself!"

"Ubi, they *had* to break away, for they were not really *us* in the first place. We are family, Ubi, *family*. They are not. We are *honorable*. We protect our connections. We do what we promise. Our yes means yes, and our no means no. That is what sets us apart from El Dragón."

Paco turned and looked into Papá Eli's eyes, and when the old man saw this, he rose and faced the aquarium, placing his hands behind his back like a field marshal surveying his parade ground.

Paco watched the fish along with him. A minnow darted away from one pair of jaws and rushed into another. Papá Eli put his thumbs in his pockets, curling his fingers into gentle fists as he rocked on his heels.

"Son, every profession has its stigmas, but *we* have an *ethic* for our business, a clear expectation of how it is to be done. Those El Dragón people are *not* businessmen. They are carnivores! They do not reason. They only devour. Nothing is sacred to them."

Paco watched the eel withdraw into his hole. The white-haired man stared into the dark mouth where the beast had been and spoke to his reflection in the glass.

"It is time I retire. High time."

Papá Eli paced the space between the desk and the fish, and as he passed Paco, the boy turned and took the wrinkled hand of his host. The rosary swung like a time piece.

"You said you would help me. I will not let go until you do." And he stared into the old man's eyes, where many creatures swam in a worried deep. There was depth in Paco's eyes too, but in those waters, nothing moved, only a soul of fierceness and repose, like gems resting on an ocean floor.

Papá Eli removed his hand from the child's as if from a hot coal. He placed three pensive fingers upon his brow, puckering his lips back and forth as several sentences competed for airtime, though at length none won, and silence prevailed. He turned to his operative.

"Ubi, verify the room is ready for our honored guest. Make sure he has everything he needs. A hot meal, for one thing, and some decent clothes while Lupita tends to the lad's original. He lacks shoes; see to it he has some. Place one of the staff on the porch for the night just in case more guests arrive uninvited. The boy needs a good night's sleep before I help him tomorrow. I want to return him well fed and unharmed."

9

PAPÁ ELI'S WISH

Papá Eli found Paco at the kitchen table with a bowl of over-sugared shredded wheat and milk Ubi had provided for him. ("He got up before the sun," Ubi explained.) But now the kitchen was alive with the savor of a true breakfast in the making: burritos packed with eggs, two kinds of cheese, and three kinds of meat all laced with flavors red and green.

They ate breakfast together: Paco, Ubi, Papá Eli, and two security guards. The boy's goodness became for the others a buoy tethering their tongues, such that Ubi and the guards could say nothing evil. So, they filled their mouths with the goodness of the food. For a moment all forgot their troubles.

Papá Eli also savored the gift. "You remind me of a time in my life when I, too, was a boy. All day long I washed cars. The hard work made every meal taste like a feast and every night's sleep free of care. Each day I crowned the cars with foamy suds, and each day I poured rivers of water down their sides, making them spotless. The work put me under constant soap and water so that I, too, always emerged clean. Then, one day, a driver made me an offer for a better life. It was the last car I washed…And here we are."

The white-haired man paused in his eating, his hands folded over his food as he looked at the child, hair fresh from the shampoo Lupita the housekeeper had poured over him while he bathed.

After a space of time, he startled from his stillness. No one was looking up from their breakfasts. He took in a breath and flashed the beatific smile of an at-ease grandpa. Then, he summoned Paco and Ubi to his office. The master of El Pequeño Jardín propped his feet on his desk and placed his hands behind his head.

"Well, my boy, what are we to do with you today? I promised I would help you find out about your parents."

Paco hopped onto the desk and sat on its edge. "I know they are close! I asked the moon about her last night at my window. She kissed my face and woke me up. I held up a marble for her to see! I reminded her of Mamá. I know the moon will tell her I am well. I know the moon will see her and see me too. Mamá told me that before the stork brought me to her arms, she talked to the moon every night about me! She said the maker of the moon listened too."

Papá Eli gave a dubious look as he touched his fingers one to another. "Well, the moon is beautiful to talk to, but far away. I do not know her language, only the threat of her light on nights when darkness is an elusive friend, and she delays my deeds. But I can help you, son. Yes, I can. And when I do, I trust I will be helping myself as well, if the maker of the moon is taking note. A Christmas gift to myself."

Paco widened his eyes in curiosity. Papá Eli dropped his feet and set his elbows on his knees as he faced the child.

"You see, my son, I have done very bad things in my life, yes, many evil deeds when the moon was not looking. So many, in fact, that it has been decades since Papá Noel has visited Papá Eli. Yes, many Christmases have passed with nothing but coal in my stocking, and every lump has a story."

Paco looked puzzled. The old man rose and gently took the boy's hands. The thick aroma of Cuban tobacco and care-filled air reached Paco as he did, as if both host and guest were trapped inside a humidor. Papá Eli spoke in a whisper.

"My hands need washing, young man, and what can I do to get rid of the stains? I can hide here in my personal *Paraíso*, and that is well, for here I will sin no more. But how do I escape what I remember? Like flies, the memories cloud my paradise. I cannot shoo them away with hands that drip—" and here he caught himself.

Paco looked deep into the old man's eyes in search of something safe to trust in. Papá Eli let go of his hands and once again paced before the aquarium, speaking a soliloquy before the fish while the boy and Ubi listened.

"Before I left Matamoros, before I abandoned my mansion there, I had an operative named Sergio—the 'Tío Sergio' who piloted your boat with sunglasses on."

Paco climbed down from the desk and looked into the aquarium. "He grabbed my arm in the cold water. He threw me a jug and an ice box. 'Hold on to these and you will float!' he said. Then he shoved me away. Then the ship went away. Then he went away too."

"Yes, he went away all right," sneered Papá Eli, "back like a skunk to its den…But before the days of his bad smell, this tío was a good man, I say to you, very loyal and industrious. When I moved here to El Pequeño Jardín, I entrusted him with the care of my Matamoros properties, knowing they were in capable hands. But he fell away, for the shine of silver proved too much for him, and he broke his oath. Now he works for my enemy. He deserves a dozen curses for his betrayal, but I will not utter a single one of them again if he serves me one last time."

Papá Eli pulled out a phone, the older of the two he carried. He dialed and waited. Six times the line rang, six rounds of ringing, six rounds of silence. No one moved.

"*Dígame*," a voice said.

Papá Eli's face darkened. "So, old salt, you dumped your cargo in the water and swam for your life. You should be ashamed!"

"I couldn't help it! They didn't give me the right GPS for the meetup point. I struck a wreck or something!"

"How could you sink a ship in such shallow water?"

"How was I supposed to know about a drop-off?"

"Did you think to look at the map?"

"It didn't show it."

"You were drunk."

"I was alert!"

"You abandoned a child on the beach!"

"I saved him from drowning! Is that not good enough?"

"Look, no more arguing. El Dragón is your master now, but I call on you to honor your old oath one last time, hear me? The oath you broke! Make up for it, *hermano*. Make up for it! Obey the code one last time."

"What is it you want?"

"I want to know about the boy's parents."

Sergio did not answer. The aquarium machinery filled the silence, the rattle of air trapped in carbon chambers searching for a way to the surface.

"Well? Tell me…"

"What is it worth to you?"

"You snake!" hissed Papá Eli. "You would never—"

"Of course I would never…but El Dragón would, and I belong to him now."

"Oath breaker! I never should have called you!"

"Then you and the boy will never know. But such news has its price."

Papá Eli wiped his forehead. He glared at the phone angrily and lifted a thumb to cut the line. But the sight of Paco before him made his thumb unresponsive.

"All right, name your price."

"All you owed me when you fled."

"Where do I deliver it?"

"Diamondback Ranch. You know the old place?"

"Of course I do. Eden's Bend just bought it but hasn't touched it yet. It's still empty."

"Exactly. Come to me there, and I will tell you what you need to know."

"Give me time."

"Take all the time you want. My news won't change."

"How do I know your words are true?"

"You called upon the code, didn't you? I will obey it one last time, as you have requested."

"All right, then. I will meet you at Diamondback Ranch five days from now. Sunrise, Monday. The old blacksmith shop. It's a meetup point I'm sure coyotes like you are familiar with."

"Bring what you have promised, señor, and you will find out what you need to know."

"Very well. Let us see if you truly honor the code one last time. I know *I* will. Let us see if Diamondback Ranch is the place where promises are kept."

The phone line cut in Papá Eli's ear. Sweat poured from his face. He breathed an anxious sigh.

"Well, son, soon you will find out about Mamá and Papá."

Paco beamed with eager delight.

The white-haired man sank into his desk chair. "We will visit the deserted place north of our neighbor, one 'Tripp' of Eden's Bend—a new ranch, the envy of kings, ruled by an Anglo whose hair is still as black as a raven's. His hunger for land is ravenous too, and last month he acquired Diamondback. That is where our Tío Sergio told us to go. That is where promises are kept."

The child glowed with a memory. "Papá showed me a blacksmith shop in Mérida. A man woke up iron with a hammer. The iron was so awake, sparks flew into the air!"

"The iron at the blacksmith shop of Diamondback is not awake, son, nor has anyone heard a hammer blow there for years. And it is your good fortune that it is fast asleep, for soon Tripp will reawaken the ranch now that he has added it to his domain. Eden's Bend is a big place, my boy, very big indeed. Big enough for the flying tower you saw and for herds of strange beasts you have never seen before. A zoo without bars that tips the scales of fate in favor of the animals. May it be that my service to you tips the scales of fate in my favor too."

Papá Eli kissed his rosary. He stared into space.

"What are you looking at?" Paco asked.

"A hope."

"A hope?"

"Yes, like a morning glory blooming inside the thorn-scrub. Too much to explain, but I see a bloom the thorns haven't choked...Come here, son."

And he did so. Papá Eli gently placed his hands on the boy's shoulders.

"Once we are done with this dirty business of Tío Sergio, I will place you with my friends at Eden's Bend who work there. They will be your new tío and tía. They will make sure you go where you belong according to whatever Sergio tells us. They are dear people to me, like family. No children, but big hearts—too big for the world I live in, which is why they moved on. They wanted a simple life, and they found it. I am sure their sleep is sounder than mine and the trailer they live in safer than my vine-covered walls. Yes, my boy, they are richer than me by far. All they wanted in life was daily bread, a roof, and children. God gave them two of the three."

Paco saddened. "Thank you, Grandfather, but I like it here at El Pequeño Jardín. I like watching the fish."

Papá Eli sighed. "I like watching them too, son. But not every fish is safe in that beautiful blue world, and not everyone is safe in my little garden either. Especially you, my son. Especially you."

—⁓—

By the time the cook rang the triangle dinner bell at El Pequeño Jardín, Paco had given a name to every fish in the aquarium. He had also become friends with Guillermo, the servant from Chiapas, who had loaned him a set of quite baggy clothes while Lupita washed and mended Paco's own. Guillermo taught the boy how to feed the fish from the trapdoor above the aquarium into the bubbling swirl below.

The next day, Thursday, Paco became friends with Papá Eli's cockatiel, who, though for a time posed in aloof reluctance in imitation of his master, was attracted to the gentleness of the boy. For no vanity was in the manchild, no pride—making the bird's own pride useless. So, the well-feathered bird left his pride behind and rested on the boy's shoulder while he played marbles and worked through a coloring book Lupita had brought him with his clothes.

Friday morning, Papá Eli instructed Ubi to bring their guest finger paint, paper, pastels, and glue, and the boy found no end to what he could do with them. This delighted the old man so much that he allowed the boy to play in his office while he worked at his desk. And Ubi, though he usually paced the porch taking care of matters on his phone, found himself where Paco was, phone on silent, push notifications off, texting at leisure while the child softly sang over his creations.

On Saturday, when Papá Eli brought him a tin box of marbles, the boy's fascination was so complete that he had trouble persuading him to stop and eat.

"The marbles are dancing!" Paco said, with a tone of resolve. "They must finish their dance, or they will forget how they began." So Papá Eli obliged, though it cost them both the warmth of their meal.

Sunday was the man's weekly day of rest, a custom his mother had taught him and, so he had heard, had been the tradition of his father, whom he knew primarily by way of stories such as these and a handful of faint but hallowed memories behind a veil of first grief.

Paco rested too. He sat in a chair before the aquarium while Papá Eli reclined in the other. The boy munched a snack called doo dads, a vintage blend of pretzels, peanuts, Rice Chex, Corn Chex, and cheesy crackers, all marinated with enough spicy butter to successfully ensure an empty bowl. Paco's shoes—a gift from Guillermo and too big—rested one atop the other beneath the boy's bare feet while he browsed the completed coloring book.

Papá Eli pondered the life filling the tropical tank before him while he savored his ritual Kahlúa and coffee.

Ubi gave the code of knocks at the door. Papá Eli called him in, and he stood before his exiled king. "You called me?"

"Yes. While I sit here, I'd like to reflect on how the arboretum is proceeding before we get back to it tomorrow. What is the progress?"

"Señor Martinez informs me the Cambodian agarwood tree is en route. We found a way around Bangkok customs."

"And the birds-of-paradise?"

"One arrived from Papua New Guinea yesterday."

"And tell me of the fountains."

"Water lines are set, señor."

"That's good. What about climate control? Were you able to work out the issue with the power line junction?"

"Yes, Papá, we are moving forward. The final section of double casement glass goes up next week. Once we seal that last area, the crew from McAllen will start installing HVAC units and humidifiers. Then we will transfer the plants from the nursery. You should be able to release the birds into the arboretum whenever you want after that."

"Very good. It would seem we can confidently set a date for the grand opening party we will give the staff and ourselves after the plants have had some time to flourish. Let us therefore choose October twenty-eighth: the Feast of Saint Jude! The patron saint of those in desperate situations! How fitting it will be! What a perfect day to make my retirement official. A golden day to finally rest in my own little Eden."

In the quiet that followed, the aquarium aerator became the only sound. Paco closed his coloring book, dropped down from his chair, and watched a pair of clownfish nestled in the midst of the swaying poisonous tentacles of a large lavender sea anemone.

"What are they doing, Grandfather?"

"They are enjoying the protection of the anemone. You see, son, that creature is poisonous. It paralyzes the fish who touch it, and the victims become its meal."

"But those two fish…why don't they die?"

"They are special fish. They are immune to the poison."

"They are friends with the anem—, anem—"

"Anemone."

"Yes, the Amen Onie. They are friends with it?"

"You could say that, for other fish dare not attack them while they abide with their poisonous friend."

The master of El Pequeño Jardín smiled as he tapped Paco's shoulder. "We all need friends, son. We all need companions even if the match is wild and strange. It reminds me of a television show I watched when I was your age. Something that made a strong impression on me, a memory so vivid I can recall it as if it were yesterday. I watched a clever man named Walt Disney play with a Bengal tiger. It was in his office, lying across his desk—a mahogany desk just like mine here! Walt laughed and shooed the tiger off his papers the same way a man chides his house cat. I thought to myself, 'Now *that* is a companion!'"

Papá Eli's eyes grew large like Gollum's as he whispered at the edge of his chair. "It makes me wonder, son. It makes me wonder if such a thing were possible in my new arboretum. What if a noble cat were there? What if I fed him pampas deer? Then I could recline in my chaise lounge and watch. Then the cat, sated with fresh flesh, would recline beside me, and we could both retire in dignity and peace. Away from the jungle. Away from the hunt."

Paco looked intently, and in his heart, he saw three who warned him: Mamá, Papá, and the good cat who had listened to his story. The boy's face showed an anxious uncertainty, as when a summer-lake swimmer dreads snapping things lurking in the gloom below.

Papá Eli chuckled. "Don't be afraid, my boy. I am not El Dragón!"

He pulled out his phone, the newer of the two he carried. "Here, look, I have something to show you. You and Ubi, come here."

Paco and Ubi came to him, stood at his right and left hand, and fixed their eyes on his phone. What they saw caused them to lean in such that their faces were almost touching Papá

Eli's, yet no one was aware of the other for the awe set before them. This is what they saw:

It was a ninety-second night scene, faintly lit. The first seconds were a smear while the videographer steadied his phone. Next, out of the shadows of ghost-shaped mangroves, a large feline with rosette spots cautiously approached the edge of a river. He bowed, kissed the water with a brief drink, and looked around—even in the direction of the camera. Apparently, he concluded there was no danger, for he descended gracefully into the water and moved in seam-less transition from walking to paddling. The cat scanned the shore before him as he swam, then smoothly rose from the water and disappeared into the brush.

Papá Eli played the video again, but this time he paused it on the frame where the cat looked into the camera eye. He opened an InfoTech Menefee app called EdenUp, which compared the image to a database and identified the genus and species of the animal. It was *Panthera onca*, an apex pred-ator of the New World with rosette spots, stocky shoulders, and jaws of strength.

Paco's eyes widened as he looked into the cat's face. "My friend!" he whispered.

"So, there is no doubt about the rumor," Ubi said slowly. "A jaguar has returned to South Texas. Roaming and free."

Papá Eli turned to Ubi. The eyes of his master filled with the wildness of a lion too old to hunt but too hungry to remain at peace.

"I wish to have this jaguar."

Ubi's face betrayed his surprise, but his words were monotone.

"Yes, Papá, you wish to have it, alive or dead."

"I wish to have it *alive*."

Ubi took a slow breath. "Of course, Papá. Alive is better."

111

"What a pity it would be if the sheriff shot it in the name of safety, and what a pity it would be if someone captured it. For they would only send it to a vulgar zoo, a place of gaping, witless people; a diversion for overfed children making faces at a nobility they cannot discern."

"Yes, Papá, it would be a pity."

"But *I* discern, Ubi. *I* can *truly* appreciate this prince! I wish to save this creature from humiliation. I wish to save him for my collection in the arboretum."

Ubi was perfectly still but for his mouth. "A noble desire, Papá."

The old man turned to Paco.

"So, you like the cat too, don't you? He's your friend, eh? I heard you utter that word."

Paco considered what to say. *If I tell him more about my friend, it feels like pouring a bucket of feed into hungry waters, just as I do with Guillermo. That doesn't seem the right thing to do.*

The boy chose silence.

A movement in the aquarium caught Papá Eli's attention. He noticed a copperband butterfly fish casually sampling a rose-colored bubble-tip anemone. The master of El Pequeño Jardín stood and bent his head toward the glass, examining the scene.

"Ubi, ask Guillermo to find a more aggressive pair of clownfish for the tank so the butterflies will leave the bubble-tips alone. I want them only grazing the *pest* anemones."

"Yes, Papá."

"And send him to Eden's Bend. Tell him to give José and Lourdes this message: 'Leave the gate open between Eden's Bend and Diamondback Ranch before sunrise tomorrow morning. I have a gift to give you.'"

"Yes…Papá."

10

WHERE PROMISES ARE KEPT

It was the dawn of Monday, and there seemed to be no
gentle prelude to the sunrise, only the hot lamp of a sun
that took more than it gave. A worn Chevy pickup crept
east along the access road passing through Bear Claw Ranch,
rolling to a stop before the closed entrance of the neighboring
property. Paco, Ubi, and Papá Eli stepped out of the truck.
The road beyond the gate was empty. Neighboring trees—
scrubby evergreens and otherwise—flailed their arms against
a warm wind, turning their backs to the two men and the
little one who stood between them.

Paco considered the gate, his hand in his pocket, his fingers
in fellowship with the first seven marbles of his life after the
sorrow of the sea: the six the raccoon had given him in the
wilderness and the one he had grasped wildly as it dropped
into the abyss beneath him.

*The tin box marbles are good, but these are better. I know their
names, and they know me, and they know a story Grandfather
Eli does not know.*

The boy considered the gate's padlock.

*It has no heart or voice. It cannot see we are in a hurry. Like
the light bulb in the hiding place filling with water. The place of
Mamá and Papá.*

Ubi tried a doorbell button to an unseen dwelling. It was
broken. He leaned upon the gate, surveying the road as it

bent away from them between two culverts where scattered bags and empty bottles eluded anyone's care. A sign sank into sumac shrubs, leaves of mottled orange, red, and deep maroon matching the rash of rust on the sign they were devouring:

DIAMONDBACK RANCH

A long silence followed. The cicadas, hidden in the wind-bent weeds, roused themselves from slumber to give a rhythm to the waiting. Paco could hear them chanting:

Rising, but ever dying
Filling, but ever draining
Greening, but ever drying
Weeping, but hope remaining

Papá Eli surveyed the sky. A shred of a cloud passed overhead, the remnant of a great vaporous bank that had assailed the flaming adversary of the South Texas sun but had failed before a single drop could reach the earth. A lone Canada goose, out of place but calm, circled above him, watching.

Papá Eli shaded his eyes. "Brass and bronze. No rain for months. This land is as weary as the one looking at it. Let's leave."

They climbed in the truck, and Ubi turned it around. But at that moment in the rearview mirror, he spotted a pickup approaching. Ubi halted the truck, leaving it idling. He and Papá Eli stepped out to greet the two men who arrived and opened the gate.

Papá Eli stretched out his hands to grasp theirs. He did not let go as he spoke. *"¡Buen' día!* I am your neighbor at El Pequeño Jardín. I have an appointment here. I am looking for help with some family connections."

"Follow us," said one with no emotion. Papá Eli, Ubi, and the boy did so, truck following truck. Both drivers drove so slowly that no dust rose, and the vehicles followed one another so closely that it was as if an invisible rope pulled them in tandem toward an inexorable center. Paco watched the nameless guides in the cab ahead of them. Their heads jostled in unison each time the truck rolled over a bump in the two-rutted road; Paco and his stewards repeated that jostle as they rolled over the same terrain a moment later.

They turned off the road and crossed a grassy field littered with abandoned crawdad mounds, causing an off-rhythm *crunch* of the dry mud homes to punctuate the silence of grass blades flattening beneath the tires. The pickups passed a place of tree stumps and branches piled high, awaiting the fire. Along their right, the border of Diamondback Ranch appeared, a rusted memorial of humbled wires leaning before a second fence, tall and stainless. On its other side was a fresh gravel road, well-made compared to the nothing-trail the trucks ambled on. Papá Eli touched Paco's shoulder and pointed.

"That, my boy, is Eden's Bend. It is where you will stay with the tío and tía I told you about. See how new it looks! Its owner, Tripp, has done a lot to tame it."

"What are those shiny buildings far away?" Paco asked.

Papá Eli smirked. "That is one of many places where the prince of Eden's Bend tries to make money. In the case of the shiny buildings, it's emus and ostriches. He fattens those proud birds and sells their meat, oil, and leather. In doing so, he can pay the bills and make a way for many a noble animal to have its place under the sun. But, as with all things in this wicked world, for life to improve, lives must be sacrificed. The foolish ostrich thinks she is queen, but she is really just quota! The profit gained from her sale helps keep the place running for Tripp to live out his dreams."

115

Ubi glanced over at them while driving. "Fine Line Farms. That's what they call the northernmost part of the ranch."

Papá Eli set his face soberly ahead. "And a fine line it is that we are traveling. A fine line indeed."

Paco peered beyond the fence of Eden's Bend from the truck window. Grassless paddocks hosted metal pavilions. Shadows moved beneath the shelter of those roofs, whose metal deflected the sun into the boy's eyes with such intensity that he had to block the glare with his hand. He could just make out the shapes of tall birds inside the shelters: some parading their broad wings, others keeping watch on their presumed domain, most with heads bent toward what seemed to be troughs. From one pavilion, a chute funneled its way to a single gate before a metal building whose sharp edges cut into a cloudless sky.

Then a new scene came before the boy's eyes. Directly on the other side of the wire wall, a host of feathered folk gathered to evaluate the newcomers. First it was emus, who escorted the trucks with cocked heads, stepping with high-heeled motions parallel to the vehicles. Soon they met the boundary enclosing their paddock, a fence spanning away from Paco at a right angle to the two-car convoy. There the emus stood, no longer able to follow, but their escorting services transferred to a gathering of ostriches in the next paddock. The ostriches, taller and bolder than the emus, walked alongside the trucks in a gaggled mass at the fence, a crowd of curious heads on outstretched, stubbled columns of flesh.

Paco considered them, and it seemed to him as if they held him in contempt, peering down from necks that knew no mercy nor would receive any.

A motion below prompted Paco's eyes. A shadow skimmed the ground. He looked up: the goose was flying along with them, her wings coming into view now and then as she leaned first one way and then another in track with the draft of warm air radiating from the earth.

Paco looked in the direction the truck moved. A thicket of pigweed invaded the road beside a clump of madrone trees, whose branches twisted up with half-withered leaves lolling in the wind. Beyond it was a wooden structure listing hard to one side as if the removal of a single rusty nail would cause the whole thing to collapse. An age-darkened iron trough, crumpled on one end and bristling with branding irons, disclosed itself among the weeds, leading the curious eye to discover other objects strewn about the place as if dropped in mid-labor: hammers and tongs. Horseshoes sealed into rusty clusters like turtle pralines. An anvil anchored in sunbaked mud of brick-like hardness. Remnants of chutes and fences, brittle with age, leaned silently away from the direction a generation of winds had beaten them. Pokers and irons long forgotten by the fire now in fellowship with rust and dust.

The truck ahead stopped there. Across from it, framed within the new fence of Eden's Bend, was a small gate of wire mesh, a door of such modest size it required a grown man to stoop to pass through it. On the Eden's Bend side, a padlock hung on a latch loop, the lock's upside-down U gleaming open in the glare above its powerless brass body. A smoother portion of the gate bolt rested outside its sheath.

The ostriches escorting the trucks stopped at that spot, crowding one another in competition for a better view. Their knees, as calloused as those of camels, banged the latch, the open lock, and the loose gate as Paco watched them.

The men stepped out of the truck to join another who stood amid the debris. He was stout, and his face obscure, for sunglasses and the shadow of a straw cowboy hat covered it. He wore a butcher's apron smudged the ruddy color of his trade, a tinge that launderers' soap could only go so far in cleaning, for the stains of the blood were as deep in the fabric as tattoo ink dwells in skin.

Papá Eli opened the truck door and dropped the tip of a cane to the ground first. It was an awkward sort of cane of knotted but polished juniper, overly thick at the top with brass vaguely resembling the head of a bird instead of the traditional candy cane curve. Then, one aching leg at a time, Papá Eli stepped out of the truck.

Paco turned to Ubi with a confused look. "Grandfather moves slower than when we watched the fish. Is he not feeling well?"

Ubi said nothing. He grabbed a black backpack, the kind that students use, except for the surgical steel thread suturing it shut. He motioned to Paco to come out his side of the truck and join him.

"Hold my hand," he said. Paco took it. A power came from Ubi that at once ignored the child and guarded him, as when one feels the shoulder of a dog sitting still but intent on the shadow of a fox slinking in the bushes. Ubi and the boy stood behind Papá Eli.

The butcher doffed his hat. The shadow of the brim departed, leaving a mustachioed face bearing the sheen of perspiration on a hair-plastered brow. He took off his sunglasses for a moment to wipe his face.

"¡Buenos días, Sergio!" Papá Eli greeted him with two outstretched hands, covering those of the butcher and shaking them with unrelenting slowness until the others were shifting their feet. Then he turned to Ubi, who offered his boss the backpack. He handed it to Sergio.

Papá Eli smiled politely. "Here you are. All I owe you. Stacked, wrapped, and counted. You can verify it in our presence, should you desire. Would you like some wire cutters?"

Sergio received the sack and handed it to one of the men, who took it to the truck. "Not necessary," said Sergio as the man returned to his side. "You always keep the code."

"And it is so good of *you* to keep the code one last time. Now, please help me in these troubles I am too old to bear. Here is the boy. Tell us what happened to his parents."

Sergio looked down at the child. Paco returned the gaze with eyes piercing past Sergio's sunglasses, like a sunrise through a window where the curtains part.

Papá Eli leaned wearily on his cane. "What is your news? Where can I find his parents?"

Sergio motioned slightly with his head, and his two companions, seeing this, began to probe among the relics scattered on the ground.

"Izzi sent them back to Mérida."

"What! That is your 'news'?"

"Señor, I am only telling you what Izzi told me. I am sorry, but I have no other word."

"What do you mean you have 'no other word'? I delivered to you all you demanded! I kept my promise!"

"Sí, señor. I humbly receive it, and I thank you for keeping your promise. I have kept my promise too. Izzi told them the boy had died in the shipwreck and that they would see the same fate, too, if they remained here and contacted Border Patrol in search of his body. So, at the command of El Dragón, Izzi arranged for their departure. And now I must return to Matamoros with the boy to send him home too."

"But how am I supposed to believe you will actually send the boy all the way back to Mérida? It's a world away!"

"El Dragón's orders, señor. An order is not a discussion. Hand him to me, please."

Sergio motioned to Paco to come, but he remained as fixed to the ground as a tree stump.

119

Papá Eli stomped his cane. "But the *boy*! How can you *do* that to him! He has no part in our deeds! No share in our darkness!"

Sergio shook his head. "He does now. Wrong place at the wrong time. His parents saw too much. So did he. I must take him and send him away."

Papá Eli placed both hands fist-on-fist atop his cane as he stared at his former operative with anger. "It is common knowledge that El Dragón cares for no one but his pet Komodos. And it is also common knowledge that the dirt beneath his feet is a much more convenient place to send people than the other end of the country."

Sergio was silent. Behind him, one of his men reached down to pick up a branding iron. He considered its end as if unconcerned about the conversation. The other reached for a poker and did the same.

The old man's heart roared. He filled his lungs and squared his shoulders, hobbling forward, a hand on his hip. With teeth clenched, his lips began to move with every word seeping through an ever-tighter winepress of wrath.

"How do I even know you are telling me the truth in the first place?"

"I said I would keep the code one last time, señor," Sergio replied as if through the simmer of a pot at the boil. "They are *not here*. They are *not coming back*, but the boy can go to them. *That* is the *truth*. Truth enough, at least. Give him to me."

"But what if the boy's parents are minutes away and not in Mérida as you claim? And why should I believe that El Dragón would go through all the trouble of sending them back to the Yucatán when it would be easier for him to send them to their gr—" and he stopped himself.

"They rode La Bestia. So will the boy. It will cost him nothing."

Papá Eli laughed in scorn. "You really want me to believe you will send the boy back on La Bestia too? No one goes back once they have ridden that man-eating train! How do I know El Dragón won't just pawn the kid off in another deal with someone worse than himself—if there *is* such a one!"

"The parents left a token," said Sergio. He reached into his apron pocket and showed them an oval stone whose blue and white hues shimmered as if a mountain stream were passing over them, as if the gem radiated iridescent beams through heavenly waters.

Paco gasped. "Mamá! Her moonstone! The gift Papá gave her that sang in the night!"

Armed with iron rods, the two stepped forward to Sergio's side. Ubi let go of Paco's hand and stepped forward too, hands at the ready, brass button loosened to the knife on his belt.

Sensing the heat of the humans, the ostriches pressed harder against the fence, their pensive heads bobbing up and down in response to the waves of strength radiating into the air about them.

"El Dragón's orders," Sergio repeated.

Paco touched Papá Eli's hand. He looked down at the child through eyes that were weary lamps burning behind a glistening veil. He touched the boy's cheek.

"Son, my words have fallen to the ground. Forgive me."

A tear touched the old man's hand as Paco spoke. "No, Grandfather, you did what you promised. You told me you would help me find out about Mamá and Papá, and you have. Thank you."

Sergio stepped forward as the men raised their iron tools. Papá Eli stepped in front of the boy as he pushed him back.

A chill passed through the air. The ostriches trembled at what they felt and threw open their war plumes with a dreadful hiss. Paco and all the men turned at the sound, and the boy's eyes fell on the backs of the ostriches, now revealed by their outstretched wings.

Papá Eli returned his gaze toward his opponents while Ubi raised his fists and took an athletic stance. The white-haired master of El Pequeño Jardín squinted at the three men with a steel-plated stare and raised an accusing finger.

"I am old, 'Tío Sergio,' but do not cross me. The boy is under my protection. One more step and I will make sure you feel it."

He tossed his cane straight upward, grasping its narrow end, and there was no mistaking now as to why the cane looked more like a club than a walking stick. His opponents looked up at the weapon as the old man circled it above his head.

Ubi threw a Krav Maga knee strike into the torso of the nearest of the distracted men while Papá Eli brought the club down into a jackstraw pileup of arms and collarbones.

The man wielding the branding iron missed his mark as he fell backward. The man with the poker managed a glancing blow onto Ubi's back, but momentum was not in the poker's favor to slow Ubi's punches. The juniper cane crashed down on Sergio's menacing forearm. He lost hold of the moonstone.

It was the space of time Paco needed. He dove for the stone. In one rolling motion, he was behind the brawl, thrusting the treasure into his pocket and springing to his feet.

The man with the branding iron wheeled around, throwing a hand toward Paco, but a crack to his head jolted him back into the fight as the boy lunged through the gate, slamming it closed on the Eden's Bend side. He thrust the bolt through its sheath just as the man with the poker threw his body onto it—the door refused him through the strength of the bolt.

Tall shadows across the gate mesh prompted Paco to turn around. There were the ostriches, stooping and crowding forward in absent-minded perplexity at the surprise they saw.

Paco grasped the neck of the closest one. Dangling and swinging, he held on as the startled bird stumbled backward with a squawk and turned to flee. The bird's stiff neck was all the help Paco needed. He hoisted himself onto the back of the beast as the ostrich picked up speed into an all-out gallop away from the fence line.

The scuffle stopped as quickly as it had started. Ubi drew his knife. Papá Eli, recovering from the shove of his opponents, swung his club in the air between himself and the three men of El Dragón.

Papá Eli shouted as he stretched out his cane like a scepter. "Come *no farther*! Be wise and call it a game, amigos!" And they did so, seeing that the boy had escaped. They watched his departure as he became ever smaller amid the dust cloud of stampeding birds.

"Remember me, boy!" Papá Eli cried out. "Remember me to your mother and the moonstone!"

Paco spurred on the angry ostrich with his heels. The tennis shoes, loose as they were, quickly fell away. Wildly the ostrich ran, and wilder still the flock running with her, half amazed at the bravery of the boy, half outraged that a manchild would commandeer one of their own.

"Run!" Paco shouted. "Run, run, run!" And the ostriches, in the strength of their rage and fear, ran as they had never run before. Only love could have made them run faster.

They passed the pavilions. They rushed through a row of Washingtonia palms. Some ostriches joined the stampede, while others remained sage observers beneath their shaded shelters.

Acres fled under the thunder of six dozen legs, and the boy began to wonder how long it would be before someone would overtake them. For there was no cover, only open sky and endless field and a sun before whose heat nothing was hidden.

But on the horizon, Paco spotted a white metal building—a stable, apparently, still and bright, adjoining a corral and half hiding some distance away a much older stable and the thicket growing behind it.

Paco pulled on the neck of the ostrich to steer her toward the closer, newer stable, but she was already correcting her course for them anyway, knowing that the sooner she reached a place where Man worked, the higher the chance the manchild would get off. And the bird ran hard, not to help the boy, but to hasten the relief from her burden.

—⁓—

Inside the new stable, the friends heard the sound of the ostrich stampede. Patch ran out and climbed to the top of a corral fencepost in the direction of the noise. There, in the forefront of the dusty cloud of giant birds, ran an ostrich carrying a son of Adam who had surprised them with his sudden rule.

Patch rose on his hindquarters. "Jiminy Crickets, what's this? A manchild at the head of an ostrich flock! And who is it but...but...Plod! Bog! Miracle is here! Miracle is here!"

11

You Go Where Your Hope Is

Miracle jumped off the ostrich and ran toward the corral fence, which featured three generously spaced beams between each post. He stooped between the beams just as Plod and Bog emerged from the stable and just as the raccoon reached him. The boy clung to Patch and Patch to the boy. They leaned on Plod, who turned his head to abide with the two as they clung. There in the corral, though neither roof nor wall sheltered them from view, there was no fear of being seen, no caution among them. Only the kind of joy that shines when, after long hours of cloud, the wind breaks up the sky's blanket to reveal the heavens with shafts of light clear and long. Such was the joy when the friends beheld one another. The joy itself was their shelter.

Bog made a song to turn that shelter into the solid stone of a memory. Here is what he sang:

> *The tangle of threads and the dangle of ropes*
> *The hanging of heads and the dashing of hopes*
> *Is over! Is over! Like mist on the pond*
> *Like fog you forget at the moment it's gone*

When sunrise appears as a wavering disk
Parading its rule amid clouds on the whisk
Until he takes on the bold face of a king
And gloom bows before him as darkness takes wing!

"I am so glad to see you!" rejoiced Miracle. "So happy we found each other! How are you? Let me see."

Patch, standing meekly, permitted the child to lift each of his fingery paws. Likewise, Plod presented each hoof to the boy in turn as he felt the child's hands touch his pasterns.

Paco felt the smoothness of the horseshoes. "My, how you have traveled far with your friends!" And the boy patted the toad's head as he spoke to him. "I have traveled far too, but with Grandfather, the one who took me from you in the palm forest. He brought me here just as he promised. And look what I have from Tío Sergio! A gift from Mamá!"

Miracle opened his hand to reveal the moonstone, which radiated the blue of night and the glow of evening in a translucent, noteless song.

Patch's eyes lit up. He drew near to behold the glory of the stone. *A mother of marbles. I must take a real good look!* The moonstone spoke of a story long ago continuing into the present moment, of which Patch's own story, and the boy's, was a part.

The call of a Canada goose prompted all to look up. Chalice descended with outstretched wings. She gave the call of her kind, a cry whose joy matched its longing, and it was the occasion that determined which one was heard. In this moment, she cheered in pure delight.

"The friends are gathered from where they were scattered! There is home again! Home among friends!

The wind-carried nest
From the hidden beach branch
Has landed to rest
On the plains of a ranch!

And they laughed with one another.

Another blink of shadow prompted all to lift their heads. The great blue heron descended.

"News, everyone! News! News from the Cat Who Remembers!"

Patch scampered to the heron. "News from my friend, the lord of the Valley! Tell us what you know, Mr. Blue!"

"He's north of here, a good three-moon's journey as your paw goes. Man has taken him captive."

"Captive?" Patch fretted. "Oh no, how'd it happen?"

The heron shook the fatigue out of his wings and folded them again. "They pierced him with sleep and carried him away in a manmachine. I followed the trail of rumors in the beaks of my black-crested cousins, traveling northward until I found myself at the fork of two rivers, the ones Man calls the Brazos and the Bosque. And there I found him, bound in a manplace with many others of the animal kingdom, kin both near and far! A great living museum called a zoo."

Bog croaked a sound of lament. "Alas, the lord of the Valley is now Man's trophy. To be made sport of is worse than death! Why did Man not slay him in battle?"

Plod neighed with a cautious snort. "Perhaps Man is choosing a better battle for him. After all, you heard what our great blue neighbor called him, didn't you? 'The Cat Who Remembers.' Now it's clear as day what the new thing is: he's a cat, all right, a cat with a long memory."

The heron nodded, his eye curious as he noticed Bog in Plod's mane. "And a cat he is indeed, oh Traveler with a Toad.

The lord of the Valley is well but wounded, recovering from grackles who attacked him in their wind-driven madness. Now he waits, walled within the borders of his manmade lair. And while he dwells there in exile under a mahogany tree, I deliver his greetings to you:

> *Oh distant friends beyond the rim*
> *Beyond the wall of what I see*
> *The surface of the tale is grim*
> *And vaulted into mystery*
>
> *No one can make unbent the grass*
> *Or circumvent the spider lines*
> *For through them everyone must pass*
> *Or trip on hidden, tangled vines*
>
> *Yet this I vow till sands have slipped*
> *And filled up Waiting's bitter urn*
> *I will endure the sharp-edged tip*
> *Of separation out of turn*
>
> *Until the open path is shown*
> *And brings a springtime to this song*
> *Until I fish with friends at home*
> *And walk the realm where I belong*

Patch rejoiced but could not speak. He recalled the feast at Garfight Pond only he and Oracle had shared while the horse and the toad pondered the vow.

"So, he likes to fish," Plod mused.

"A friend of the pond, it seems," Bog commented.

Plod flapped his lips and tapped a hoof on the ground. "Yes, but the biggest apple to chew on is that last thing he said: 'walk the realm where I belong.'"

"He means here," Patch said with awe. "I don't know how it'll happen, but he means to come back. We need to make room for those words until he does. And room for him!"

The heron continued. "The lord of the Valley found the tree he had been searching for—the Lonely Tree—with the help of the night songs of the quail. And the Lonely Tree is now no longer Lonely, but Lovely. She bloomed as if in spring at the arrival of your friend. I had a good while to ponder what the Cat Who Remembers said about the Lonely Tree as I headed back here, and somehow all that pondering turned into a song. I think his breath had something to do with it, if you ask me. Now, I can't sing to save my soul, but I can at least tell you what I'm singing on the inside:

> *Where she has ended*
> *She will begin*
> *Where she was stranded*
> *She will graft in*
>
> *Foliage of color*
> *Branches of fruit*
> *Starting another*
> *Tapping a root*

The friends let the words rest upon them. And in that quiet, a feeling also came upon them, the same feeling one has at the distant sound of migrating birds, whose call marks the end of one season and the beginning of another. A rest on the move.

The heron turned to Patch. "Now, let's see. What nickname did he give you? Hmm...Ah yes! 'Fair Bandit.' That's what he called you. He smiled when he said it. He had a special message for you." The heron lifted his beak:

Carry the knot you can't untie
Carry the knot before you
For every seed of hope that dies
Seedlings will sprout behind you

Council I'll hold when I return
Council for those in hiding
Meanwhile be brave with friend and foe
Courage in heart abiding!

Patch lifted his head in response to the message, for his heart had become stout at the hearing of Oracle's word, and the raccoon made room for it.

Chalice stretched her neck skyward and gave the call of her kind. "Wise and wonderful words that cover like a mother's wings! Yes, words that cover until the promise of return is fulfilled! For I see that friends are gathered again, and their waiting will not be lonely. I can rest from my watch with a full heart, for I have seen the manchild escape a trap and find a sheltered nest. Another of the flock will come to take my place in watching. Until my turn comes again, I bid you peace. Farewell!" The goose rose and glided above them in long and silent circles until she veered away toward the sea.

The heron bowed to the friends. "And if you please, I, too, must retire now to Green Island to recover from the long journey. Chalice and I shall exchange many a tale while we rest among the branches of our refuge. We shall return when the time for each of us comes to it. Until then, keep your

feet wet and your wings dry. Goodbye!" And he lifted his
frame and departed.

—◠〜◠—

The friends watched the sky where the birds had departed.
The horse whinnied softly and almost shook his mane—until
Bog reminded him of his presence with a croaky clearing of
the throat.

Plod stilled himself. "Sorry, partner. I was a little preoccupied with what just happened."

"So am I, my equine comrade. Looks like you and I have
something to ponder from the friend who prefers fish to fur."

"Yes," replied Patch. "Words as fresh as strawberries on
a summer day. Now let's finish this errand the lord of the
Valley gave us!"

Patch lifted his face to the manchild Miracle. Before the
barefoot prince he stood, quiet and unwavering, knowing that
in that silent space a word would form between them that
would translate to the place too deep for words. He waited.

Miracle glowed with the knowledge of what Papá Eli had
told him.

*There are two on this ranch who are 'like family.' The two
who left the gate open. The two who will take me in.*

He looked upon his friends with a smile. "We must find
Tío and Tía. We shall ask Mamá's moonstone where to go.
We shall ask her where their home is."

On his outstretched hand, he set the moonstone before
the steady rays of the sun. The friends gathered round while it
shone back to the sky a fierce and glowing fire. But to the boy,
the light was neither unfeeling nor demanding; it returned
the light in such a way that a direction formed in the boy,

an instinct and a leaning, until he looked in the direction it seemed the light of the moonstone was pointing.

He spied rows of trailers just visible on the horizon, flickering behind the heat radiating from a weary plain. The trailers seemed asleep in the haze, but to the holder of the moonstone, they nonetheless signaled a clue to where to search.

The boy the birds named Miracle pointed toward the trailers, marshaling hope as he did, like one directing soldiers into the breach of battle.

"We shall go to the sleepers." He mounted Plod with the help of the fence, and, with ankles bare and tender, gently guided the horse toward the distant trailer park.

Oracle's words sang inside of Patch. True, the words had been delivered through the great blue heron, whose reedy voice could not carry much more than a dry sense of humor, let alone a tune. But the words had a life of their own—a song of their own. A song causing Patch to remember his name, the name given him before he had been called Patch, before the Powhatan had called him He Who Scratches with His Hands. The name Adam had given him during the Days of First Things.

Patch tapped Plod's fetlock. The horse turned to the raccoon, ears ready to hear. "Your mane, please. I must carry this knot."

The horse obliged. The raccoon climbed and sat in the space between Miracle and the base of the horse's neck while Bog moved forward and sat between the ears, the place called the poll. The boy and the toad welcomed him.

The air of Eden lingered, and by it, Plod lifted the latch of the corral with his nose. "Let's see how far we can go before Man brings us back."

"Onward!" Bog croaked, "for a glory greater than last stands and iron pots! A new exploit my ancestors would be proud of!"

And as they went, a song overshadowed them like an invisible cloud, which, though not seen, made the heat of the day bearable and brought the fresh air of spring to the companions: Patch, Plod, Bog, and Miracle, the boy whom Papá and Mamá had named Paco and then Little Colt for joy. This was the song in the air the friends breathed:

> *You go where your hope is*
> *You follow the clues*
> *The home that you seek is*
> *Revealed in the hues*
> *Of what is before you*
> *A stump showing green*
> *You go where your hope is*
> *Till orchards are seen*

To reach the trailers, the friends had to walk a dirt road winding southwest between corrals and cattle chutes. They passed a barn whose door was wide open. Inside, Men bent over a circular saw piercing the air with precision cuts. They did not notice the friends as they passed. Then the four crossed a broad, dry plain, whose grass was no more than stubble from the double devouring of drought and cows who had grazed it before Man had moved them on. The cattle were moving south, leaving nothing behind them but dusty air and fresh droppings for the friends to step around.

Finally, they reached the trailer park. Before them, in the blur of heat-bent light, were rows of wheeled, rounded boxes the color of sun-beaten turquoise. Each one featured a door on the same side, and from each of these mobile manplaces, tarpaulins or aluminum awnings stretched out, creating squares of shadowed relief. Potted plants grew at the foot of the stairsteps leading up to each door, and folding chairs awaited their owners. Behind some were plots of pumpkin, sunflower, and other private gardens. A slight breeze blew, a motion of warm air that sighed, then ceased.

Patch sniffed the air. "I smell the same spices of the manchild! The same flavors that are in the air around Miracle and his clothing!"

They approached. All was still. A host of small air conditioners gave a collective hum as they labored to negotiate an exchange of warm air for cold inside each blanched box. A chihuahua yipped from within one of them.

Patch frowned. "It looks like no one's home."

"It's the time of day when Man is at work," Plod replied. "Only the weary will be home."

At that moment a work-weathered Man in a straw cowboy hat and wrangler duds opened his trailer door. He stepped out toward a pickup truck parked under his canopy. He saw the friends, and his puzzlement gave way to pleasure as he realized the horse carried not one but three companions.

The vaquero laughed and smiled. "What can I do for you, little one?"

"I am looking for Mamá and Papá. We came here from Mérida, but the sea became angry with our boat. I lost them in the dark cold, but I know they are here. Look!" Paco showed him the moonstone. "The Grandfather with many fish told me to come here. His name is Papá Eli. He said he has family here who will help me find Mamá and Papá: a new tío and a new tía. Do you know them?"

The vaquero opened his mouth, arrested by a thought that hovered on his tongue. He marveled at the boy, who gazed back into his eyes with a hope shining like the polished precious stone he held out.

"What is your name?" the vaquero asked.

"My name is Francisco del Nombre, but Mamá and Papá call me Paco. Have you seen them? Tío Sergio said they left for Mérida on La Bestia. Where is La Bestia? Tell me so I can go there too."

The vaquero popped his hat back as if a sudden gust of wind had struck him. With his other hand, he ran his fingers through his graying locks.

"¡Increíble!" he whispered.

A woman in a cotton dress appeared behind him, her eyes squinting from the light of the open door, her disheveled auburn hair overdyed but for the stripe of gray at the roots. She was tying apron strings behind her back, but the sight of the boy made her pause.

"¿Qué pasó?" she asked.

"It's *Paco*," said the vaquero. "The one they thought had perished! He has come back from the grave! *This* is the 'gift' Papá Eli has sent us! *This* is the one we left the gate open for!"

The woman gasped and tossed off the apron. "¡Ay, Dios mío! I can't believe it! How?"

"He came on this horse with these two little friends!" He pointed to the raccoon and toad.

She clasped her face with her hands. "What? How? ¡Es un milagro!"

"Yes, my love, a strange wonder. Now we know what Papá Eli meant! 'Take the gift in,' he said, 'and tell the authorities. You will likely keep the gift until they figure out what to do.'"

The man made the sign of the cross and stepped out of the trailer. He lifted his face toward the boy.

"Come with me, son."

12

THE MOONSTONE FINDS A HOME

The vaquero took the horse's halter and led the friends west down a row of trailers. They passed through ranks of residences ready for the return of those who would sleep well in them that night. The sun blazed behind them, and the chorus of window units created an off-tune fanfare for the entourage. Paco beamed like a morning glory flower.

Patch sniffed the air, peering past Plod's mane for any sign of the parents. "The smell changes here. Like a path whose tracks are cold."

Bog glanced back at him, speaking quietly. "No Man cooks *here* like they do back *there*, where we met our new guide. These are empty abodes."

They reached the final manplace. There was no covering beside it. The air conditioner was mute. No potted plants guarded the steps. The ground was chairless, the door shut. And though it looked no different than any other, the trailer seemed as barren to Patch as an orange without the rind whose fruit has withered before a cheerless noon.

And just beyond this, planted at a right angle to the last trailer, was a cruciform marker, like those along highways and on street corners; not graves but reminders of a moment in time when the turn of the wheel had been fatal. Here was one such marker, but this was no road, no corner—only a spot as blank as the surface of the sea. Affixed to it were sequins and sand dollars in a pattern. A wind chime hung on one arm of the cross, whispering light tones as the summer breeze passed through it. On the other arm hung a pulsar bracelet, its threads of seven colors wound in a tight handmade pattern. Cloth poppies, wilting on a faded green wire, wound their way from the end of each arm, and in the center, where the two arms met, the flowers gathered and bowed their faces toward names written on a porcelain tile:

EN MEMORIA
JUAN Y MARÍA DEL NOMBRE
Y SU HIJO PACO
SIEMPRE EN NUESTROS
CORAZONES

The boy stared at the letters. "What do they mean? They do not speak." He looked around. "There is no one here." His face searched the elements of the marker, as when one gazes upon a puzzle where the last and central piece is missing, but none are left to work with: only an empty box bearing witness to the perfect picture of what should be but is not.

Paco slid off Plod and stood before the marker. The shadow of the vaquero rose before him and covered the marker as he approached the boy in sensitive silence from behind.

The vaquero turned to the sound of his wife, her footsteps a rapid shuffle, for she had not changed from her indoor slippers in her haste to join them. She clumsily lowered herself to her knees behind Paco and placed her hands on the lad's shoulders. Then she turned her face up toward her husband with a watery gaze through hair the hot breeze would not leave alone in her speechless sorrow.

"So, it falls to me," the man said, rubbing his beard stubble at the sideburn. He glanced to the right and to the left, as if on some wild off-chance an angel or Saint Francis would step forward to intervene. But he saw no one at his side, only a lantern in the dark, called Courage. So, having taken hold of that lantern, he took in a breath for the words he knew would blow out the candle of the boy's heart. It was the slowest breath he had ever taken in his life. But the time came to exhale and extinguish. He beheld the child, full of life but tender, like a fresh leaf springing from a branch. Bright but easily bruised.

He bent down before Paco and placed a hand on his shoulder as the boy continued to stare with pain-filled perplexity at the marker. The man's fingers touched those of his wife, who nodded to him to speak. He looked the lad in the eyes while his own burned in protest to the words he knew he had to say.

"Son...dear son...There is no need to ride La Bestia. No need to go to Mérida. They are not there, son. They have left, and they are not returning. The sea took them, and where they have gone, you cannot follow now. The day to follow is another day, but not today, son. Not today. I am sorry."

Pools brimmed in Paco's eyes. Pools that glinted like shattered glass piercing bare feet. Pools that effused an untranslatable steam of anger at the iron door the flooding sea had sealed behind him after his parents had thrust him out of the sinking hulk. Pools of words he had wanted to say to them but for which there were no longer ears to hear.

Paco flung the moonstone and wept.

"No, no, no!" he wailed. "Mamá! Papá! Take me with you! Take me with you! Don't go! Don't go! Don't leave me here! Don't leave me!" Paco quaked, his body folding upon his feet. He crumpled against the place beneath the names until the marker leaned under his weight.

Grief eclipsed the day. Patch, Plod, and Bog bowed their heads. The vaquero took off his hat. The woman pulled Paco close, her arms, though flesh, more like a broad covering of wings in how they felt to the boy. But his mind could do no more than take note of this good feeling, for it was cordoned off by a grief the boy had never known. Heart and spirit wailed in pain while the boy's mind abided mute, aware of the comfort the woman gave, but unable to convey it to the rest of his being. Only in reflection some later day could comfort descend upon the rest of Paco. But for now, there was none.

All remained in the present space, wordless and waiting, for hope had fallen and silence needed to return. Only in silence could a new word of hope be found, like a seedling springing from the ashes of a forest floor after a fire has consumed it.

And in the silence, a wind passed over. Not a gulf wind of weather's routine, nor a cool front out of season, but a wind that at one and the same time was a stranger and a comforter, a witness to the grief and a messenger from a griefless realm. A song.

In the generations to come, when waves and floods brought sorrow, many among the animals took up this song at the hour of their own lament, such that the greatest tragedy in the boy's life became a treasure for many whose names he never knew. And the death of his parents became a living word causing their shadow to stretch far beyond the brief and narrow space of years they had walked the earth.

Cold and loveless mute sea bottom
Shortens life and breath and years
Pulling like a turning column
Winding threads of grief with tears

Tightening its rule of nature
Heightening its reign of dark
Till the time when all things shatter
Till the moment angels hark

That the sting of death is broken
That the law of night is done
When the oceans open coffins
When the sea is in the sun

—∭—

The sound of feathered flapping broke in, followed by the sound of a light brushing of talons across metal. A ferruginous pygmy owl had landed on the roof of the empty manplace. He looked on with solemn eyes.

"Greetings, Friends of Miracle, I am Salt the owl of the Colony of the Lost. Mercy be yours in your loss. It is a thing each of my flock knows well, both the loss and the mercy."

Patch sighed in relief. "Salt! How good of you to come! I'm Patch of Palo Verde—but I'm sure you know that from the goose and the great blue heron and everyone else in your flock who's watched us. Sir, I don't know what to do! My friend the lord of the Valley told me to bring Miracle to his parents, but this looks as if it's the end of the trail! His parents aren't here. They've gone where I cannot take the boy!"

Salt sang a single, clear tone and spoke. "Take courage, Treasure Keeper. You have done what you could do. You have brought the boy to the border of your strength and found a mercy at that border, a pair who are now a mother and father to him. Yes, Patch of the Order of the Ring-Tailed Secrets, you have fulfilled the errand completely, in *value* if not in

141

strict definition. The catastrophe has turned a corner into creativity. The Man and the Woman will cover the manchild from here."

Patch looked about for the moonstone but, not immediately seeing it, replied to the owl. "It was Miracle who led us to the Man and the Woman with the help of a moonstone, not me. None of the rites of my tribe speak of such a thing. The moonstone carried the secret of which direction to go. How did Miracle know that secret?"

The owl considered the boy—body still facing the raccoon. "I doubt the manchild could explain to you how he knew. He is not self-conscious enough to second-guess and not sophisticated enough in his own eyes to require lengthy explanations."

"Maybe the moonstone bent the sunlight just right."

"Perhaps, but I doubt it."

Bog piped up. "I would say the hearts of these two souls comforting the manchild pulled the sunlight hither. There is a trustworthiness about them, like when fresh rain fills the pond and the dragonflies hum that all shall be well."

Patch turned his head to one side, laboring to understand. "Or maybe it was the other way around. Maybe the sunlight pulled the moonstone in this direction because the sun saw the Man and the Woman."

Plod flapped his lips as he exhaled. "I can't speak for the sunlight and the moonstone, and I can't speak for the Man and the Woman the child trusts on sight, but a breeze blew when he stretched out his hand with the moonstone back there at the new stable, and it was like the breeze that just passed through here. A wind so gentle only the tips of the hair on my muzzle felt it."

Salt moved his shoulders in a circular motion, feathers rising and falling as he turned to the horse—body still facing the raccoon. "Yes, oh Seer of the House of Equus, what is gentlest is often what is greatest. Perhaps the gentle breeze touched everything in that moment of waiting—the moonstone, the sunlight, and all of us gathered here. But beyond that, we have no words to explain how Miracle knew where to go. Only a love from another world could articulate such mysteries."

The owl sang seven notes as he turned his head toward the raccoon again.

"Servant of Miracle, again I say to you, take heart. You have done well, and I am sure that the gentle breeze Plod speaks of was with you in the doing, helping you fulfill what was asked of you. And it is no small thing that you fulfilled it, for a yes means yes to very few in these Last Days, be they in your House of Procyon or any other house for that matter. Many *aspire*, but few *do*. Yes indeed, very *few do, few do*, oh you whose deed is a life-giving scent in the animal realm! Very *few do, few do*!" And the hooting sage stretched out his wings in honor.

The bird's call awakened the air about him. The horse raised his head and gave a gentle whinny while the toad grasping his mane gave a call in harmony with the hooting owl above.

—⁓—

"*Maravilloso,*" whispered the vaquero. "The animals: It's as if they are singing."

"Why does it remind me of Sundays?" his wife wondered.

"Sunday mornings," he whispered. "I can't explain why, but it's as if the matins bell has sounded."

"I know. It is a sign. We had best accept it."

"No, *mi querida*, even better, we had best appreciate it."

And so, the vaquero and his wife took comfort in the song.

The raccoon dropped from the horse and went to the place where Paco's knees met the dust. The wife looked in alarm at her husband as the furry pest approached the child.

"It's okay," the vaquero whispered. "I think the creature knows it's a time for mourning and not mischief. Let him be."

"This is so very strange," said his wife. "It's like I'm seeing something that is not foreign."

"That is because it is not foreign. It is from the future."

"A future we have never seen but is still familiar?"

"Sí."

"How can that be?"

"I do not know, mi querida. I only know it is so."

And the couple reverently watched the raccoon abide with the boy.

—⟪⟫—

Patch set the weight of his frame upon Miracle's lower legs, feeling the rising and falling of his body as he drew in jerking measures of bitter air followed by long vents of lament.

Leaning there, Patch mused upon the cross.

I've seen this in the great green parks where Man sleeps among the scripted stones. I've seen this on the roadsides where the manmachines roar. But here it seems more like a trail marker. The print of a path I can't follow without Man going first.

In the pattern of sequins and sand dollars, Patch noticed a peculiar empty spot, blank yet occupied with a smudge of what looked like stiff tree sap.

Hmm. The more I look at it, the more I can tell something goes there…Oh! Yeah, that's it! The mother of marbles belongs there!

He searched for the moonstone the manchild had flung. It lay beneath the trailer. Patch took it in both paws, raised himself on his hind legs, and placed it upon the smudge; it fit perfectly. Since it would not remain there (the sap or whatever it was now being dry), Patch lay the gem in the tear-marked dust beneath the face of Miracle.

The boy noticed, and, without lifting his head, slid his hand across the earth until his fingers touched the stone, enveloped it, and brought it to his heart, where it whispered to him words only he could understand.

The stone also radiated a memory, and that memory—wordless though it was—spoke to the vaquero and his wife.

He turned to her. "I will call the man."

He searched his wallet until he found a business card, the bright white corners of which still stood at sharp right angles among the many smudged and worn ones. He read the card:

TRENT FREEMAN
DEPUTY US MARSHAL
FUGITIVE TASK FORCE

He called the number written there.

"Marshal Freeman speaking."

"Señor, I am José Benavides, one of the hands you spoke to at Eden's Bend."

"Yes, sir?"

"We have found him, señor. We have found the child. He is alive. He is with us."

"That's great news! Give me time to call CPS. Keep him safe until we get there. It will take a while. I'm out here at El Realito with Sheriff Gibson on the trail of the men behind the shipwreck. Border Patrol's here too. We found evidence where the boy had been. Footprints and a place he had slept."

"I see. We will take care of him, sir. Rest assured."

"I'm mighty relieved in light of what I'm looking at this very moment, Mr. Benavides: the tracks of a big cat, the likes of which locals haven't seen in a good while. The pugmarks on the front paws push five inches wide! They're all over the place, even mixed with the boy's own footprints. Sometimes the tracks are right next to each other, going the same direction! They must have missed each other by only a few hours, maybe minutes. We were worried he was in harm's way. He's lucky he didn't get hurt."

The two men continued in conversation. The woman raised Paco to his feet for the short walk back to the trailer, her arm around his shoulder.

"There, there, *mi hijo*. It is good that we found you, but not good what you found out! Cry all you want, little one, cry all you want. Cry until the river runs dry. We will take care of you for now. We will take care of you. And oh, how sweet it is to learn you are even *alive*, son! Yes!"

She pulled him closer as they walked. "But my sweetness is bitter to you, I know. Your heart is broken, dear one, broken and scattered. Scattered like pigeons in a plaza when a dog runs through it. But the dog will go home, and the birds will gather again. Yes, they will! You will see! But until then, my little one, we will comfort one another, eat lots of good food, and hear about your adventure. You are not alone, son, not alone. We are here. All shall be well."

The woman sat in a folding chair beneath her trailer's canopy. She set Paco in her lap. The boy poured out until he had nothing left to pour. Weeping settled into sniffles and sighing. Then he grew silent. He fell into a deep sleep. The woman rocked him back and forth, humming bars of the calmer cantina songs she could recall.

Her husband, meanwhile, who had lingered before the marker, came with the horse, whom he tethered to the truck's side mirror in the shade. The toad was quite still in the mane, and the raccoon quite still at the horse's feet as the Man considered them, shaking his head in mock disapproval mixed with pleasurable acceptance. He brought fresh-squeezed lemonade to a small table beside his wife, then he brought water for the animals: a bucket for the horse and the dog dish of their late pet for the raccoon.

"Señor Sapo," he said to the toad, "You are welcome to hop into either one, provided your friends are fine with your choice. *Bienvenidos, amigos.*"

He turned on a standing fan, its stiff and circular frame giving off a rattle like a Sopwith biplane, a sound forgivable for the relief from the heat it brought. Then he sat down beside the lemonade.

The vaquero contemplated the woman and the child; it was difficult to discern who was the more comforted of the three.

As they waited for the arrival of Marshal Freeman, the calmness of the boy's animal friends did as much for them as the fan and the lemonade to bring refreshment. Perhaps more. And the depth of Paco's sorrow-borne sleep anchored everyone in an interlude where all else, animals included, could safely abide.

After a time, the wife lifted her eyes to her husband.

"How long do you think we have before El Dragón knows?" she whispered.

Her husband gave a sigh and pinched his chin in thought. "Not long, I am sure, for the man who brought us the marker and took its stone is beholden to him. But we have a good while before it matters, mi querida. A good while. A snake has to wait for the cattle drive to pass before it can come out of its hole, and many a bull will be at Eden's Bend to inspect the child and to inspect us to make sure we are not guilty of any wrongdoing. No serpent will move among us while the bulls are on the move. Yes, we have time. We can be patient. And patience will conquer every thorn. You will see, *mi tierra*, you will see."

The vaquero made a feed bag for the horse and rubbed him down.

"This neighbor needs his hooves shaved," he whispered.

Paco awakened to the gentle sound of Plod munching on mash and the vaquero cleaning the beast of burden from the sweat of his labor.

The boy rubbed his eyes and looked up at the woman. "Thank you for holding me, Tía. What is your name?"

"I am Tía Lourdes. And there with your animal friends is your new tío, my husband José. I call him *mi gordito* because he is so handsome and so wise!" She winked at him. He winked back. "Well, he *was* handsome in his day, but he is still wise!"

She looked at the child. Her face shone.

"We will be your family, little one. We will be your family while many come to visit us. People will come to ask you about everything that has happened. They will come and talk with you and talk with us, not once but many times, and I am sure that after all of their talking and watching and writing words down, they will see no better thing to do than to place you with those from Mérida like you! For we also are from your hometown, and we had heard of your mamá and papá. It will take a long time, as long as it takes the moon to become new ten times over. But we will foster you until you are like a firstborn to us!"

13

ORACLE AND THE HEDGEHOGS

It was two hours past midnight when the waning half-moon peeked over the horizon to see the trailer where the boy now slept. Sweeping her beams across Texas, she found the Bosque River where he flowed into the Brazos, far to the north of the manchild Miracle. There, along the Brazos's southwest bank, the moon found the great manstone garden, where animals from every continent dwelled in well-fed captivity. The lamps of Man cast their mercuric glow across the zoo.

The moon rejoiced to see the lord of the Valley, whose masters had returned him to his habitat after two nights and three days in the infirmary, careful as they were to make sure no infectious malady had set in from the fight with the grackles.

During his absence, Man had anchored several stout branches, each as thick as a trunk, radiating from the small rise at the center of his exhibit, a bare bouquet of wood like a leafless tree. For, in the wild, jaguars recline in natural watch posts such as these.

The cat of the House of Panthera Onca lay along the highest spot. From here, he could see across the half-empty pond to the bamboo curtain behind which Crash the tiger lived. He saw the dwelling places of other animals too, whose barriers of fabric-covered fence and pampas grass usually forbade a sighting of the animals themselves. The exception was the buffalo and her newborn calf, who lived in a carefully simulated open prairie behind a double fence of rigid wire. Through it, the cat could see the mother buffalo chewing the cud in calmness, and her calf, though not yet weaned, mimicked the calmness of his mother until hunger prodded him.

The cat of the Ones Who Remember could also see the giraffe, for her head rose above the barriers to survey the dwelling places about her with an air of authority, as if she were the night-shift supervisor of what she saw—a look the elephants did not appreciate. They trumpeted comments to the giraffe, who responded in whispers (for giraffes can only whisper). Oracle listened to their antiphony:

Long neck I have to see where others go
Long nose we have for wind and bath to blow

Long sight I have to take in all that moves
Long mind we have to never memories lose

I see you are a walking story long
We see you are a whispering tower strong

I see you are an ancient silent song
We see you are above the dusty throng

What exodus drove you to shadowlands?
What closed the welcome way to Adam's hands?

How do you know the name he gave you then?
We do not know; we can't remember when

And the cat explored these words as one searching for a path through an uncut jungle.

Oracle heard a crumbling of earth. Searching for the source, he rose and hopped down. Not far from the mahogany, his eyes fell on a small spot of wiggling ground. From the rippling soil emerged a whiskered nose testing the air. Satisfied, the nose proceeded upward, and out followed a hedgehog. Behind her poured a brood of offspring, quietly scurrying in a circle around their mother. The hedgehog turned to the jaguar. She came near, eyes alive with fear and courage, the motion of her feet hidden beneath her wobbling patch of spines. Her nose twitched inquisitively beneath her quills. Her children gathered behind her. She bowed.

"Greetings, Cat of the Southern Jungle. I am Miriam of the House of Erinaceus and the mother of these, my children. We have heard about you from the pigeons, who say that when you breathed on them, they remembered the story of the Namer naming them in the Days of First Things. The pigeons cooed you are of the Flock of the Lion, and your jaguar tribe is called the Ones Who Remember. We know it is true, for when they flapped their wings over us, we, too, remembered Eden. The wind from their wings took two broken tales our tribe carries and made them one."

"Greetings, Mother," Oracle replied. "Welcome to my manmade lair. I am surprised by your arrival. I did not sense your coming until the earth gave way. How is it that you roam this gated place so freely?"

"We hedgehogs have lived under this land since long before it was ever a park or zoo. We came in the covered wagon of a Man named Ross, whose many children kept us as pets until his daughter Kate set us free. We lived under their gardens, and we made dwellings under the crops of maize the native mantribe planted here after he had escaped the warrior's arrow. 'Waco' was the name of his tribal band, breaking away from the Wichita in the great grasslands of the north. The Waco tribe withered, the House of Ross prospered, and many families of Man crossed over our realm—and our backs—with their labor: foot and hoof, plow and tire, shovel and steamroller. Even so, the tunnels have remained. Through them, we carry messages between our captive neighbors, and through them, we have come to you. Yes, it is the hedgehog, along with the opossum and the squirrel, who freely roam the zoo when Man sleeps.

> *Quiet, constant, daily digging*
> *Opens up a better way*
> *Than the sweat of clever rigging*
> *Man constructs to rule the day*
>
> *Underground and out of sight*
> *From machin'ry's growl and scratch*
> *Undercover through the night*
> *Tunnels bend where Man can't catch*
>
> *We are working while he's sleeping*
> *We create a humble mound*
> *Though he's busy zoo a-keeping*
> *We're a city never found*

Oracle savored the words, which smelled like freshly upturned garden soil, the scratched-open clue to a world he did not know.

Mother Hedgehog drew closer. "There have been tunnels under your dwelling for a very long time, and in the places where we gather, they are as wide as they are long. But for you, they cannot grant passage, for you are a creature of the surface, too large and strong for our paths to carry."

Oracle nodded, his face sober. "Yes, Mother, when one is large and strong, a gentle path is hard to find. But it is the only way, requiring time, enough time to become a friend of weakness. Because I am strong, I must wait long."

Mother Hedgehog listened, smelling this new thought as she would an unanticipated bloom beneath the ferns.

The jaguar sat and twitched his tail. "You carried two broken tales, you say?"

"Yes," Mother Hedgehog replied, "each one a clue, each one a fragment of a bigger story that had drifted apart in our memory. But the breath of the bird wings brought them both together. Now we know the first story, and it has made the broken stories one. We have come to say thank you."

"You are welcome, Mother. Tell me the two tales."

The hedgehog lifted her face and beheld the stories before her mind's eye. "Long before our tribe came here, yes, long before we made a home along the river winding through this land, we carried a story about the first hedgehog. It is said he had no spines but a strong back on which he bore precious stones. He grew proud of his gems, and he boasted to the roses he was more beautiful than they were. The sun heard his glowing words and burned with displeasure until the stones on the hedgehog's back had become as hot as the beams touching them. The hedgehog fled beneath a rosebush to hide from the sun, but the roses refused to help him without a price.

"'Give us your stones, and we will give you our shade,' they said.

"The hedgehog pleaded, 'I will give them, but do not leave me naked! What will I do when the animals gather, and I have no coat of arms? Who will I say that I am?'

"'We can help you,' the roses said slyly, and they gave him thorns in place of gems. And that, so the hedgehogs say, is why we have quills on our backs. But this is a broken tale, for

153

it does not tell us why the hedgehog carried gems in the first place, nor does it explain why the roses had thorns."

Oracle's tail danced. "Nor does the story continue far enough, for it does not reveal how the weakness the roses gave you has turned into the strength of your tribe, such that even my kind, the Great House of Panthera with its five tribes and fierce teeth, is loath to fight you. Your quills are greater than our jaws. Though you are small, behold, you are one of the freest of creatures, even here in the garden of mazes Man has made. Your weakness has turned to strength."

The eyes of the hedgehog sparkled. "That is what we saw when the birds brought the Breath of Eden to us!"

"Yes," replied Oracle, "and it is only the beginning of what you will see...But tell me the other tale."

"Gladly, sire." And the hedgehog beheld the other story, which flickered before her heart like a welcome winter campfire.

"There was a time when the hedgehogs lived inside the rocks of a mountain. They did not dig but made their home where the stones had already worked for them. And they sang a hymn to their fortress:

We praise the stone
We call it home
We are our own
We are alone

"One day the earth groaned, and that evening a great beast came to the mouth of the cave, a monstrous creature with skin like flint, a tongue like a serpent, and wings like a bat. No quill could pierce him. For three days it stood at the cave mouth and demanded that half of them come out to be swallowed alive, lest all of them be devoured at once. They were trapped in a double snare: both the snare of no way out and the snare of no clear conscience, for the hedgehogs knew it would be lifelong misery to survive at the expense of their kin, yet all were equally miserable because none could muster the courage to sacrifice himself to the terror of the beast. But at length, hunger and thirst compelled a prayer from their lips.

"So, they cried out:

Oh rocks, fall on us!
End our starving and our dread!
Blot out dilemmas in our head!
For the beast will not budge
And our spines do not prevail
Against a foe we can't assail
Tumble down till terror stops
Oh crags who crown the mountaintops!

"All the rocks were silent—save one. He fell, but not *on* the hedgehogs as they had prayed. No, he fell *before* them. Then words came out of the rock, the first words ever recorded from the mouth of a stone:

You call
I fall
I give
You live

"And with that, the stone turned to soil, and the hedgehogs discovered soft earth where the rock had been. They dug, and as they dug, their paws grew strong. They bored a hole and followed one another through the way of escape the rock had made for them. It became a tunnel taking them far from the monster but remaining too small for him to enter. He could only utter threats that echoed off the tunnel walls. At first, the echoes caused the hedgehogs to freeze in fear, but they reminded one another it was only the *sound* of the beast and not the beast itself.

"They kept digging until they reached a valley of rich loam and tender roots on the other side of the mountain from where they had dwelled. And this, so we hedgehogs say, is why we are graced with the skill of digging: because the rock received us."

Mother Hedgehog returned to all fours and cocked her head. "But this tale, too, is a broken one, for it does not tell us why the earth groaned under the claws of a strange new beast, nor does it tell us why one rock listened while the rest remained hardened to all but themselves."

"Nor does the tale go far enough," Oracle said, "for it does not lament how the rock fortress that protected you became a stone trap that doomed you, nor does it rejoice in how the soft earth, so easily broken, feeds you with roots from above. Strength became weakness and weakness strength."

"Yes!" Mother Hedgehog rejoiced. "The Breath of Eden showed us what you say! The Breath of Remembrance! Only the rock and the beast remain a mystery."

Oracle lowered his body and stretched out his forelegs such that his face drew close to his guest. "They are a mystery to me too. Something only Man can know. Now tell me, Mother, how did the Breath of Remembrance make your two tales one?"

Her eyes glistened. "By telling us the tale before the tale. We remembered the day the Namer looked upon the first of our kind, the day he looked upon us in the Garden."

"What did the Namer say to you on that day?"

"He did not *speak* to us only. He *sang*. He sang words in the tones of a world beyond our whiskers, a world known only to him, but making a home in us *through* him. He sang to us who we were:

> *A gem with fur that under me is hidden*
> *A stem of air beneath the rose forbidden*
> *A stone that moves at homely garden pace*
> *A home that proves a deeper resting place*

"He sang these words and many others too, singing of things so wonderful I can only say them in the heart of the earth as I lean on the bosom of my closest kin. When the Breath of Remembrance moved over us, we remembered the Namer's song that had come before the two tales we had always told ourselves. Yes, long before them. Oh, how those two tales seem mere echoes compared to the Namer's voice! And now we taste not only the root of the two tales; we taste the fruit to come. For our own two tales leave off in mid-telling and do not say where we are going. But the Namer's song has within it both where we have been and where we will be, both who we have been and who we will be."

Oracle's whiskers touched those of the hedgehog as both looked heavenward. There was no fear in the touch, so great was the wonder that had come upon them. The lord of the Valley spoke.

"This is truly how things are, in spite of every tangle your kind and mine fall into. The first story is always the key to the new one, and the path to the future always begins with a memory."

And the jaguar and the hedgehog mused upon these words. The songs of the creatures of the night accompanied their thoughts until, like the bow of a canoe gently grounding on the shore, they came to rest.

—ᛖ—

Mother Hedgehog rose and tended to her children, who, in the presence of the grown-ups' conversation, had become sleepy or were already slumbering. She returned to Oracle's side.

"How did you come to be here, sire? On the morning of your arrival, watchers from my tribe posted in the pyracantha hedges told us how the rulers of this mangarden rejoiced at your coming. The giraffe whispered to them a rumor she had heard from the flamingos that Man captured you as you explored one of his ranches. It is clear you were not born in a gated cell like some folks are."

"You perceive truly, Mother. I am not from a manplace such as this one. I came from the wild because I had a prayer to answer. A prayer from the last jaguar in this realm under the sign of the Lone Star."

"But you are a cat from the distant Southern Jungle. How is it you know the prayer of the last jaguar who walked under the Lone Star?"

Oracle sat up, his ears touching the leaves of the mahogany as he turned his face toward the hibiscus. "I know it from a windblown, queenly traveler who lay exhausted on my jungle floor. With the help of the hibiscus, I nurtured her, and when she had regained her strength, she told me the Tale of the Last Jaguar, Kahoo the Grave, who led the animal kingdom seventy springs ago in the place under the Lone Star which Man calls the Valley. He led the creatures in paths of honor, and he made decisions just and fair.

"But Man could not host a rival lord, so he brought the jaguar's reign to an end at the top of a wild olive tree, the Lonely Tree, where Kahoo prayed for a successor as darkness

158

met his eyes. He lifted his head, and the olive blooms listened as he prayed:

Oh moon, hear!
Oh stars, listen to me!

I depart the earth this night to join my fathers
But you remain, and you keep watch
Do not leave this river delta bare
Do not leave it unled forever

Watch in my place, and wait with open eyes
Until another comes to lead the kingdom
From the north and from the sky
From here to river's end!

Oracle reclined before the hedgehog. "And so, I came to the Valley with the help of the Lady River and trees whose roots still held on to ancient wisdom. I found the animal kingdom leaderless and adrift from the memories of Eden. But dim as the eyes of that realm were, I still found bright hearts, and I made friends with them. Though different from each other in our kinds, we found fellowship together—even the fellowship of a manchild."

"A manchild?" asked Mother Hedgehog as her quills rose and fell. "Tell me more. For our kind has no friendly dealings with the children of men. They hunt and torment us."

"The manchild I befriended was of a different spirit. He was baptized in the grief of gulf waters before I had met him. No desire was found in him to trouble us, but rather to treasure us. Indeed, he himself seemed a rare treasure, for the birds known as the Colony of the Lost had discovered him at dawn, washed up on the beach with no Man to help him, and they vowed to watch him the duration of his journey since they, too, had been lost at one time. And they chose for him the name Miracle. He welcomed me and the fishing friend I had made, and he told me his story of sorrow in the sea."

"Ah, sorrow," the hedgehog reflected, "a gift both marvelous and dangerous, and only the opener of the gift can decide which one it shall be. Sorrow at so young an age can work for good or for ill the rest of one's life, like a land creature tossed into the water before he is weaned. Either he learns to swim, or he drowns. It can go either way."

"I know, dear Mother, which is why I tried to guide the child out of sorrow. I sent my friend to help him find his parents, and he gathered others to help him in his quest, but Man's restless ways have driven them from the boy on separate paths to separate places. They abide apart from one another. Now here I am, also separate, apart from my friend, apart from Miracle—a broken piece of Kahoo's prophecy."

Oracle dropped his head to the ground beside his paws and let out a long sigh.

Mother Hedgehog moved to where Oracle's head now lay. She, too, reclined with her head resting on the ground beside his. "You sound discouraged."

"I am discouraged."

"Why so?"

"Because the word of Kahoo is not complete, Mother. I put my paw forward into it, but I did not walk the length of it. I am not from the north, nor have I ever swum the sky. And Kahoo's prayer said nothing of a manchild. My fur is caught in briars I cannot pull myself out of."

Mother Hedgehog considered the cat's words. She rose, turned toward him, and saw his eyes were clouded with a vision of a sign without meaning. She touched his nose and looked him full in the face.

"Do not give up your paw. For no prophecy is complete in the words alone; only the one prophesied about can complete it. And no prophecy tells the full story; there might well be an unspoken part that has as much weight as the spoken. Therefore, though Kahoo called for a jaguar 'from the north and from the sky,' it does not rule you out as his helper from the south, nor does it forbid a manchild joining you from the gulf. Yours is not a broken piece of a single prophecy, but a puzzle piece to a greater one.

From the sky and from the north
From the gulf and from the south
Both are equal in their worth
Both come from the Maker's mouth

Oracle's eyes filled with tears. "Thank you," he gently growled. "You have cracked open a dawn for me. For all that is in the dark, one thing is in the light: the thing I know I can do."

"Yes," Mother Hedgehog said, "to give the animals a new story that is the true story, the one coming from the name Adam gave them. Through you, they can remember. Even within the barred gates of this place, your gift remains and takes wing beyond the walls."

"It does indeed, as both you and the pigeons testify. Thank you for reminding me. I will impart to the animals the memory of the first story. In that seed are the branches of their true tale. And such branches grow regardless of where I myself am planted. It is the same for my mahogany companion, for he, like me, dwells within a confined place, and yet he stretches out his branches. No walls can limit the life the root gives."

A gentle breeze passed through. She caressed the fur of the four-footed ones and stirred the sleeping branches of the trees, mahogany and juniper, ash and oak, tallow and cottonwood.

—ᴧᴧ—

Oracle looked into the hedgehog's eyes. "Mother, I seek the knowledge of another puzzle piece: the jaguarundi of the Valley, a feline who all say is gone, save a rumor I heard from my cousin the tiger across the manstone pond. I need your help to bring that rumor to the light of day and see what it speaks when it is no longer in the shadows."

Mother Hedgehog trotted to the place of Oracle's paws, though her feet were unseen, such that it looked as if she hovered her way to the spot. "How can I help you? My children and I rejoice to find that puzzle piece for you."

"Where can I find a coral snake? Does one live here?"

"Yes, she is in the manplace called the herpetarium. She lives behind a sheet of glass placed among many other serpents, I am told."

"The glass is good, for she cannot bring you harm in the errand I give. Ask her for the riddle of the jaguarundi. If she is of a certain brood of corals the tiger told me about, then she will speak it to you. When you have learned by heart the riddle she asks, carry it to me, that I might hear it and give an answer for you to take back to her. If I answer well, then the coral will give a password for you to speak to the turtles, who then may tell you the place of the secret lair of the jaguarundi in the Valley."

"We will go," Mother Hedgehog said. And with that, she awakened her children, who formed a gathering of quills and sank back into the earth through the hole like a pool of water receding into a drain. They hastened to the herpetarium.

But when they arrived, they found the entire building consisted of a manwork so impervious that the hedgehogs could not penetrate it. Its foundation granted no sufficiently sized fracture or portal for passage. And though they pleaded with many a gecko and cockroach to carry their request inside, none were willing.

"For the sight of a snake is the same as the bite of a snake to us," the gecko said. "Glass or no glass." And the cockroaches muttered the same.

For a night and a day, they looked for ways to enter—abandoned badger lairs, forgotten drainpipes—but when night fell again, the hedgehogs returned to the lord of the Valley and asked his forgiveness, for they could not carry out the quest he had given them beyond the barrier of Man's granite defenses.

Oracle blessed and released them. "All you can do is all you can do, and you have done all. Go in peace." And they departed.

The cat of Sian Ka'an lay down on his side, his back between himself and his hopes.

I shall turn my heart to gratitude, lest despair be my companion in the sleeping hours. The Bermuda grass beneath me is soft and green, for Man apportions water to it in these days of drought. And I shall know my portion in these dry days too. The crickets calm the sleepers all around me with their gentle chants, and they shall calm me too. The far-off murmur of Man's mobility does not disturb the circuit of the stars, and it shall not disturb me either.

Eyes closed, Oracle took in the air. The faint scent of slumbering neighbors drifted by, such as the buffalo who had come into her milk for her calf. The scent of nurture mixed with the natural oils of the buffalo's burly mane. The smell of the giraffe also strode by, carrying with it a slight sting of half-decayed straw in a spot between her cloven hooves. Then passed before him the vapors of the elephant, a cloud of gathered memories stored for the days of thunder. Then came the aroma of the jaguar's proud but ailing cousin behind the bamboo. Oracle beheld the images the aromas carried to the eyes of his heart until all of his neighbors had gathered before him. His body rose and fell as he meditated upon the assembly of animals, his coat's rosette spots gently moving like lilies on a pond move when the wind blows and the waters are stirred.

14

CRASH LANDING

The great manstone pond was dying. Man had chosen not to supply it in his attempt to conserve what water remained for the living things of the dwelling places he had created for them. On the night the hedgehogs turned back from the herpetarium to tell Oracle of their failed quest, they used its empty quarter as a shortcut. Over the next six days, the pond dwindled until only a drab pool remained, saturated with urban grays and browns, a shallow sheet that bore the heat each day and passed out each night weaker than before. The fainting waters disclosed a yawning mouth on the bank that widened as the surface receded. In time, the waters retreated enough to reveal a tunnel, dark and uncaring, unnaturally naked to the sky, harboring secrets that were no longer there.

On the night the August new moon hid behind the horizon and the tunnel could open no wider, Mother Hedgehog visited Oracle.

"Crash the tiger greets you. He says, 'A great sign appeared in the heavens today! Surely you saw it! At noon the moon passed in front of the sun and took the lion's share of his rays away. And now, behold, this night the moon is altogether gone and the heavens wide open! This means a way of escape will soon come to us. And behold the great mouth opening at the bottom of the manpond! This is a confirming sign, for it is a passage hidden from both moon and sun. It is dry and empty now, and it leads to another empty manpond and the riverside edge of the zoo.'"

Oracle rose, tail curling with excitement, ears angled in sober readiness. "Very good. Thank you for the message, Mother. But what are we to do when we reach that edge?"

The hedgehog rose on her hind limbs. "He says you must leap a great moat and climb a gate. 'The smell of freedom will give us strength,' he says. 'Then I will go to the realm of the well-fed deer, and you will go to your beloved Valley.'"

Oracle surveyed his dwelling place. "Man has tamed me here. His barriers forbid me passage. Your tunnels that have coursed under me long before foot and paw trod this place: These permit you to pass freely under the walls. But, as you have said, I am too large and strong for your secret paths."

"Yes, you are," Mother Hedgehog replied, "but I can call upon my tribe to try to make a way for you, one deep and wide enough to bring you to the other side of the walls. Only I cannot promise what the earth will do. For the soil has broken its covenant with the roots of the trees in these days of the deaf sky. We have heard the earth whispering to the roots as we pass through. It gasps, 'We can no longer hold you, but you may rest here among us if you can until the sky hears us again.'"

"What have the roots said in reply?" Oracle asked.

"Nothing yet, in part to save their strength, in part because it is not yet time to speak. For roots, though always there, seldom speak, even though they uphold the entire tree."

Oracle wondered at Mother's comment. "Your words are deeper than the roots themselves."

She bowed in gratitude. "I will gather my tribe in a chamber called the Listening Place. Its entrance is a tunnel deeper than the ones we use to pass between these dwelling places. We have made a room there, a hall spacious enough for one from each household to be present. I cannot tell you where it is, for it belongs only to the hedgehogs. No one knows of it except our tribe and the face of limestone holding up our feet there."

—⟊—

Mother Hedgehog traveled the common passage of her tribe until she reached a place where another tunnel branched downward. She descended so deeply she reached a place where the soil still carried the faint aroma of a single drop of rainwater from the time when all things had been green. Here the hedgehogs had widened the passage to form a room: the Listening Place. Here the earth had promised the hedgehogs, "We will remain in place for the sake of the raindrop. We will not fall on you so long as he remains. You may come and go freely, for one drop is enough for us. He is a promise of downpours to come."

—⟊—

Six more nights passed. On the seventh, the moon waxed at her first quarter while the Texas August breathed her last days upon a realm of forgotten leaves. The humid air touched plant, seed, and soil, but weak was its encouragement, and it did little more than stir in creation the discomfort of a fitful slumber, for none had drunk the cup of rain ensuring pleasant dreams.

Oracle reclined beside the young mahogany of his dwelling place, which Man still watered with careful allocations, but which felt the loneliness of the land reaching for rain. The lord of the Valley leaned against the tender bark, and the mahogany found strength as the life of the jaguar touched his.

"Thank you," the mahogany said. "You have awakened my roots. And if the roots are awakened, the fruit will come. Yes, in due time, it will come."

"You are welcome, Sage of the Captive Forest. Your roots shall grow deep, and your trunk tall, such that your whispered wisdom will move across this barred garden like runners of wild ivy."

The mahogany moved his slender trunk in gentle reply. "And may it be that your paws, oh Cat Who Remembers, run just as wild one day."

The soft crumble of earth announced Mother Hedgehog's arrival. She came panting and was so out of breath she could not speak until the space of time it took for the tail of a gossamer-thin cloud to pass before the moon.

"We have done it," she finally said. "The way is ready, and may the earth show mercy on you as you pass through."

"And on you," Oracle replied, "until the days of the deaf sky are ended and the heavens once again give ear to the cry of the earth."

"Crash the tiger awaits. He has unlocked his lair through a bribe to the spider monkeys. He is at the moat near a gate of the mangarden, the one closest to the river. 'Make haste, for it is open!' he commands."

"I am grateful, Mother. You have done what I could not do so that I can do what you cannot do. Therefore, all the good that comes through my paw from this day on is under your tribe's paw as well."

"I delight in that inheritance, Lord of the Valley. But I did not do it for that reason, though what you say is true if you escape. I cannot tunnel around or beneath your words, for they speak what *is*. Nevertheless, I dug for your sake, for you are meant for the Valley, and I dug for the sake of all on whom you will breathe, for then they will remember what we remember."

And Oracle bowed to honor her heart. He followed Mother Hedgehog to the mouth of the tunnel. Five pairs of eyes greeted him in silent but gleaming welcome.

"We could not bear the thought of you pawing like a fox," said the hedgehog closest to the cat, "so we have widened the mouth for you." And he whispered a boast:

On the surface searching out
Man and manchild scratch and shout
Eating up the marked-out grass
Building with more steel and glass

But the city underground
Makes a path Man's not yet found
Secret portals shrewdly dug
Underneath his landscaped rug!

The hedgehogs circled the mouth of the tunnel and bowed to the lord of the Valley as he dropped his forepaws into the entrance.

Oracle smiled. "Thank you," he said, and he touched his forehead to Mother's while she smoothed back her quills to keep the kiss gentle.

—ɯ—

The cat descended into another world, a secret one of slugs and crawling things afraid of the sun. But the scent of the hedgehog was there, as was the aroma of the mole, who, after much prodding and the persuasion of a store of truffles, had consented to help the hedgehogs—but only for as much time as it would take for their truffle-filled stomachs to grow empty again.

Down Oracle went into the hole, deeper and deeper at an incline so steep the cat had to brace his legs to keep from sliding. The air was good, but light was utterly absent.

Oracle's eyes dilated to the fullness of their round and clear capacity but saw only imagined shapes faintly crossing his vision in the same way a turtle faintly appears to the lolling, boat-bound fisherman but disappears the moment he throws his startled gaze in earnest on the mysterious moving thing. In that pitch-black tunnel, Oracle's eyes finally humbled themselves and rested.

It was all paw and whisker now. But Oracle was a great cat from a tribe who ruled in the night, and his whiskers were long and many, and they touched the sides of the tunnel with such lightness and dexterity that in his mind's eye he composed a perfect vision of the tunnel from the touches.

Down he went, and farther down, and farther still, and it occurred to Oracle that the way was so narrow he could not turn around, and the passage was so steep he could not back out. There was nothing left to do but go forward. In time the path leveled slightly.

I am past the wall. Soon the tunnel will begin to rise to the slope of the manstone pond.

But even as he concluded this thought, he felt a groan in the earth and heard a crumbling behind him. He hurried.

A muffled burst of heaviness struck at his hind legs. He felt the top of the tunnel fall upon his tail. Oracle urged himself forward.

More earth, asleep and forgetful, fell, this time on his haunches. Again, the jaguar escaped, but it seemed the faster he moved, the faster the soil dumped itself down, oblivious to the living thing it pursued.

The tunnel turned upward. Upon the cat's blank eyes fell a small patch of night sky. The star Vega, a burning torch of bluish white, hung like a prize.

He lunged his paw upward—the earth overtook him, covering the sky, the paw, and his face. Oracle pulled back as a block of dead gumbo clay dropped where his head had been. He took another step back and found his hindquarters pressed against a mountain of fallen loam. He pushed forward again, holding his breath, thrusting his paw at the unyielding clay. Nothing moved before him.

His lungs burned, scouring every last space within themselves for air—and found none. He was sealed in the earth like a tomb, like a body forgotten to the land of the living.

All was lost.

Oracle prayed.

Tunnels deep will bend to love
As tender branch will bend to dove
When Gardener who formed the earth
Bends down to form a way for birth

Remember prayers from Lonely Tree
Remember words from Kahoo free
Do not forget what star and moon
Have heard and seen is coming soon!

And with these words, he fainted and waited to turn into the dust around him.

In the silence, Oracle felt himself descending, not rapidly but as one moving through water, drifting toward a place of shadows. It seemed that deep beneath him he could hear the shadows whispering. The voices were indistinct, as when someone in a cavern speaks a memory of a long-ago story, and farther up the passage the story echoes in an unintelligible form somewhere between a moan and a song.

There was a moment of unutterable aloneness. A place of no footing, no song. A void over the deep, where even the whispers faded away.

Oracle felt a tug. His descent ceased.
There he hung in mid-darkness.

The cat's nose twitched in response to a tickling feeling. He winced, for his snout itched but he could not move his paw to scratch it. The tickling grew stronger, and Oracle found he was no longer suspended above the shadows; he was in the tunnel again. Air poured into his body.

A shuffling sound filled the earth around him, and when Oracle opened his eyes, he was staring into the face of a mole, whose soft and tender features were pressed against his face. The mole's eyes, small and embedded in velvet-like fur, stared into his own with a blend of fear and wonder.

Oracle felt the dirt moving around him while other moles dug with their flipper-like arms. They worked in a silent and unceasing rhythm, scooping and shoveling, dissolving the earth. Only the one pressed against his face did not dig. As for that mole, though his spades were at rest, his eyes took in the lord of the Valley with the steady watchfulness of one carefully gathering memories.

Ah, I see. The others are depending on their brother to relate to them the stories dwelling in me!

Brother mole withdrew and the wink of Vega reached Oracle's eyes. He struggled to the surface.

When he turned back to thank the moles, they were gone. He heard their squeaking whispers of joy fading in the tunnel, but none bid him farewell. They did, however, decorate the mouth of the tunnel with truffles in honor of their guest.

"The hedgehogs have breathed upon the moles," Oracle concluded, and he rejoiced.

—ᙡ—

The cat leaped into the manstone pond. He bounded across barren concrete and splashed through a thin sheet of water, all that remained of the time before the drought, but enough to free chunks of clay from his claws. He reached the drainage pipe. Into its gaping mouth he dove, and the dank air refused to receive his aroma, remaining stale and aloof to his presence. But the cat moved forward nonetheless, head pitched downward in caution, ears turned forward, feet at a pace one step short of a run. Oracle emerged in the basin of another empty pond. He climbed to the rim of it, following its bank near the homes of the giant Galápagos tortoise and the sloth.

Beyond these, he found a narrow corridor skirting the edge of the meadow of the buffalo, who stared at him with wide-eyed silence. Once through the corridor, Oracle moved down a culvert and around a corner. He bounded northeast across a sidewalk between two kiosks, climbed a fiberglass rock formation, and ran along the top of the brick border of the aviary.

He emerged in an open space gently sloping upward. At its crest was the striped back of his friend Crash, who sat at the edge of the dry moat bordering the zoo, tail twitching at the thought of the Red River woods. Oracle joined him.

Crash nodded a greeting and returned to adoring the vista before them. There, beyond an empty road and an open gate, wound the Brazos River. Neither cat said anything, but both looked at the inviting arm of water with wild surmise.

Stealth was on their side. The Tribes of the Underground had disappeared, and the buffalo had not called out. The spider monkeys, watching from their quivering tightrope, squeezed their hands over each other's mouths. Besides these witnesses, none yet knew the place of the jaguar and the place of the tiger were empty. None yet knew they had reached the waterless moat near the boundary line between the zoo and the outside world. None yet knew that the Men who had clocked out of the day shift had left the service gate open, expecting a late delivery truck at any moment. The truck had never come, and the Men of the night shift had never known it was expected.

Crash growled resolutely. "If there were ever a moment to make a run for it, it is *now*."

"But the edge of the moat is alive with fire," Oracle said. "Listen to the crickets warning us. If you are still, you can hear the flames humming in the wires."

The tiger rose and poised to spring. "I'll go first, then. I still have my circus days in me. Jumping through a ring of fire was as easy as licking my paws back in the day. It can't be much different with the invisible fire. It will just sting for a moment, if at all."

Crash jumped across the moat before Oracle could stop him—before Oracle could offer him the Breath of Remembrance that could have lent the cat a strength deeper than a self-made tale. He landed with all fours at the lip of the moat and pushed his way between the stinging fence lines.

But as he did, motion-sensitive flood lamps threw an unnatural blast of light upon him. The tiger urged his body forward. The firestring burned, but not for a moment as he had thought; it traveled into him like an angry liquid seeking the center of his bones. He shouted, twisting involuntarily in pain, tangling in the lines. He fell backward, and his heavy frame pulled the firestring with him, ripping it away from its posts. He hit the bottom of the moat. The firestring died.

There he lay: the tiger Crash. The fall had knocked the wind out of him. He stared at the constellations above, distant lights in an ancient dance, where the swan and eagle circled, each lending their light to the Summer Triangle. And there, too, he saw Vega, the jewel of a harp, as some saw her, but to others a vulture plummeting to earth with a burden too heavy to carry. Crash saw the vulture. He watched it fall.

The spider monkeys shrieked in alarm, swinging in frenzy through their trapeze.

"We won the bet!" rejoiced a monkey. "*Told you* he wouldn't make it! Give us our share of the tiger's bribe!"

Another gnashed his teeth. "Curses! A bad break, that's all. He was as good as free!"

"Sore losers! We won fair and square. Give us the loot!"

Meanwhile, the flamingos cried out through a flutter of flapping wings. The buffalo moaned her long call of warning, and her calf cried out as if forlorn. The elephants trumpeted, and the giraffe stomped in anxious uncertainty. Every animal in the zoo awakened.

Oracle beheld his blundering friend suffering at the bottom of the moat. He considered the Brazos, its flat, wide waters moving away. Oracle looked again at the tiger, who was wincing as the last of the invisible fire dissipated in his body and new pains from the fall took over.

The sound of an electric manmachine whined at high speed up a path. Man had come.

"Go!" cried Crash. "Go, both for you and for me! Greet the cats in council you told me about! Greet them with my courage and my roar!"

Oracle glanced in the direction of the manmachine, then the river, then Crash. "What courage is it for me to leave you behind? To leave you and put my paw forward would be a half-lived life—the very thing we're fleeing!"

"But the *council!*" shouted the tiger. "The Valley *calls!*"

The manmachine rushed into view, a crate in tow. Men leaped out before it had fully halted. They came running, arming their weapons as they advanced with a *click-clack-click*, steel rods spitting either needles of sleep or bullets of death, and which ones would ultimately pierce the animals they almost never knew until the piercing itself.

But be it sleep or death, I know what to do.

Oracle remained. He reclined at the edge of the moat and kept watch over his friend below, speaking to the tiger through the look on his face.

I'm not leaving you.

Crash saw and a look of comfort fell across him as his eyes replied. *Thank you, Lord of the Valley. Truly, you have conquered.*

Footsteps prompted Oracle to turn his head. Two Men and two Women skidded to a halt, weapons at the ready before the cat of the Yucatán.

"Why ain't he in a hurry?" said one.

"I don't know!" said another as she aimed her weapon. "I'll keep my sights on him in case of a sudden move."

Oracle considered what to do. *These Men and Women need guidance. First things first.*

He peered over the edge of the moat, fixing his eyes downward as his tail waved in a nonchalant curve. The Men and Women followed his gaze to the tiger.

"Holy camoly!" shouted one. "Call Chase! Get the vet team here pronto!"

A Man phoned while aiming his revolver at the cat. Two others positioned themselves to defend him, one with a tranquilizer rifle and one with live ammunition. The fourth reached behind him for a catch pole on the crate while he leveled his dart pistol on the animal.

Oracle remained still.

The best thing I can do is impart peace. It is the one thing requiring neither paw nor voice. Just breath.

And Oracle did so. He watched the Men and Women respond to his peace as, one by one, they lowered their weapons. And yet none replaced their lowered weapons with raised phones, unlike what the cat observed daily at the observation glass of his exhibit, where Man's one predictable habit was the raising of the slender box to capture him in images.

And so, with both the weapons and phones of Man at rest, the cat of the Southern Jungle enjoyed a space of harmony between himself and his masters, the sons of Adam and the daughters of Eve, who wordlessly acknowledged along with the jaguar that none should disrupt the sacrament of the present moment. And none did. All remained in that moment until it became a door to a promise both fully true now and not yet fulfilled. A word from a distant oasis to the barren desert of daily routines.

Oracle's thoughts turned toward the manchild whom the birds had named Miracle. *Perhaps the seed of the present moment will take root in these Men and Women like it has in the child. I hope it will. But now it is time for me to clear the way for them to help my friend in the moat below.*

With that, he rose, yawning as he did, his tail curling and uncurling in the fluid fashion of a feline. Then he placidly walked toward the crate and sat before its door. He turned to the Men and Women, yawning again.

"Incredible!" said one. "It's like he knows!"

"He *does* know," said another. "You can see it in his eyes."

"Open the crate!" shouted the one who seemed to Oracle to be in charge. "Have the pole and rifles at the ready! Then let's get to work on that tiger!"

No need for anxious speech, oh Man. No need for fire rods. I will remain in the captive realm of Crash until a way is made that is clearly of the Maker's doing and not the work of a desperate paw. For—as long as I remember my name and the Maker—I am free.

Oracle reclined inside the crate. As they transported him, he noticed the Men and Women only whispered, and, because of their muted voices, he could hear the serenade of the cricket and the mourning dove.

The zookeepers returned the jaguar to his place. The young mahogany stirred before his smile.

"Welcome back, Lord of the Valley. The doves told me you preferred delay with a wounded friend to departure for your destiny. Sit under my branches and recall the Days of First Things. This will comfort you."

And Oracle did so while he breathed the predawn air, free and clear.

15

THE GARDENER OF EDEN

The stars of September and October passed while the hedgehogs brought news of Crash's slow recovery.

"The Woman who leads the zoo sits with him daily in the manplace called 'the infirmary,'" Mother Hedgehog said. "The fly told us so. She says the Woman speaks to Crash in her native tongue. She even sings to him when they are alone. But when the physicians are present, she is silent."

"Have you ever heard of such a thing before?" Oracle asked.

"No, not among the tales of our day. But in the tales of First Things there are many stories like this, as you know. The Breath of Remembrance has revealed it."

"Then the Woman, too, remembers something of those First Things."

"It appears that she does," Mother Hedgehog said. "But there is more. Today, the lizards of the magnolia trees outside the infirmary told us the Woman took the tiger in a manmachine to a realm of stout oaks and tall grasses north of here called Cross Timbers. She released him in a place where the fences are far off, the deer are nearby, and the creeks flow to the Red River. Now the cat runs free until the sun sets on his days."

Oracle stirred the air with his tail. "What good messengers the tree lizards are."

"Yes," said Mother Hedgehog with an eager nod, "and courageous too. One of the House of Anolis was brave enough

179

to hop on board the manmachine, disguise himself with the color of the crate, and watch it all take place. The lizard went there and back again with an eyewitness account. We know the lizard's testimony is true, for he lost his tail on the return journey by the hand of a Man who tried to catch him. The lizard had posted himself on the seat where the Woman steered, desiring to learn all he could. When the Woman saw the lizard and startled, the Man assisting her tried to seize him, but the lizard escaped with his life, though not with his tail."

Oracle smiled. "Well done for the House of Anolis, and well done for the daughter of Eve, who remembers something of the First Things; enough to act on them. Enough to make her life and the lives of others a sign the First Things will return after the Last Things have had their day."

Mother Hedgehog rose on her hind legs. "You are comforted by the news, then? Not sad that you are left behind?"

"I am comforted, Mother, and my sorrow finds a resting place in it. Crash has received his final wish: a place to roam and be a tiger before the last leaves of his tree fall. He will be content, and therefore I will be content. And I know he will remember me, even as I will remember him. His story shall not fade as long as I have breath to share it. As for my own fate, I do not know if it will be like that of the tiger, whom Man chose to set free to a great degree. For there are other choices Man can also make concerning us, the animals. We shall see which one he chooses for me."

—ᴍ—

The stories of November's constellations reached their prime. Perseus, the intrepid prince, leaping off his winged horse, raised his adamantine sword to cut the chains of

Andromeda, the beautiful maiden bound to a rock before an ocean behemoth rushing to devour her. King Cepheus and Queen Cassiopeia, her parents, looked on in amazed relief at the hero's intervention while a charioteer stood ready, upon the slaying of the beast, to carry the newlyweds away.

But another swam these heavenly waters too, passing right between beast and maiden: Pisces the double fish, united by a fishing line. They were the offspring of the one called the Great Fish, known for its lifesaving graces in many nations, from Babylon to Egypt, and even to Roman Palestine, where one day a Man would take two fish, bless them, break them, and give them away, shattering more chains than the sword of the demigod ever could.

Beneath that struggle and the sign swimming through it, the earth groaned in thirst for rain. Trees creaked in the breeze as the soil beneath them loosened its hold, drained of the grace that gave it strength. The wind brought with him news of the Great Plains he had blown upon and news of the mountains he had buffeted. But no one listened, for he brought no news of storm clouds. His words were hollow. The zoo preferred to sleep and find rest from the worry of another rainless night.

Oracle slept too. And in his sleep, he dreamed.

He found himself in a place where no drought reigned. Thick grasses flanked a path so fresh no tracks preceded him. The soil smelled so new the scent of it imparted a kind of food, a living breath entering heart and bones. Occasionally the path wound through bushes rich with aromas of comforting herbal cures and flavors fit to savor at many banquets to come. There were no thorns.

The path curved past the low-hanging branches of a pome-granate tree burdened with the weight of unplucked fruit of such pristine ripeness Oracle could smell the juices of every sweet seed within. He walked beneath great palm fronds dripping with dew and fragrant fuchsia flowers so vivid in their hues the colors vibrated through the air in a wave that struck the cat's eyes like a high tide splash.

The ground rose. The leaf-covered incline gave way to open sky, where Oracle beheld carefully crafted terraces, each hosting a pool where rice plants rejoiced to join the elements of water below and sky above, the green sheaves aglow with the sunlight passing through them. Clouds paraded upon the pool's smooth surfaces, while above them sailed their mirrored originals.

Oracle continued farther up, and from that elevated place, he surveyed a cultivated realm, bush upon branch upon tree stretching out in every direction, even to the horizon, where the lush land blended with a grand and indistinct terrain.

Light and air mingled with a fine mist. The three elements diffused one into the other, until the three, though distinct in their beings, became one full-fledged mantle covering the garden estate like a comprehensive canopy, impossible to grasp with the paw and yet touching every living thing.

The scent of a Man reached Oracle. Instinctively he searched for the source, discerning the direction the smell came from. He put his paw forward and gently pursued. As he walked, the branches harbored the scent he sought, a sign of the one who had been there. The aerial trail continued until it was no longer a trail only but an invisible cloud surrounding him, affirming each step.

Oracle heard the cloud speak. Each step released another word—word upon word woven together into a wind moving with him. Here is what the wind proclaimed in rhythm to his stride, a burst of words growing and overgrowing each other like shoots of jasmine and overflowing with first fruits in each sound:

Green slopes frosted with lavender harvest
Curve the pathway where fulsome frankincense
Salutes the seedling cedars soon to host
A palace on galbanum-bearing bluffs
Who greet great terebinth orchards below
As strong as bronze made tender by the doves

Plane trees planted at brook's bank meander
Water bound with tall palms cov'ring roses
In cool shadows where myrrh mixes with cane
Sweetening the onycha and stacte
Growing while greeting oaken arms outstretched
To host feathered broods of avian song

Cypress succors spices with her shroud
Of mossy gowns while leaf-laden branches
Woo cassia cradling sweet odors
And evergreen boughs raise rich harvest hopes
From frail cone to pine, from full vine to wine
Foretelling outpouring after mourning

Acacia blooms along with bright myrtles
Sending cinnamon in scented breezes
Ahead of kings exploring for their source
Now First King hides within his fields cachés
For the crowned ones to come, reserved for when
Servants reign and songs renew the earth

The cat came to a clearing, and there before him knelt a Man whose back was to him. His arms were bare. His outer garment lay on a nearby tree stump around which fresh shoots rose from living roots. A broad straw hat cast a disk of perfectly cool air upon the place where the Man worked. His face was indistinct, for the shadow of the brim obscured it.

Oracle approached the Man, who glanced briefly at the cat with a smile but continued his work, knees in the dirt, hands piercing holes in the soil, fingernails full of fresh earth from the labor. Within each hole he placed a slender stick and gently plugged the remainder of the space with a tender plant so green and fresh the color and the smell thereof permeated the air, and Oracle could not tell whether the scent came from the seedlings, the gardener, or both.

"Greetings, Cat Who Remembers," said the gardener.

"Greetings, Maker…What are you doing?"

"Planting a garden."

"For whom?"

"For my children."

"Where are they?"

"They are asleep in the wild. But I will wake them and bring them here once all is planted."

"How will they know the ways of caring for what you have planted?"

"They will know, for I myself will walk with them."

Oracle stretched out his body and watched the gardener with that signature feline mixture of curiosity and aloof repose. He groomed his coat in unselfconscious diligence, licking in careful succession one patch of fur after another, his supple body at rest like a throw rug, colorful and still.

Oracle paused, for he observed the gardener draw two fingers through the soil beside the row of seedlings, creating a cut of earth. Chattering waters flowed into it from the ground below, and from another cut flowing into it swam dozens of small silver fish whose mint-condition scales flashed in the sunshine. They darted through the plants, the reflected light from each fish filling the cat's eyes with life-giving insight, instant and new. The waters laughed as the seedlings grew strong, and Oracle thought he could hear the leaves laughing too, but in the silent code of rooted things. He watched the stems rise in verdant delight.

"These will be good tomatoes," the gardener said. "Thin of skin but thick of flavor! They will splash in the mouths of my children and play with other flavors gathered there. They will color our garden along with the pepper and the citrus."

"How great is your garden?" Oracle asked.

"Three days' journey," he said, reaching for another seedling to plant.

"Are there places for my paws and the paws of my kin?"

The gardener smiled. "Oh yes, plenty—every place your Namer names for you across the whole earth."

"Across the whole earth? Not just the garden?"

"This garden is the first fruit. In time it will grow across the face of the wild. It will expand to the home of every wind. And your kind will be tamed along the way."

"Tamed for serving him?"

"Yes, for serving, and, in time, for befriending. He will show you friendship from being with me."

"What if he forgets to be with you?"

"Then he will show you that too."

The gardener took a handful of dark soil from a sack beside him and mixed it with the fair-colored earth around the seedlings. Then he took a hand spade, broke up new ground, and did it again.

"When will you bring your children here?"

"In the cool of the day. When the shadows of the pines reach the walls, I will bring them."

"Very good," the cat said. "I would like to see them. I shall remain here until they come."

The gardener rose. He stepped ahead a few paces and surveyed the realm from the vantage point of the hill where he was. Oracle also rose, stretching his body, his forelimbs straight as rods, his back curved like a ski slope, and his tail a gentle hook. In a smooth and noiseless gait, he came to the gardener and sat beside him, making his presence known with the brushing of head and back against the Man's leg.

Oracle followed the gardener's gaze, and he noticed that when the gardener's eyes fell upon a certain distant feature of the estate, they lingered there in solemn meditation. Oracle lingered there too. Beyond an orchard of alternating apricots and almonds sloping upward and away, two trees loomed above the line of innocent boughs: one with promising colors peeking through the leaves—the other a deep, desirable green, steady and still.

"What are those two trees?"

"Those are the center of the garden."

"Two trees?"

"Two trees. I planted them there."

"Is that where your children will make their home?"

"That is where my children will make their choice."

"They will grow strong there, then."

"Yes, they will. One way or another."

"If they are strong, they can take your garden to the ends of the earth more swiftly."

"Yes, dear friend, more swiftly, but perhaps more forget-fully too."

"That is not good, for if they forget, they will lose their way back to the center."

"If they lose their way, I myself will become the center."

Oracle looked at the gardener's hands, and he noticed that they also, like the soil of the garden, were pierced.

The Man has prepared his body like the garden he works in, Oracle observed.

"Yes," the gardener replied, though Oracle had not opened his mouth. "Fruit will come from this planting too. It will be a long time in coming. And though it is the first planting, it will be the last to be harvested. Yes, this planting will be both the first and the last."

Then a light came from the holes and went through Oracle, a light so bright there was no thought for him to do anything other than to close his eyes and be still. The light continued to shine. He perceived the brightness of it resting on his eyelids, the touch of the light like the wing of a dove. And all was pure, and Oracle felt himself lost and found again at the same time, dust and spirit, with both past and future before him. He inhaled, and it seemed the whole of creation passed through his lungs like a song.

"I must see the gardener's children," he groaned. He resolved to open his eyes even if the light would undo him. "It is worth the undoing, for what other reason is there for living than to look upon life? And if it indeed turns out to be the last thing I do, it is a well-done last thing. Come now, oh heart, rally yourself and command these eyelids to lift! Behold, the children of the gardener!"

But when Oracle opened his eyes, he awoke to the slumbering zoo, where the crickets were greeting the dark before the dawn. On the southeast horizon, just visible among the cottonwoods, three planets peeked at him as they ascended into the waking sky where, one by one, the sun blew out their glory. Mars, Venus, and Jupiter each flickered a farewell, each departing like a candle melted down to its brazen base when the flame is more vapor than light.

And the cat longed to know the end of the dream.

16

LOVERS' LEAP

Winter arrived after weeks of fitful hesitation. During those arbitrary evenings of warm or cold, the moon ran her course from waning to waxing again. She reached the winter solstice, the longest night of the year. A single cloud ran his silent errand before the moon, clothing her for a moment with a whisper of new-crescent glory before she sank behind the horizon.

Bathed in that departing glow, Oracle slept.

In the path of his sleep, from dream to dream, Oracle heard a sound moving along with him. In the first dream, as he swam the silent, overgrown canals of the Mayan city of Edzná, a faint moaning rose from the deep blue beneath him. In the second dream, he was a cub again, curled up in the bosom of his mother while his father recalled the story of Onca the Pathmaker, the first jaguar, in the time before things were forgotten. In that dream the moan grew to a groan, and the groan grew unceasing.

But in the third dream, while the stars sang to a strange forest lashed tightly to the earth by molten bands of earth now hardened, the groan became a roar shattering the dream and filling his ears with a rush of active panic in the zoo. The spider monkeys were screeching like banshees.

"The tree has fallen! The Grackle Tree! The tree has fallen! Fallen!"

Oracle shot up. Animals great and small were lowing the calls of their kinds. Then he saw it: The glass barrier through which Man observed him now stood split open in a jagged V shape among torn mock stone. And lo, on the other side of the fracture, the old cottonwood—that same towering sentinel where the grackles had formed their attack through the spell of the spirit—was down. Its great ball of roots splayed into bare air, roots harboring the whole of the tree's memories now wafting free from their hiding place to poles unknown. Oracle could hear the roots' recollections:

> *Native Man reclining 'neath me*
> *Seeking healing from the springs*
> *Graybeard soldiers on me leaning*
> *Telling tales that made them kings*
>
> *Secret courtships in my shadow*
> *Blooming in the midnight rain*
> *Broken grackles fresh repenting*
> *From the cat who brought them pain*

The ancient tree lay across a manpath of the zoo, flattening pampas grass and a fabric-covered barrier. Beyond that lay more exhibits, and beyond that the whole world.

The lord of the Valley poised to leap through the V, but its edges were sharp, and the jaguar perceived that the space of air between his fur and the unforgiving glass was less than the space of a sparrow.

I cannot look at the broken glass, or certainly it will slash me as I leap. I must look to the place I will land. Only then will the glass demur and honor my passing free of trial.

He fixed his eyes upon the place he desired to land: the roots. It was enough to do just this one thing. Oracle passed through unscathed.

Clear of his lair, he turned toward it.

"Farewell, young mahogany."

"Farewell," the tree replied. "I bear the mark of your claw gladly. I shall retell the tale of your abiding here to your future kin who find this to be their dwelling place. The tale will give them comfort and courage, the mark on my bark testifying my tale is true." And the tree pronounced this blessing over the lord of the Valley:

> *Be drenched with rain and sun*
> *Be strengthened on the run*
> *Where e'er your paw may go*
> *May life behind you grow*

Oracle kissed the bark with his whiskers. "And may you harbor life as well. Among your branches, beneath your boughs, and to your deepest root."

He looked at the living things around the tree. "And likewise be blessed, oh palmettos and blades of grass and gentle hibiscus, reminder of the monarch who birthed my journey through her story. Thank you for your company. Like the trees who guided me on the Trail to the Lonely Tree, your memory shall remain planted within me."

And all the living things of the lair bade him adieu.

Oracle turned and traversed the tree, gingerly stepping through its confused mass of branches until he reached a place where they were too crushed together for him to easily pass.

He left the trunk for the ground, and out from the leaves he emerged to find himself on a service corridor where a double fence of rigid manmesh stood guard. The path reached a T intersection.

I have been here before. To turn right is to reach the moat and the troubles on its other side. I will not try that again.

He turned left, pursuing the way past the backside of several exhibits. The corridor came out at a high point, and from that place it afforded Oracle a view stretching across the simulated prairie and other habitats to the base of a steep slope beyond the zoo. Ashe juniper trees—or "red cedar" as Man calls them—covered the slope.

It is the realm beyond this mangarden! I shall survey it from the height above, and from there choose a way to the river below.

Oracle climbed the prairie's first fence, claws leveraging its face of steel squares. He sprang from its top to the second fence, where he used the dexterous skills of limb and tail to remain balanced for a moment on the precarious edge until the momentum of the leap had played itself out. He chose a place to land in the prairie below and jumped. His body gracefully absorbed the landing through the springlike flexing of his limbs, which distributed the weight of the impact across his whole frame rather than jolting it through the paws only. Then he silently sped across the prairie.

At the far end, before a hedge of purple sage, the buffalo stood with her calf half hidden in the bush behind her. She stomped the ground, lowered her horns, and prepared to fight; for there is no fear that shakes a mother from defending her child. Her eyes were wild with the expectation the jaguar would attack.

But Oracle did not attack. Instead, he breathed. The buffalo caught the scent of the air, raising her head to follow the aroma as it moved through the night. Oracle waited. He let his peace remain upon the space of silence. The calf sensed safety and came from behind his mother to smell the aroma as well.

That same air released such a hope among the sleeping buds of the purple sage they took it as a sign of rain and blossomed forth deep lavender hues in the dead of night, a barometer foretelling the undoing of the way things are. And the scent of the sage mixed with the scent of the breath.

The buffalo remembered something she had not realized she had forgotten: a word spoken to her in a pasture so fresh that to nuzzle the tender blades was to become sated and to smell the soft lushness of the field was to become a spry yearling again, leaping for the sheer joy of it. She remembered her name. And she reclined before the jaguar, unafraid, with this song in her heart.

Adam's first word is protection enough
A child of his coming will smooth out the rough
He'll pass right between us, both hunter and prey
And blaze a way back to the Garden's first day

The sound of Man reached them. Electric motors in motion on zoo paths rushed along out of sight, screeching and braking. Lights swung about in the air and on the ground. Footsteps sounded. Three zookeepers appeared at the edge of the prairie and hurried in, one almost tripping over another who had stopped suddenly at the sight of the jaguar, the buffalo, and the calf at perfect peace in one another's presence.

"What is going on?" a Man said. "Call Chase! Call the cops! Holy cow, this is serious!" The Men drew their firearms and dart rifles.

Oracle dashed past his bovine friends and disappeared into the compressed tangle of sage. The Men went after him, but the buffalo followed. With her great size, she pushed them into the leafy arms of the bushes such that two were unable to raise their weapons and the third could not aim. Thus, the sage and the buffalo worked together to pin the Men long enough for Oracle to escape. And the calf leaped with delight at the sight and mooed a joyful sound that both frightened and amazed the captive Men.

Reaching the next exhibit, Oracle found that the animals there, a family of Arabian oryx, had fled to the refuge of their concrete feeding stalls, too aghast at the possibility of anything other than the predictable routine of eating, sleeping, and being admired. But the giraffe was looking over the fence at the toothsome predator. Her legs shook with terror, but her neck was stiff. She lifted her head high.

"What have we here?" whispered the giraffe. "A cat who leaps to freedom! Welcome, fine prince."

Oracle tried to speak as politely as he could while he struggled to recover his breath. "Brave neighbor, thank you for your word of welcome, but I need wisdom to go along with your greeting. Behold, your neck is long and your gaze far. What do you see? How is the way? Where is the place I can most easily climb over?"

"You have one last field to cross, my own, and though the bamboo on its far side is thin at its rim to the outside world, the ironthorn is not. You will find yourself hard-pressed to get through it without ribbons of red flesh trailing behind you! And now what I see is Man closing in. They have entered the elephant's home on our flank and the oryx gate behind you. You have only moments, sire, you whom the hedgehogs call Lord of the Valley."

Zookeepers burst upon the oryx field to see the jaguar facing the giraffe on the other side.

"Quick!" yelled one. "Knock 'im out!"

But even as one of them raised her tranquilizer rifle, the earth gave way beneath her, and she found herself falling backward into a ditch three feet deep—the work of the hedgehogs, who the week before had built a storehouse just beneath the surface on a patch of grassless ground the oryx had given them for stockpiling kibbles procured from the petting zoo in exchange for a percentage of the take.

Then another zookeeper fell forward into holes of the moles, fresh conference halls they had rejoiced to make in secret meetings after their chosen one had beheld the face of the Cat Who Remembers and told them many a wonder he had seen in the jaguar's eyes.

In that instant the other zookeeper found himself preoccupied with the new emergency of coming to the aid of his teammates as the earth opened up and blocked their way.

The delay was all Oracle needed to climb the barrier and jump to within a foot of the giraffe. Startled, she darted back a step, her sense of dignity still preventing outright flight.

Oracle's eyes burned in earnest as he appealed to her. "Good neighbor, lend me your aid! As in the days of the Long Sleep, above the many waters in the Tomb of Fallen Trees, when your ancestor allowed the leopard cub to climb her neck and see horizon's end—please, may I do the same? For certainly, if you allowed me to climb, I, too, could see the way out."

"There is no way," she said. "My palace is also a prison. It is the way things are."

"The way things *are* is not the way things have always *been*. Oh friend, be thou now one who remembers the way things *were* before the time of death and ironthorn!"

And Oracle lifted his head and breathed. The breath rose as a living cloud, dew-like but traveling heavenward until it abided before the nostrils of the long-necked queen. She inhaled, and the breath settled on the field of her memory, baptizing what was planted there in a tenderness she had not known since the day she had been a wide-eyed newborn. And now she beheld a thing that, though invisible to the eyes of her nature, was still vivid before the eyes of her heart. She saw the Namer standing before her. He spoke:

What you see and come to know
Vision for the folk below
What you do and when you act
Makes up for the others' lack
In your heart is wisdom's store
You yourself become the door

And the giraffe knew what to do. No longer imperious in attitude but still royal in manner, she cantered to the opposite fence and beckoned the cat to come. Men were in the exhibit now, shouting one thing and then another, rifles clicking, spotlights darting this way and that, but the giraffe was unperturbed as she stretched her head high, just beneath the coiling razor wire at the top of the fence.

With careful moves and velveted paws, Oracle hopped to the giraffe's back, climbed her neck, and reached her head. He placed a back paw between the horns, and with the thrust of that leg jumped upon the bamboo just above the razor wire, its merciless rings quivering from the near miss of the cat's body brushing by. Grasping the green, leafy poles with his claws and jaws, Oracle clung in midair as the bamboo swayed wildly with the unexpected burden.

For a moment it looked as if the bamboo could not decide what to do: fling the cat back to the feet of the giraffe, receive him as a guest, or drop him upon the razors below. But when the bamboo stopped swaying, the jaguar remained. He clamped the next bamboo with his teeth, swung, and clung to it. Parting the bamboo with a foreleg, he saw the base of the juniper ridge.

He turned to the giraffe. "Thank you, queen of this captive garden. I will tell your tale in song. As for you, go tell others what you have seen by the Breath of Remembrance now abiding in you. Remember your name, and remind others who they are! This is your royal service!"

The giraffe threw her head back in delight. "Thank you, oh Cat Who Remembers. I feel a gallop coming on into the midst of the pursuers. My, how Man shall be surprised by this whisperer's new greeting! Farewell!"

She departed, and a swell of human shouts followed. Oracle leaped to the ground beyond the zoo and plunged free into the forest.

—⦙⦙⦙—

He found a path made popular by mountain bikers, one battened down by bulwarks zigzagging up a steep and cedared slope, but in the dead of night no one was there save the creatures dwelling along its borders. They watched with amazement as the lord of the Valley bounded past them.

The birds of the day let out chirps of surprise in the dark, and the squirrels, for the excitement of it all, found themselves compelled to scamper from one tree home to another. (Indeed, it was such that by the time Oracle had conquered the switchbacks, every squirrel of the hillside had ended up in the home of another, and it took the turn of four entire seasons before the squirrels, argumentative and covetous over what they had discovered in their neighbors' nests, could agree with one another for a complete return to their original homes with their original property.)

Up Oracle ran, leaving the trail and leaping between red cedars where cricket and caterpillar alike felt the sound of his bounding paws on the soil around them. Farther up he ran, past dormant picnic tables on terraces, through grasses, and back into thick foliage again, slaloming elm and oak, feeling the land rise, desiring to reach the highest place from which to spy out where to go.

Suddenly—as when an electric light flashes before eyes in the dark—the jaguar reached a break in the trees to find a completely different world that could not carry him: a cliff edge and starlit sky.

He scrambled in hard reverse upon crumbling limestone. Pebbles, dust, and a shell from an eon-old ocean tumbled, bounced, and disappeared into the void.

Regaining his balance, Oracle crept to the edge and surveyed the sight. Far below his feet stretched a land of oak, cedar elm, sugarberry, and Ashe juniper. Beyond the trees slept the farms of Man.

A river, the Bosque, flowed into the spacious bend of the other, larger waterway, the Brazos, whose wide arm he had seen on the night he and Crash had made their ill-fated attempt to escape. The water of the two rivers lingered in a triune pool before curving away as the lone Brazos to the southeast. Park lights cast a glimmer on the most distant visible bend.

The jaguar arose, alive with understanding. "This is where I shall descend and enter the waters. I will swim them as they seek the coast, where I can follow the shore home. For that is the way the great blue heron traveled when he delivered to me news of my friends in the Valley."

Oracle lowered his body and spread his weight across his paws, head, and tail. He picked his way down the side of the limestone cliff, treating each stone as if it were a hot coal before assurance would cool his caution into a confident step, for the stones of the cliff wall were unfaithful to the sand and gravel about them, and all three lay in a state of fitful dreaming about the ancient cataclysm that had thrust them from beneath primordial waves toward the heavens while their tectonic counterpart beyond the river had plunged to the depths. The dream was vivid and left the earth on edge.

I cannot afford to wake it.

Oracle snaked downward toward the tributary river. There, in furtive steps beneath the ferns, he reached the Bosque's bank and drank.

—⁂—

Chase bypassed the zoo and stopped her vehicle at the place the jaguar had disappeared into the forest. She turned on a red-beam flashlight, searching the ground. There they were: fresh tracks at the trailhead. The paw prints of *Panthera onca*. She touched them.

The strength is still in these prints. He is not far.

She clipped the flashlight to her cap, turned on her senses, and awakened the ancient ways that had trained them. Throwing an intense glance at every bent leaf and broken twig, she ascended the trail, flipping open the holster of her tranquilizer pistol as she did. She commanded her body to breathe quiet breaths, though her lungs burned for more. Stealth was the call of the hour. At the top of the trail, she paused, careful to step over the eroding soils that would betray her presence through their crunching.

There is a current of warm air. He was just here.

A tall grass called a broomsedge bordered a dark wall of trees. She brushed her fingertips across the stalks, discerning where they leaned away. Then she felt a place where the fine hairs of the seed heads turned in a direction different from the rest.

He went toward the cliff.

Chase followed the witness of the broomsedge until she came to the high cliff called Lovers' Leap, overlooking the Bosque and the Brazos. She discovered a place where stones were freshly stirred and gravel had just poured over the edge.

He went down here. He's headed for the river.

Spreading her weight on all four limbs, she began her descent. She went as one imitating the jaguar, slow and sure, testing each place twice and thrice again before entrusting her weight to it.

Halfway down, she assessed the way, above and below. The time was short and her progress slow. Each second weakened the hope of overtaking the great cat. She pored over every shape and shadow along the bank.

And lo! There, in the midst of the ferns, delineated as when one finds a single jigsaw puzzle piece right side up among others upside down, was the coat of a jungle feline. The stars besilvered his ruddy-gold fur in the hues of the night sky as he drank water at the river's edge. His rosette spots revealed a pattern of patterns, a map corresponding to the stars above, a mystery no longer far off. And yet the jaguar remained unreachable, as when one awakens from a long-sojourning dream only to have every last element of it—plot, place, and word—evaporate through the very act of trying to remember it.

With eyes fixed on the wonder below, she reached for the pistol and placed her foot on a portion of rock. But the stone had not expected her and broke loose, sending the noise of its surprise down the cliff along with a pile of dirt and scree. She lost her balance and thrust her arm into the space above, grasping at whatever was there. A juniper sapling touched her fingers. She gripped it—a yanking halt pierced her arm's tendons and ligaments with needles. The pistol tumbled away.

Oracle looked up from the river and saw the Woman.

Chase's body stretched out under its own weight, feet touching nothing but dust dancing in empty space. The sapling did all she could to help. But her strength was meager. She broke.

Chase fell. She fell as a leaf falls from an autumn tree, face up, turning slowly. Below, the drought-stricken bushes were unaware, stooped in preoccupation with their search for survival. But Chase's presence announced itself soon enough as she crashed through ten thousand twigs, which, between the ten thousand bruises they collectively endured, diminished the effect of her fall and cushioned her impact upon the weary earth. There she lay, stunned and breathless, the wind of her lungs blown far from mouth and body.

The stars, brighter for the absence of the moon, witnessed the fall and beheld her. Ursa Minor, the little bear, turned her head in curiosity for a closer look. Her mother Ursa Major also turned, fur bejeweled with two guardians who, in the she-bear's turning, still remained ever pointing to Polaris, the North Star. The tribe of the Skidi Pawnee, bitter enemies of Chasing Eagle's Cheyenne in a former age, called Polaris the Chief Star, for here, at the celestial campfire where he ever stood, he called the moves of the dance about him. The stars of that dance filled the wide and breathless eyes of the Cheyenne chief's daughter.

Chase saw, or thought she saw, a shower of ten tiny stars sprinkling briefly from the back of the little bear, as if the cub were calling out, offering to receive her arms. But the Woman could lift neither arms nor alarm in response. No voice came to her lips. No motion. No call.

Now, it is said that suffering slows down the sands of the hourglass and lengthens the sundial's shadow. At that moment, Chase waited one full year.

And during that year, the face of the lord of the Valley eclipsed the stars above her. The jaguar, eyes of beryl green, looked into her. The cat's whiskers brushed her face. He took in the scent of the daughter of Eve. He beheld the story in her eyes: the journey of the First Americans. The tragedy of hosting new peoples. The song that disappeared in the shouting match of competing voices. The trampling of the tribes.

Then the Woman's own story came before him: the blessing of her parents. The grief of mother's departure to the Far Country. The blazing of her own trail. The long walk alone.

Oracle breathed.

A sound entered her, the sound of many waters. Above her, the cliff was no longer a clumped-over maze of traps, but a rock face covered with foaming waves, the cliff itself growing taller and taller to reveal a host of waterfalls, each one cascading over or blending with the other, their spray ascending into one rainbow-catching mist. Beyond the cliff, snowcapped mountains ascended into a deep and sun-drenched sky where birds circled at the peaks, not to prey upon the dying but to celebrate the living. She could tell by how they flew. And she could breathe again.

For a moment both the cliff face of the night and the vision of the day abided together so that Chase saw both at the same time. Then the vision faded, the starlit cliffs returned, and she realized the jaguar was no longer looking at her. She could not remember when he had departed.

She found strength in her arms and raised herself on her elbows. All was still. The waters of the Bosque moved obediently toward the Brazos. And if Chase had known the voice of the Bosque, she would have heard him say that the fish whispered rumors of a great prince who had treaded his waters on the way to the horizon.

17

THE KING OF THE CATFISH

O racle slipped into the river. The winter water shocked his body, but the energy of having broken free fended off its frigid hold with a counterbalancing warmth. Beneath his paws, deadwood gave way to an aquatic path. He passed the place where two rivers joined and entered the lone one, waveless and wide.

I shall swim down the center, for the dark thickets of either side hide unknown dangers, and from the center, I can reach either bank with equal ease to forge a path away from whichever side the danger may come.

The face of the water betrayed faint ripples as he moved forward.

The spirit of the river is an old man who sleeps, unlike the Lady River, who, though weak and near fainting, carried me such that her waters remained as smooth as the sky while I kissed her. But not so here. I am on my own.

Along each bank slept trees whose trunks leaned over the water, their outstretched branches creating tunnels of shadow. A dry breeze caused a faint and creaking motion. The muddy bottomland of the noiseless Brazos kept the roots in their places, holding them down with the heaviness of the ages saturating the soil.

The cat passed beneath the cold concrete columns of a bridge. The free-tailed bats at roost beneath it watched with unblinking angst, but they did not utter a sound, nor did they descend to meet him.

On his right, he passed the zoo, whose lights marked its location and whose noises spoke of the calamity the cottonwood had created. The sounds drifted away as he swam on.

Farewell, Mother Hedgehog. May the city you build in the hearts of your neighbors rival what you have done in the heart of the earth.

The stars grew faint before the manmade haze of urban lights effusing their energy into the sky. Before him, Oracle saw another bridge. A manmachine crossed it with the *clickety-clack* of tires striking the seam of each slab. He passed under. Above him, mud daubers hibernated in vast numbers in their aerial catacombs, unharassed by Man in the hidden eaves of the belly of the bridge.

Before him yet another bridge arose, but this one ruled over the waters with great iron bars, an angled monument to the age when locomotives were the workhorse of Man's ambitions. The girders loomed above Oracle and gave not the slightest hint their days had been numbered, nor their glory gone, for Man had honored the bridge with a second life through a thick coat of paint and a road instead of rails.

Next came two broad stone pylons rising from the water, testifying that another bridge was no more. Peeking over the top of each pylon were tortillas tossed by daily tourists.

Ah, I have heard about this place! The ravens say they artfully arrange the flat flour to encourage Man to try his hand at a game they call 'tortilla toss.' Man throws the discs of bread from the bridge beside it. And he does so daily. I have watched the ravens wink at one another and say, 'Those empty pillars have become our constant fullness.' But for now, all is still. The ravens are sleeping, preparing their strength for the games of the morrow.

Beside these bridgeless bases stretched the tossing platform—though no one but the ravens called it that. It was, in fact, a smaller version of the Brooklyn Bridge, intentionally so designed by the architect of that New York City icon. Suspended, sturdy beams spanned the river. Thick cables christened with lights stretched in two great dipping curves over the beams. Ironworks framed the beams, and on each bank, double towers made of three million stuccoed bricks anchored it all.

A park secured the beauty of each end of the bridge. On one side a group of bronze statues preserved the memory of the cowhands of the Chisholm Trail who had crossed there: Larger-than-life cattlemen of two languages, fatigued and anxious after the long journey from South Texas, drove colossal longhorns to the bridge. On the other side, in a park named after Pearl Harbor's Black hero Doris Miller, a vivid mural remembered Dr. Martin Luther King Jr. dreaming with open eyes and fluent words on the steps of the Lincoln Memorial. That double beauty served to buckle the two sides of the city into one—age-old wounds notwithstanding.

A couple cooed on the suspension bridge, aimlessly eyeing the pylons and intentionally eyeing each other. Then the woman saw movement in the water.

"Tyree, look!"

"Huh—what?"

"That creature! Look at that thing! What is it?" She clung to him.

"Hold on, hold on, now. Let's not—Wait—Whoa! It's a panther or leopard or something! That ain't no tomcat from

Jasper's Barbecue! That thing's wild and bigger than anything I've ever seen!" He pulled out his phone and videoed.

Oracle glanced up at them as he passed under, and the bridge lights reflected off the shining layer at the back of eyes, causing them to glow.

"Did you see that?" the woman asked.

"What do you mean?"

"He *knows* us!"

"Chantelle, he's just makin' sure we ain't hunters or nothin' like that."

"No, you know what I mean. A soul, baby, a soul with a flame. He done looked *into* us. I saw it! You can't be tellin' me no different. That cat got more than *cat* in him."

"All right, all right, that's cool. Just don't bump me while I video this bad boy. The post will get too many likes to count by mornin'! Ooh, are we lucky to see him! Now give me some sugar, baby—a Christmas gift done come early to you! You're the queen of the night with your own sabertooth tiger paradin' right before your eyes! Ain't nobody gonna top this tale, honey! Nobody! At Jasper's party tomorrow night, you got *thee* story to tell!"

They moved to the other side of the bridge and watched him to the utter exclusion of all else until the distance and darkness shrouded him from their sight.

—◊◊◊—

Oracle passed under a derelict railroad bridge, each end clumped with boxelders and black willows rising from the shallows, their branches unwillingly holding knowledge of the disposable deeds done beneath them. The bushes of the snailseed whispered laments.

Then above him, he saw a bridge bigger than all the others, four bands of manstone with manmachines roaring over them. Proud illuminated towers guarded the bands with long-reaching cables radiating from their sides like half-opened umbrella spokes.

As he passed under, Oracle's eyes filled with a sight dominating the horizon. A curved edifice rose from the riverbank bathed in the glow of green and yellow lights. A bridge, legs spread low in the water, tethered it to a well-manicured complex of manplaces on the opposite bank, where twinkling candy canes adorned a walkway passing through them.

But it was the edifice that drew Oracle's attention. It opened to the river like a colossal magnet, and within it, overlooking a striped field, rows of seats ascended around a cavernous space. A large screen, the kind of "reflection pond" Patch and Bog had described as hanging on the walls of manplace dens, stood exalted on a pedestal. The back side of the screen, which faced Oracle, bore a giant wreath made of evergreen branches, red baubles, and ribbons. Marching out from both sides of the pedestal in the form of a huge ellipse, some forty pairs of columns strengthened the structure, which hosted large panes of illuminated glass. Mars and Venus had gifted the arena with their blessings, for the cat of the House of Panthera Onca discerned their influence resting upon it like invisible banners hung from balconies.

Oracle marveled. *What an important place of worship this must be! I have come upon the Mayans' ruined holy places in my home of the Yucatán, but to behold a great temple where the children of Man still come to lift up their voices to tribal spirits—this is a sight my eyes have never seen!*

Oracle crossed under another bridge and reached a place where the river broadened considerably. On the banks loomed mounds of freshly moved earth above great sleeping machines.

Wreckage of manstone stained with the river also lay strewn along the marshy edges. Boats rested at wooden docks so new they still exuded the smell of turpentine from the treatments Man had used to preserve them.

Some great dam used to be here, but Man has chosen to liberate the waters.

He swam on. The sounds of the city, with its rushing tires and roaring trucks, faded away.

The glow of urban lights no longer dimmed the heavens, and they revealed the witness of watchful stars, a cohort called the Winter Circle. Rigel, Aldebaran, Capella, and twins Castor and Pollux communed in one gaze upon the lord of the Valley, as did two other stars, Sirius and Procyon—that same star the raccoon House of Procyon honored in the Rites of the Rings, one rite for each ring of the tail. Sirius and Procyon shared their vigil with the star Betelgeuse to form another group of watchers, the Winter Triangle, who communed not only to consider the cat of rosette spots, but to nurture the nebulae hovering in their midst, the Rosette Nebula among them.

A snapping branch signaled the presence of another—a fox in awe of the prince who swam past his red-oak den at a bend in the Brazos. Oracle swam on, moving his legs in confident cadence and welcoming the waters around him.

The river became colder. The sense of the closeness of the muddy bottom fell away, as did the shore, which seemed to shift beyond the easy reach of limb or paw.

The water deepens to a home here. I have entered the realm of another.

There was a noise and a commotion below, murmurs and voices in words unfamiliar to the cat of Sian Ka'an. A conference of catfish scurried about his legs, bobbing up and down, bumping into one another, thronging in anger and fear at the intruder who swam above them. Then, before the jaguar a large, slimy mound arose, water running off in rivulets, revealing bulbous eyes and leathery spines: Ogg, the son of Broog, king of the catfish, a descendant of Longfin the Linebreaker of Lake Texoma, whom Man released into Lake Waco at the time of the Second Dam. Ogg gurgled in an unknown tongue and lunged forward with neither warning nor parley.

Oracle threw a paw onto the side of Ogg's head and turned the momentum of the beast such that the lunge missed him.

Ogg wheeled about, breaching as he charged again, and in the starlight, Oracle perceived how huge he was: as long as a log laid by campfires for sitting, mouth wide enough to swallow a gilled swimmer whole. A nightmare to the "noodlers," as Texans call them: precocious teens who grab catfish by plunging bare hands into gaping mouths. A monster from the deep, elusive to fishermen in their flat-bottom boats, hiding in the hollows of once majestic oaks now sunk out of sight.

But here the king of the catfish made his stand, for a rival cat—a cat o'land, as the whiskered fish called him in his native tongue—had trespassed. Ogg lunged again, but this time he dove before Oracle's paw reached him. Up he came flexing his dorsal side, and the spine of his proud back pierced the jaguar's right foreleg, spearing the skin and sliding upward deep into the muscle, the bone of Oracle's limb deflecting the point only for it to travel farther up with the thrust of the fish. A flash of torment ran through the cat.

Oracle brought both paws down upon Ogg, dislodging the spine as he pushed the fish away. Then the jaguar of the Yucatán went after him: teeth and terror. He bit the fish's back at the place where it met the fin and snapped the spine off.

Voices beneath the waters let out an aquatic gasp. Then, humiliated and amazed, the uncrowned king fled, and his followers floated in mid-muddy water, gazing through the murk at the one who had freed them from their fierce-backed older brother.

—⋙—

The night sky shifted to early dawn. The morning star delayed her rising to accompany the sun, and in her place rose a mysterious shade of pink and blue, that elusive in-between hue the artist pursues in his paintings. The light revealed the water as it mirrored the sky. An egret caught sight of the coming cat, dropped her crawfish breakfast, and flew long and slow above him before departing.

The pain of Ogg's greeting shot up his leg and would not relent. Oracle searched the shoreline and found an alcove beneath broad water oaks in whose shade grew red mulberry trees. The leafless limbs of both bowed like curtains over a bank of earth bordered with a veil of bare eastern redbuds. It was not quite dry but was at least firm enough to recline on. Here, Oracle lay down, his spotted coat blending with the mottled shadows of the trees.

All that day he rested.

That night, while he fished, the cry of an aplomado falcon echoed upon the waters.

"What is this?" Oracle asked. "The call of one friend seeking another."

Oracle released the call of greeting, what Man calls chuffing. Neither melodious nor tonal, it is the sound of one content in his labor, a grunt of a growl with no ill intent, made several times over. Were a Man to hear it, he would say he heard someone sawing wood in one direction, not back and forth, but rather a single, repeated, methodical move forward between brief interludes. But when an animal listened, he knew the sound said, "Here I am."

Sent the falcon heard and descended to a water oak.

"Hail to you, Lord of the Valley, free but far from all that is familiar. I greet you in peace."

"And you as well, Bold One, you who remember your name and the radiant sun who kissed your forefather in the Days of the Naming."

"Thank you, my lord. I reached your lair in the great manstone garden on the same trail of night-crowned rumors the great blue heron had followed, but I found your place empty with a great tree down and Man at work repairing the damage. The hedgehogs told me of your escape, as did the buffalo and the giraffe. I searched the river, where a fox and an egret told me they had seen you swim by. Then I found a school of catfish breaching for joy, laughing and playing and singing in an unknown tongue. Though I did not understand their speech, they mimed to me a drama of someone freeing them on his way downriver. I knew it had to have been you."

Oracle grimaced in pain from the wound of the catfish king. "I am grateful my passing through has worked for good in the school of another. And now, oh Brave Messenger, what news do you have from the Valley?"

"I have news of the manchild Miracle."

"How is the friend of Patch and Plod? How is the one Bog scouts for?"

Sent fluttered down from an oak to a mulberry branch. "He is well! A great menace tried to seize him—Men who desired his life—but a white-haired prince became his servant and sequestered him through hidden paths to an aunt and uncle who now call him their own."

Oracle stood—but winced in pain. "The great blue heron told me of the Man who helped Miracle, but your tidings of an aunt and uncle are new. What of the lad's parents? Did Fair Bandit not find them?"

The aplomado closed his eyes in the way unique to falcons, first with a translucent eyelid moving laterally as when one closes a curtain, then with eyelids above and below. He sang a series of high, mournful notes, which a cold breeze carried away the moment he sang them.

"The raccoon and the manchild were separated for a time, but when they rejoined as one flock at Eden's Bend thanks to the help of the white-haired prince, Patch found that the manchild's parents had gone beyond trail's end; their path was cut short, and neither he, nor the manchild, nor his friends Plod and Bog could follow. They found it so before a marker of manstone speaking of the parents' departure to the Far Country."

Oracle dropped his head. A tear touched the earth.

Sent dropped to the bank before him. "But take courage, sire, for no sooner had the boy lost heart than a heart-wise Man and a heart-worthy Woman embraced him, the aunt and uncle who guided him to the marker, so that he did not fall to the dust in despair only but fell into grace at the same moment."

Oracle mourned in silence while the stars moved, and the crickets harmonized with the lament taking place beneath the winter branches.

"So," he said slowly, "the boy's salty tears became fresh-water springs. The trail's end became a door. Ah, that is the way of our Maker! He continues to make. He continues to unbend the crooked paths of His children, so that, no matter how winding they become, there is somehow always a way back to Eden, if a heart be humble enough to find it."

The aplomado stepped closer. "Yes, sire, the manchild has indeed found such a path. He is in the arms of a new mother and father, and all are comforted, including the raccoon and his traveling companions. His sorrow lingers, and so it should, for it honors the loss of his loved ones. But his sorrow now pairs with joy like the wings of a bird. Together they lift his life forward."

Sent stretched out a wing, touched Oracle's paw, and lowered his voice. "Even so, my lord, I regret to inform you that the peace the manchild enjoys is a fragile one, for the sleepless malice seeking the child's life still moves Men of stony hearts. Rumors reach us through the whip-poor-will, our fellow member in the Colony of the Lost far from her eastern home. She listens to the whispers of the geckos and the bees, who say there is one who still craves to devour the child, a Man who watches like a hungry boa slowly encircling his prey. But the time of his striking is not yet, the whip-poor-will says, for in these days, too many come and go at the manplace where Miracle abides with the couple who have become a family to him. The whip-poor-will says we have time."

Oracle paced the bank, his paws marking the damp earth. "Nevertheless, time does not stand still. The shadows slip ever forward, even if in a single moment all seems at rest. May the Maker speed me on, and may the Prayer of Kahoo shape the journey."

—∾—

Sent departed at dawn. Oracle's body ached as it fought the filth of Ogg's injury. The cat from Sian Ka'an remained still as the Texas winter sun passed through mid-morning.

But at noon Oracle heard the voice of Man not far off, the brush protesting as dead branches cracked and radios squawked.

213

Whoever they are, they are not careful, for they speak freely and step carelessly. I can track their movements.

"Private property here," a Man said. "We can't reach the bank. Let's try downriver a piece on the other side. Lots of thickets yonder the zoo team hasn't checked yet. Maybe we'll spot clues there."

"Yeah, we're hurtin' for clues," said the other Man. "That viral post is the only thing we've got to go on, but all we know for sure from it is that the cat passed under the suspension bridge. He coulda gone in any direction after that."

The conversation gradually faded away, and all returned to stillness.

Oracle whispered to the water oaks and mulberries. "The voice of Man and the mark of the catfish king forbid further slumber. Both command me to watch. Both thrust me farther into this unknown realm. The great blue heron told me this river leads to the sea, and the coast will lead me back to the Valley. It will be a long journey on an injured limb, but there is no other way. I will let the river provide me with a trackless path while Man sleeps and my leg heals."

The trees responded with a sigh as a slow breeze passed through them.

And so, when the sun set and the stars of the Winter Circle rose, he entered the river and swam through the night. The crescent moon sank behind the trees, curved and burdened like a loaded bow.

—⁓—

Early the next morning, ruddy banks appeared around a riverbend, places where floods had left their legacy, scooping out huge chunks of land from farms and ranches to reveal red, rusted earth, dirt with too much iron for a garden but not enough for a girder. Green ground cover tumbled down the slopes thanks to Texas's fickle winter: the round-leafed herb of the Carolina ponysfoot and the nectar-rich evergreen of the turkey tangle frogfruit.

The river's course curved back and forth in its journey to the sea, and as Oracle swam, the river bottom rose and fell beneath him, at times brushing his tired paws, at times falling away to submerged, hidden lairs.

In one stretch the river became unusually shallow, and he discerned beneath him not mud, but limestone, a sunken memorial to the wagon wheels crossing it above a long-forgotten waterfall before the river had changed course. What remained were falls a fraction of the former ones, some two feet high. Oracle descended them and fished at the plunge pool as the cascading waters washed his wound.

Rounding another bend, Oracle found that the river turned briefly south in its overall southwesterly journey. Here silt deposits wallowed unapologetically out to the middle of the Brazos, pushing the western riverbank away from the swimming cat and bringing him near the eastern one.

There at the eastern bank, Oracle rose from the river, his leg protesting the pain from Ogg's anger as he placed weight on it. He surveyed the shore. Tracks of deer, bobcat, and wild hog showed where each had taken their turn to drink in the night. The mark of a mouse tail wound its way through the footprints. A raccoon had organized empty shells into a line.

Oracle smiled. "Patch, dear friend, I wonder when I will see you again. You have remembered your name and shared your prized treasures with the manchild named Miracle. You have made friends along the way. You have learned to carry a knot you cannot untie. Well done."

Oracle passed through alligator weed and Brazos rain lilies as he surveyed more tracks and spoor. He found another place where the riverbank had left a record of those who had traversed the soft soil. As he read the history of who had walked there, the lord of the Valley came upon the tracks of a cat, large and strong. Oracle placed his nose into the impressions.

"This is another lord of the animal kingdom, but a wounded one. For the depth of the one foot is different from the other. He is limping as I am. Who could he be, and where is he resting? A limping cat cannot travel far."

The dull ache of Ogg's wound threatened to overcome his ability to focus, but Oracle strengthened his heart.

The pain calls me to attention. I choose it so. Otherwise, all I shall hear is the pain, and I shall become deaf indeed.

A whisper caused the cat to pause. He looked up, body tense and alert. Who was it? *What* was it?

18

THE MEMORY KEEPERS

The land cries out from a faraway memory," Oracle said quietly. "It beckons me to listen, for I perceive I am in a forgotten place whose story has fallen to the ground."

The whisper continued. The jaguar leaned into the sound.

It is not one, but many whispers so low and so faint that I must honor them with perfect stillness to comprehend them…Ah! The voices do not come from the riverbank, nor the air, nor the trees, but from under the water.

Oracle approached the edge of the bank where a patch of Texas toadflax grew. He brought his ears close to the water's surface.

There, in the place where the submerging soil faded into the invisible bottom, were river mussels, their shells half revealed above creamy sand. They spoke in half moans, as when one talks in his sleep. Here is what they said:

Mud and murk
Here we lurk
While the dawn
Passes on

Foe and friend
Have an end
We remain
Live again

Tongues have talked
Feet have walked
Boats have passed
We are last

Yet we hold
All we're told
Find no fault
In our vault

Not to judge
Nor to budge
But to keep
Till we sleep

Oracle listened to the words of this other world. He drew closer until his whiskers touched the surface of the water. Rings rippled.

The mussels perceived these, though they could not see the jaguar—for without eyes, they divine who is present with senses other than sight.

"Hail to you, oh Royal One," said a river mussel, one called a Brazos heelsplitter in the tongue of Man. "Yours are not the whiskers of the coyote or the dog. Nor are you the timid touch of the deer. There is returning and rest in your way. There is quietness and strength. We greet you, oh Cat of the Southern Jungle, large and far from your native home.

Your kind has not walked here since the dawn of the age of the Lone Star."

"Thank you," Oracle replied. "I am grateful for your greeting. I see you keep the tale of this river. Please tell me, for the river himself has not spoken. He is asleep."

The oldest mussel, one Man calls a threeridge, spoke. "The river is weary and seldom speaks, but we will tell you his tale."

With a gentle jet of water from his shell, the threeridge slid across the sand and drifted to a stop before the jaguar's whiskers. "In the days when the First Nation walked here and piled our remains outside their encampments in shelly mounds—'middens,' they call them—a new mantribe appeared. The snake known as the water moccasin tells us the first Man of this new tribe carried the flag of his king, which lifted up the royal lily, while upon his own flag a greyhound and eight-pointed star ran their courses. LaSalle, they called him. Then to the surprise of all came a barefoot Man from another new tribe dragging a holy tree that gouged the ground as he carried it, a scar speaking a riddle of healing to those who followed the trail he blazed—the Gospel, they call it.

"A season passed. Then other Men came on horse with the power to conquer. They came with long-seeing eyes and tools anchoring points in the heavens to points on the earth. They drew lines across the land and granted each portion to a family of Man whose names remain embedded in the story of this realm. For no Man can buy or sell a tract of earth without mentioning the names of those to whom the conquerors first granted it."

"But not all the names lie in their right places," said another mussel, a mapleleaf, "not even the name of this very river."

"Tell me the story of how that came to be," Oracle whispered.

The mapleleaf opened her shell, stretched out her rubbery foot, and pulled herself closer to the surface. Then, without motion, but in a silent moan that translated to the mind of the cat, she spoke.

"There was a mantribe under the colors of the House of Castile who explored this place from the presidios of the south. Desperate for water and mad with thirst, they pressed through the thorn-filled thickets until their eyes fell upon a sparkling river whose banks sang as the waters splashed blue-green between smooth and stately rocks. Great was their relief. Great was their joy. 'This is the river of the arms of God!' they exclaimed. And they named him so: *Río de los Brazos de Dios*. It is the river one night's journey south of here. Then they came upon this river, where we are now, and they saw how he blushed with the mud of the bottom and the soil of the banks. *Río Colorado*, they named him: the ruddy one. The homely one."

The mapleleaf drew closer, her scored shell rising just above the water's surface.

"But the naming was not always remembered this way, nor did those who put the memories to maps in faraway Castile always understand the original tales. Therefore, by the time the mantribe known as the Old Three Hundred had come, and the sons of the House of McLennan had built their loggy manplaces, the names had been traded. This river became the Brazos. The one to the south became the Colorado. And so it came to pass that the beautiful inherited the name of the homely, and the homely the beautiful."

Oracle contemplated these words. "Alas for the river to the south and amen for the river I place my whiskers to, for there is justice in the trading. I taste it in the waters."

Cat and clam reclined in the afterglow of the story for a time while an invisible love moved the vault of sky and clouds.

Oracle reclined and placed his face at the water's edge. "Tell me what is downriver, for that is where I must go, even as far as the sea and a realm south of here Man calls the Valley. I am lord of the animal kingdom there, and I must return to pick up the trail where I and the one before me left off. But I have never traveled this river before, and I am unfamiliar with the path that leads to the sea, the south, and the Valley. My paws do not know the way."

"Nor do *we* know the way," said a mussel called a yellow sandshell, "for we have never left this riverbend. But the keeper of this land has surely been downriver, and he surely knows of the Valley and the sea. Brazos Ben, they call him. He wades our waters and cares for us, lifting each of us from the river bottom, measuring our frames, counting our numbers, taking note of the stories on our shells, and placing us back again. He knows us by name. We have not known another Man like him who abides in our waters to learn whether our world is well or ill. For all are in a hurry. All pass by in a motorized moment. But not Brazos Ben. He wades, waits, and watches. He is the keeper of this riverbend. He is the keeper of our names."

A pimpleback mussel piped up from behind the sandshell.

"And when rumor reached our ears from a rogue fatmucket of a pernicious horde coming to choke our waters with their greedy shells—zebras, they call them—Ben spent a moon searching out the bottom to keep them away. No one had ever done that for us before. And, just like the Old Man of the Brazos, he is weary and seldom speaks, but his service to us is a long and living word without words."

Oracle raised his head. "How beautiful this word is. It is a hidden beauty shared only between you and the Man who knows you by name. It is a buried treasure you have permitted me to discover. Thank you."

"You discovered it because you watched and listened," said a Tampico pearly mussel. "Buried treasures are unearthed that way while they remain invisible to others even as they pass right over them."

The cat abided with the mussels. The longer he looked, the more of them he saw, and he did not know if this was because his eyes were becoming better at seeing the mussels through the murky water or if the mussels were gathering near the surface, moving as imperceptibly as the moon on her course across the sky. Whichever it was, Oracle saw more of the folk of the river bottom.

He rose and considered them all. *In a gathering such as this, perhaps there is one among them who could aid me in my quest.*

"Thank you for the hidden treasure you have shown me," he said. "I seek another treasure too, a lost tribe of the House of Felinae called the jaguarundi, whom the coral snakes call the shadow cat. Has he ever passed by on these banks or swum your waters? For I learned of his disappearance while I was in the Valley, and in the great enclosed garden upriver, where I resided for a time, I heard rumors that his paws still touch the trails in the dark."

"We have neither heard nor seen him for ourselves," said a mussel called a Texas fawnsfoot. "But we perceive that the turtle knows of him, for the turtle, like you, is patient enough to listen. She is not of those who run and fly, but like us retains the grains of everything she hears, never letting go of them until the day she returns to dust, and her shell becomes a memorial to what she knew."

Oracle slowly curled and uncurled his tail. "Your word confirms what a cousin told me in the gated realm upriver. But a password guards those grains of memory in the turtles. They will not speak about the shadow cat without it. Perhaps here, on the land of the Man named Brazos Ben, I shall find the sly, striped keepers of that password. I will abide here, therefore. My thanks to you all, oh Eyeless Sages, for giving me eyes to see the river, the land, and the Man. May the Maker bless you."

He kissed his right paw—stiff though it was with pain as he raised it to his lips—and he placed it in the water until it rested upon the fawnsfoot in reverent farewell.

—◦◦◦—

Oracle turned inland. Grasshoppers scattered from ironweed and rustweed as the great cat made his way to a flood-gouged bluff guarded by cockleburs. He passed through and climbed the bluff, where he paused for a time, cleaning the burrs from his fur with his teeth. Before him was a meadow of Texas bull nettles and—in a spot where Man had dug up the ground—horse nettles. But a faint path showed itself, and the jaguar snaked his way through with only a few stings.

He continued until the path faded away at a dry creek bed. Crossing it, he came to a place where the ground sloped upward again past a row of camphorweed-covered mounds, each a stone's throw apart, which disappeared into forest overgrown with sorrelvines.

These must be the middens the mussels talked about. Here the first mantribe walked.

Crossing a carpet of bristlemallows, he entered a forest, where he climbed over fallen elms, some freshly down, others rotting from their collapse seasons ago. Cottonwood mingled with Osage orange, and Chickasaw plum with post oak. Ants worked their long trails along the ground while termites ran their circuits upon silent, anxious trunks. Poison ivy abounded, but its presence was harmless to the jaguar, as it is to virtually all mammals besides Man, and indeed for many of the animal kingdom its leaves and fruit are food.

Oracle passed a tangle of mustang grapes. He paused and smelled them. "Oh vine, you remind me of when the manchild Miracle offered your bounty to Patch. Fair Bandit received them, and he offered his precious gems in grateful return. Ah, it is a sweet fruit to savor this memory."

The vines of the mustang grapes climbed a thicket of bur oaks behind them. Oracle reached the other side and saw through its outermost growth a paddock with an enclosure for goats. He went around rather than through the paddock, planting each paw with careful precision behind a curtain of frostweed and basket grass. The goats, though they did not see the jaguar, sensed his presence. They stood with heads erect in watchfulness, each finishing a mouthful of grass, chewing with gusto in case it was their last.

Oracle came upon a field of freshly watered earth hosting sweet potatoes. Its border of black-eyed Susans and shrubs of snake apple vines lent the cat of rosette spots camouflage, from which he caught a glimpse of a coyote with a fresh catch of a field mouse for her den. She scampered by and disappeared behind a cloud of dust. The jaguar reached an aging windmill. Its base disappeared in a tangle of sumpweed, smartweed, and Santa Maria feverfew, all of which grew in bold sprays that had gone to seed. The blades of the windmill complained as they turned. No water flowed, nor was a tank to be seen, only a pile of rusted cans discarded so long ago that the factories from which they had come were themselves rusting sleepers.

The windmill stood at the edge of an orchard of pecans, their crumbling bark betraying their age. Within their shade stood an old fisherman's cabin, a gray and sagging relic.

I shall go there.

On the cabin's porch lay the remains of fishing gear. The tackle box was open. Rust had welded hooks and lures into unwieldy masses bonded to their compartments. A blackened bait bucket stood beside, and, next to the bucket, a dust-covered fishing rod. The reel bore the mark of the Men who had made it.

FOUR BROTHERS
ÉGALITÉ
MADE IN U.S.A.
1903

A rocking chair with a broken under-arch sat motionless, waiting to support her master, undaunted by her brokenness. Above that chair on a rusted hook hung a dust-covered kerosene lantern.

Oracle paced the wooden porch.

The scent here is full of weather and water, storms and floods of long ago. But the scent is also oiled with the life of the Man, deeply rooted and mixed with wild onions. It feels as if at any moment he will return, for it appears as if he has just set his gear down while he retrieves some forgotten thing inside his dwelling. But the stillness testifies that he has not returned.

As Oracle passed through the pecan orchard, he found that almost as many branches lay strewn on the ground as those lifting their bare arms to the sky. He picked his way over the fallen limbs and emerged into yet another clearing, this one landscaped with mown Bermuda grass.

Before him was another home, but it was not like the fisherman's cabin.

I have never seen a manplace like this before.

It was set in a towering southern live oak and supported by metal posts, some of which shone with a new layer of paint, while others still showed a dull primer coat. Retractable stairs rose from the oak's foot to a cottage nestled among huge branches some twelve feet above. From the cottage rose steps under a slanting roof to another small house and farther up another, each with a covered balcony, three stories in all. Ceiling fans dispersed warm air. A light bulb burned in a window. PVC pipes jutted between each floor, and another set of pipes branched between rain gutters and a bright-blue reservoir tank at the foot of the tree.

A faint sound of music reached Oracle's ears, a melody flowing from small black boxes fixed at the balconies. A Man named Johnny Cash sang "Give My Love to Rose."

Nearby, a caliche road hosted a Ford pickup. And beside the truck, from the slightly open door of a large metal barn, came the sound of a Man at work: the clink and clunk of nuts and bolts.

Oracle crept to the barn. He peered in.

19

BRAZOS BEN

A maroon manmachine bearing the symbol of a mustang rested on a pair of raised ramps. A license plate displayed the logo of Texas A&M University above the epithet *Classic Auto.* The sound of the Man at work came from beneath the machine. His arm appeared, stretching out for a socket wrench, a burly hand with ringless fingers.

The jaguar stepped just into the barn with the Man unaware beneath his pride and joy. He considered what he saw. Grime-sprinkled boxes conditioned the air to a cool and dehumidified quality. The roof carried a host of specially reinforced windows, as did the walls where they met the roof, giving the barn an open feel as the sky poured in. Along one side of the barn were stalls, and along the other were rows of tools for projects in mid-stage. At the back, behind glass refrigerator doors, were the heads of oak barrels. Names and dates were Sharpied on each one, and before the barrels stood a table of wine bottles, glasses, and the tools of the sommelier.

The cat of the Long Journey gently circled the manmachine while Brazos Ben labored beneath it.

I shall leave the Man to his work, for it is day, the time of his labor. I shall explore the place where he rests before I, too, find a place to rest.

Oracle turned to the tree house. He ascended the stairs to find himself on a pine-plank balcony. To his left, through

227

a narrow door, was a galley kitchen, compact like one might find in the heart of a small ship. Rows of dried herbs and cooking gear hung from the ceiling.

After climbing a steeper set of steps, he entered a room with two chairs made of cherrywood, whose leather bore tanning to match. These faced each other over a small coffee table of the same cherrywood. The walls hosted a taxidermy of antlers, wide-mouth bass, and wild turkey. A rack lifted up two compound bows hanging horizontally, while the phalanx of arrows loyal to them stood at attention in rows behind.

Oracle ascended a set of spiral stairs to the third floor, where he found a cedar draftsman's table with plans pinned across it. Reams of blueprints, rolled like scrolls, lay on a side table and scattered on the floor among pencil shavings. The smell of ink, shavings, paper, and cedarwood filled the room and the Cat Who Remembers.

This is where the Man dreams. It is sacred space.

He moved slowly about the room, taking in the atmosphere. An olive drab filing cabinet occupied one corner. A bed hung vertically upon a wall, anchored by two wheel-shaped sockets, ready to be lowered at night. A nightstand stood next to the space for the bed.

Oracle's eyes lingered on the nightstand, where a single framed photo rested. The colors had faded, but the image was clear: a Woman and a manchild squinting in the summer sun. The Woman's brunette hair cascaded down in equidistant locks on each side, flowing over slender shoulders and framing the small sapphire of a delicate pendant. She wore a white décolleté blouse with embroidery of southwestern patterns. Both blouse and patterns curved over her pregnant belly.

The manchild, a boy, leaned into his mother's side in a hand-me-down shirt from someone's favorite baseball team, the letters still bold but tattered, the stripes still there but worn.

His mother's arm was draped around him, the wedding ring on her finger paired with the marquise-cut gem her love had chosen for her when she had said yes to his plea on one knee.

Oracle considered the room. It was for one.

On the balcony he saw a ladder with safety rails. He climbed it to a small platform on the roof. Shingles sloped away from the branches of the massive tree. Fastened to the platform was a swiveling lounge chair, and anchored next to it, a table holding a potted aloe vera in an inset at its center.

Oracle smiled. *Ah, the aloe, the healing plant Patch brought me for my wounds at Garfight Pond.*

He touched the aloe with his nose, and amid its succulent leaves he smelled another plant growing, a tiny vine holding up a single lavender bloom. It was a passionflower, whose five petals and five sepals hosted three nail-shaped styles with five stamens bearing witness to the three instruments of pain. Crowning all these were fragile purple strands radiating from the center, glorifying the communion of the bloom with the nails.

The sound of a Man reached Oracle, and he peered over the edge to see Brazos Ben walking toward the house, speaking into a thin black box at his ear. His beard was white with a hint of red. His hair just covered his ears and bore the same final shade of red as the beard. A cap greased with the belly of the manmachine covered his head.

"It's quite all right," said Brazos Ben. His voice was deep and accent thick. "I appreciate the Season's Greetings. Besides, your call makes me take a break. I've been at it all mornin', making sure the Mustang is ready to roll for the Christmas Day car show tomorrow. The county courthouse loans their parking lot to it every year so folks have a place to gather after family festivities.

"This Mustang's a beauty, a '66 with its original eight-track! But I think the former owner must have poured Blue Devil or some other sealant in the engine to mask a blown head gasket. I flushed the radiator till it was clean as a whistle. No luck. Replaced the thermostat too, but that didn't do the job. Only thing left to explain it is that darn liquid glass trick. I'm headed to town this afternoon to look for a good low-mileage engine to switch out for the old one if I can get there in time. They close early today for Christmas Eve."

Oracle listened to the Man ascend the first set of stairs. A glass clinked against another in the kitchen.

"Yeah, everything else here is fine. The goats have been spooked lately by something stalking 'em. It's not a bobcat. The tracks are too big. Likely a cougar. Haven't actually seen it, though."

Oracle heard ice tumble and a stream of water pouring. Footsteps sounded on the second set of stairs.

"Sure, I'll take a look at those readings. Old oil wells like that can be fracked pretty easy. You just have to make sure there's enough still down there for all the trouble of running the rig. I've been doing that kind of detective work over in Midland County for the last month. Usually doesn't take but one good shot down the borehole to get the seismic read on whether or not it's worth opening up again. I won't do anything about it today of course; no one's workin' on Christmas Eve except myself and the salvage yard."

Oracle leaned his ears into the air, listening. A chair gave a sigh from bearing up new weight. There were no more footsteps. Barely audible was the thin sound of a Man speaking. Brazos Ben replied to the faraway voice.

"Thanks for asking. This drought's been the worst anyone remembers since the fifties. The weather stats say so too. It's been tough, but I've managed. When the rainwater reserves ran out, I set up a better softener for the groundwater. It's so full of metal here in Falls County, you might as well be chewin' on a horseshoe. My water system ain't perfect, but I have enough for myself, the goats, and the crops."

There was a pause while the other voice sounded. Oracle heard the thud of one boot, then another drop to the floor as Brazos Ben spoke.

"No, just some sweet potatoes on a little bit of dirt my neighbor's leasing from me. And space for the goats.

"But to be honest, for most of my sixty acres, I just let it grow wild. I catch a few feral hogs now and then for meat or for auction, but other than that I just let Mother Nature look after most of it. Folks come on tours for that sort of thing these days, watching wildlife and snapping pictures—a kind of hunting where nobody gets hurt, and everybody wins. Hunting's fine and all—I've got an ol' Aggie buddy with a great deer lease over in Kimble County—but for my part, I plan to leave this land to itself as much as I can and let it grow the way it would naturally if we humans weren't walkin' all over it. I do just enough to make sure nature stays in balance and there's space for me to live. That's the closest we'll ever get back to Eden, I figure."

As the conversation continued, Oracle rested his head upon a paw.

While the Man is at peace in his home, I shall not disturb him. Only if he ascends to the roof and sees me shall I depart, for then the noise of my claws on his dwelling and tree would be of no consequence. But for now, I shall remain here while he remains there. For he is the ruler and the steward of this place.

Brazos Ben bid farewell to his caller, and there was silence. After a time, he let out a long sigh. Oracle heard movement, then the sound of boots on stairs as the Man descended. After a sound of water flowing down a pipe, he saw the Man walk back to the barn and return to his work.

Oracle made his way down, anchoring the move of each paw with the claws of the three others set solidly into house and tree. He walked along a huge branch, lowered himself to another, and dropped to the ground—the pain of Ogg's injury jolting him sharply. Then he limped into the forest, seeking a place to recline, for the fullness of the day was beginning. The cat clambered over fallen trunks among living ones of dogwood, Shumard's oak, and black hickory. The spiny shrubs of the gum bumelia obscured the view with their zigzagging branches. Then he spied a place ahead where a stand of sand post oaks grew close together, creating a refuge obscured by the bumelia.

Here I shall rest.

But as Oracle was about to enter the spot, a fly buzzed past him, carrying the scent of blood in her trail. He picked up the scent and turned. In the distance, he saw a strange object differing in shape and color from the trees. The jaguar fixed his attention on the oddity, which seemed to be suspended in midair. He took two cautious steps toward it, then another.

The carcass of a goat hung off the lowest branch of a gnarled blackjack oak, dripping blood.

The lord of the Valley tensed and turned his head in every direction, seeking a glimpse of the predator who had made the fresh kill.

Either the cat is away or in the undergrowth ready to strike, poised like lightning on the edge of a cloud.

Frozen at attention and alert to danger, Oracle waited with breath held back. He took in every sound, every beetle underneath a leaf, every bird flitting from tree to tree in branches too far away to see. But no sound of a feline came. No evidence at all.

Like a ghost, the cat has soundlessly departed, leaving his prey for a meal later tonight.

As Oracle turned, his paw touched a hollow shape. He looked down. The pug mark of a cat of great size and weight was before his eyes. He looked in the direction of the print. Here and there among the trunks of the bumelia, the jaguar saw the tracks continue—one paw making a deeper impression than the others. The tracks disappeared among a mob of honey locust trees, whose trunks and branches bore thorns long and thick, stretching out as if grasping the air, the ground, and each other.

He has limped away to his daytime lair. If he sleeps, then I, too, shall sleep. But the night comes, and it will be our time to prowl. The time when our eyes may fall upon each other, and perhaps our claws.

20

THE SIGN AT THE RIVERBANK

Orion the hunter glared into the woods below. It was Christmas Eve, but the constellation gave himself no reprieve. Instead, with belt tightened and club held high, he searched the forest, passing through a matrix of spaces between a score of twigs and branches until the light of the Pleiades and seven other jewels on his studded scabbard struck the closed eye of the jungle cat.

Oracle awoke in his post oak lair. The shadows about him hosted blotches of residual light from the night sky, giving no coherent sign of the heavenly point from which each had originated or if they had retained their power to guide in such disjointed fashion.

The jaguar took in the air for signs of who was near. The smell of wild hogs foraging among toadstools came to him, but no sound carried with the smell, indicating the hogs and their pungent feast were some distance away. He heard moles swimming through the natural mulch of the forest floor and an armadillo burrowing his snout in the dirt for grubs among the roots.

The night is benign for now. I shall explore the riverbank for a place to fish. Oracle made his way out of the bumelia only to find the way thick with gumweed and bindweed. Navigating this, Oracle came to a line of Mexican plum trees, and finally the Brazos.

He found a fishing spot at the riverbank where possumhaw and silverbrush provided seclusion, and the moonlight shining on the waters aided him. He fished and drank, watchful of the shadows. Blanchard's cricket frogs called to one another, for the drought had compelled them to sing out of season. Some called from the one bank and some from the other in an hour-long antiphony.

It sounds like the tapping of countless tiny stones. Or the first drops of rain.

The frogs ceased as if on cue. All was silent. The cat of the Southern Jungle rose and waited.

A voice reached his ears. A Man was humming a spiritual song, "Walk in Jerusalem Just Like John." Oracle turned toward the plum trees, and, beyond them he saw a middle-aged Black Man walking toward him. He carried a fishing pole and a bait bucket in one hand and a tackle box in the other. He wore a comfortable cap, and his jacket, of a cut and design from a century before, featured pockets with expansion pleats called bellows pockets. His trousers were baggy, held up by a leather belt at its tightest notch. His shoes, worn but well maintained, matched the belt.

The Man seemed pleased and continued to hum as he drew near. He approached smoothly, as if the gumweed and bindweed were no trouble to him. No twig snapped, nor did the ground make a sound, in response to his footfalls.

The Man was close to Oracle now. He did not seem to see the jaguar—or if he did, the sight brought him no fear. He passed by and took up a place on the bank next to the cat. He baited his hook with a minnow and cast the line into the sleeping waters of the Brazos. The baited hook made no sound when it struck the surface, the bobber no *plop*, the water no ripple. And yet the Man fished.

Oracle reflected. *Here is the place he always stands. It belongs to him, for his way tells it so. But why does his spirit continue to come here though his body is gone? Why is there no rest from his labor? My father taught me to be silent before ghosts, to let them be, and to keep our paths set apart from theirs, but this is a ghost of a different spirit. There is no fear, no craving. Only contentment. What then keeps him captive to the earth? What prevents him from joining his fathers in rest? I must know. I will follow the trail where he walked.*

Oracle entered the trees at the place the ghost had emerged from. Referencing the feel of the wood from the day before when he had explored it, he made his way to the fisherman's dilapidated cabin. The undergrowth brushed against him as he moved—witchweed, devil's claw, and crow poison—each whispering an unintelligible word as he passed.

On the porch of the cabin, the items he had seen the day before remained in their places, the fishing pole frozen in time, the tackle box hosting rust, the bait bucket a trophy of decay. The same smell of weather, weariness, and deeply rooted routines reached him.

Oracle noticed the cabin's front doors, both screen and wood, stood slightly open. He tapped them mildly with his paw and entered. The once-lived-in manplace was now empty of the Man himself, but home to the small creatures who make nests in the corners of unoccupied places such as these. Oracle saw the holes to their dwelling places.

Finding nothing but stillness, he returned to the wooden porch and reclined. He looked out on the grounds of the house and the pecan trees beyond them that hinted the way to the river, leaning at mournful angles.

"This is what the Man saw each day when he came out of his manplace," Oracle said.

"Ye*ss*," a whisper rose from beneath the porch's floor-boards, lacing a hiss into each word. "And he saw what could have been, if the truth had been served."

From between Oracle's paws at a space in the floorboards rose glistening skin: stripes of red, yellow, black, yellow, and red again. A Texas coral snake. It took a full minute for her lithe body to come curving out of the darkness beneath the cat. And as she did, she curled her form into an even coil to make a throne for her head, which rose to meet the jaguar as he, in turn, rose in caution and readiness, claws extended, beryl-green eyes penetrating the shadows to discern two cool portals that were the creature's gaze.

"He owned this place," the coral snake said, "but the rulers of the county never gave him the title deed, for another Man coveted the land, a Man whose eyes were white with greed, and he saw to it the fisherman remained only a squatter here the length of his days."

"How do you know these things?" Oracle asked.

The coral snake remained cold in her demeanor, as if it were nothing to her, and yet she spoke.

"The mussels of the river bottom keep the memory. They tell of Men from the other side of the Brazos who would cross by boat at night to threaten the fisherman. He knew if he ever left this property for so much as an afternoon to appear before the courts of justice, his neighbor would be given word by those of that same court, cross the river, claim the land, and bar him out. And so it is that even in his death, he lives here to guard it from loss."

"What was his name?" Oracle asked.

The coral snake uncoiled and recoiled as if rolling a memory out of its storage place and onto her tongue before returning to the place before the jaguar's face.

"Shiloh," the coral said. "Thaddeus Shiloh, the son of Octavius the sculptor, the son of Philip the carpenter, the son of Peter the laborer, the son of Sonnamaijem the war captive thrust across the sea and dragged from the swamp of Igbo Landing in the manrealm called Georgia. He was left for dead among the marsh weeds, but breath was found in him, and so the slaves who found him named him Lazarus. He was the son of Obiora the sage of the Last Great Council east of the Niger River; and Obiora was the son of Onuora the elder born in the month called First Moon during the days of Obi Ezeudo, the priest-king of the manrealm called Nri."

Oracle took in the names and their stories, the eyes of his heart seeing them as a slowly moving mural fading into the shadowed past.

"You describe a tale not unlike the hieroglyphs in the ruined, sunken corridors of my Yucatán home. Your words are the hidden epic of glory and dishonor that had led to the ghost of the humming fisherman. Tell me, when Shiloh died, did the Man whose eyes were white with greed take the land?"

"No," replied the coral, "for there were also rulers whose hearts were made of flesh and not stone. They required the fisherman's unclaimed title deed be put in order before a new owner could purchase it. And while those days passed, the greedy one came to walk about the land in pride, confident that what he coveted would be his. And he pitched camp on this side of the river.

"But the mussels say that one night, while the Man skipped stones on the Brazos, he saw the spirit of the fisherman appear at the bank. He fled to the middens the first mantribe had made, and he did not come out from beneath a pile of those empty shells until his family came to get him. He never returned, and the land was given to another for a fair price, who gave it to his son, and his son's son—the one whose manplace you explored yesterday after you visited here. For the coyote told me that you explored his dwelling after treading the boards above me."

Oracle's face clouded with thought. "The fisherman had no heir, then, for if he had had heirs, the land would have passed to them."

The coral glanced at the cabin as she swayed. "True, it would have, but he had no heir, no nearby family, save the one love he strived to win a kingdom for, this bottomland with its fish and hogs and savory soil. He worked this land to woo her heart, but the Woman perished before she could embrace him. For there were those jealous of the favor she enjoyed and envious of her beauty. They set fire to her reputation, and another Man took her life. Instead of justice, the court gave the murderer a ticket to Tulsa, where no one knew his deed or the name he left behind. Therefore, when the fisherman died, he had no wife, no children, no kin who could be called upon through Man's imperfect diligence and the law's weak limits."

Oracle looked at the rusted gear. "He died alone, then, on a day he was preparing to fish."

The coral curved toward the tackle box and back again. "Yes, he died alone, but not lonely, for he held on to the hope that all was preparation for a day when he would be given land no one would ever take from him, a day when he and those like him would be heirs of the world, and dust would be my food while clover yours."

The coral ceased her story. Oracle tried to discern her disposition.

I cannot tell if she is approving or uncaring in regard to what she has just spoken. Her face betrays no preference, only an aloofness that leaves me grateful for the message but wary of the messenger.

Oracle spoke. "Thank you. Your story is both a sad memoir and a noble memorial. His ghost will go when the greed goes, the greed cloaked in ways that force rags on a Man in place of his royal robe."

And the cat and the coral communed in the fisherman's hope, wondering how it would come to pass and what food they would eat on that day.

The snake's pleasant bands of scarlet, sable, and canary yellow led Oracle's thoughts away from his contemplations until he found himself preoccupied with how the coral's lovely colors contrasted with the drab boards beneath her, even in the night shadows of the porch.

She is beautiful.

For a moment, the time it would take for a moth to flutter past a face, the stripes of the serpent caressed his mind away from everything but the pleasure of her appearance. But then he recalled what Crash the tiger had said about her kind and shook himself out of the hypnosis.

"Oh Storyteller of Man's Patience and Man's Evil, I am told you are a keeper not just of histories, but of riddles. Riddles unlocking secrets."

The coral snake rocked back and forth. Her tongue flickered like a dark flame.

She is more charming than ever, yet at the same time, it is as if all her charm has melted away and her true colors are revealed.

The serpent spoke. "Yess, oh curious cat, so it is. How does it come to pass that you know this secret?"

"A great striped cousin, fallen far from his proud continent, told me your tale. He told me of a brood of corals who know the lair of the jaguarundi, a feline forgotten by Man and unknown among today's four-footed fur under the Lone Star. But the jaguarundi is well known to you, if you be of that brood's descendants."

The coral's tongue wavered as if touched by a hair. "I am."

Oracle's eyes sharpened like lamps. He leaned forward until the tip of his nose felt the smooth tongue of the coral, whose steady eyes betrayed no fear before the beryl-green gaze of the Cat Who Remembers. He filled his breath with the air of Eden's memory—but no breath transferred to the coral. Oracle deliberated.

The door of her heart remains concealed through an act of the will I cannot decipher. Even so, this is the one whom Crash told me I must encounter. There is no bypass on this narrow trail.

He spoke. "Your foremother discovered the jaguarundis' secret den, and upon threat of death they compelled her to swear an oath that neither she nor her descendants would ever tell the location of it to another living soul, lest the destiny of eating dust come upon the coral early."

The serpent slowly reared her head. "*Ss*o many senseless speculations like this are brought before me. *Ss*o many tiresome inquiries to the hurt of the inquirer. Save your strength, oh Cat of the Southern Jungle, and move on from here."

"I will not move on until you have made your move. For the tiger told me that though you are under oath, the turtles are not. They are free to tell me where the jaguarundi is. And they will tell me if I give them the password. You, oh Coral-Colored Guardian, are the keeper of that word. For the jaguarundi bound your ancestor with this oath:

Bind we now your tongue to silence
Bind we head and stripe and tail
To the sharing of this knowledge
To the showing of the trail

Just the turtle knows this secret
Only he our dwelling place
Had discovered ere you came here
Only with him is there grace

To discuss this darkened knowledge
To disclose the hidden lair
Only with the turtle present
Can your secret see the air

21

TOOTH AND CLAW

The coral turned her head sideways in semi-charmed attraction to the litany of the oath, as when a favorite song from one's youth disarms by the nostalgia thereof. She drew near to Oracle's right eye, her tongue teasing his eyelash and making him blink unwillingly. Then she raised her head over the jaguar's, poised like the cobra of a pharaoh's crown.

"Several have sought this before and failed. The price was ice in their veins. You must answer the riddle, and answer well, lest poison sink into your skin and you sleep the long sleep of death. Such are the dark waters you drink for failing to solve the riddle."

Oracle arched his neck. "I know the risk, oh Cunning One. I also know the gain. I accept the game of riddles required for you to disclose the password to me."

Oracle stretched out his right paw, wincing as he did. He retracted his claws and rested the limb before the coral snake. Calm and seemingly blissful in demeanor, she rested her head upon his paw while, at the other end of the long convolutions of her form, her tail tensed upon a floorboard, building strength to strike like a spring compressed.

"You are honor bound as I am honor bound," she said. "According to the ancient custom we are both submitted to, I shall speak the riddle, and you shall answer. If your answer strikes the mark, I shall remain docile, your paw for a pillow.

But if you miss the mark by so much as a word, I shall set my teeth into your flesh until my elixir begins its creeping journey to your heart, and there is no return."

"Agreed. In accordance with the ancient law we both are bound to this side of Eden, speak the riddle and I shall answer, be it true to the mark or be it the final marker of my sojourn under the sun."

The lord of the Valley opened wide his eyes, ears, and the storehouse of his knowledge.

This is the riddle the coral snake asked:

Who has trails without a marker?
Who has feet that tell no tale?
Who has hiding places darker
Than the chambers of a snail?

Oracle considered. His mind and heart held counsel. He communed with memories. He recollected words from the gatherings of the wise among his tribe in the hidden glades of Sian Ka'an. He called to mind Eden. He remembered his name. And in that part of him too deep for words, his spirit hovered over them all, aspiring to take them in at the same time, brooding over the broad face of possibilities as a pelican broods over the waters, watching for the swimming schools of promised catch that reward the watcher.

Looking up at the void above him, the space beneath the overhang of the porch on which the coral snake and the jaguar lay, the faint edge of the derelict lantern caught his eye. The crescent shine of the moon reached its curved, dust-covered glass. A sliver of light traveled its surface, and Oracle considered how the path of the light from heaven to earth to glass was an invisible one.

The analogue was discovered. He spoke.

Shooting stars have blazing trails
That neither post nor sign can mark
Nor do their cuts through starry kingdoms
Leave behind a line to hark

Birds in flight rejoice in walking
Mounds of air with swung-back feet
Yet their paths are never talking
Never showing who they meet

Shadow cats have hiding places
Umbrous inner courts for speech
Shadow cats in contemplation
Dwell in rooms beyond our reach

The coral snake's head sank into the fur of the jaguar's paw. Then it was as if a warmth emanated from the creature, cold-blooded though she was, and whether that warmth was originally from the coral, the jaguar, or some other mysterious source, Oracle could not tell. But a motion followed the warmth, a motion within the smooth-skinned creature. There was no visible sign of reaction upon the face of the snake—but there was no bite to the paw either.

She slithered across Oracle's foot, down the worn-out steps of the porch, and onto the ground below. Finding a place of bare earth, she began to move in a repetitive pattern, deepening the mark in the dust beneath her until it became an unmistakable shape: a hollow diamond with a sign of Man's speech in its middle, a backward *B*:

Oracle's face brightened. "Ah, so the password is a picture, not a word with breath! This sign pulls upon a memory from the Valley I cannot fully comprehend, like a voice too distant for me to distinguish. But the voice is speaking nevertheless, and I shall put my paw forward to find the speaker, though the trail be a long one."

The coral snake's head moved like a palm frond caressed by breezes. "Ye*ss*, oh Cat of the House of Panthera Onca. You have answered well. I have kept my oath, and you have kept your course. With this word placed before the turtles, they will speak. They will tell you where the shadow cats live."

Oracle bowed. "Thank you for abiding by the ancient custom. My quest now has a bridge to its next destination like a tree trunk across a plunging stream: from the turtles to the home of the shadow cats, and from their home to a Council of the Cats, where the jaguarundi will, for the first time in living memory, be present, and the stewardship of the Three Tribes restored in the Valley."

The coral snake began to lean away from Oracle as if swooning from the slosh of too much drink. But as soon as her head reached the floor, she immediately became agile, sidewinding her way across the porch to a knothole. With neither farewell nor blessing, she entered the hole, descended, and disappeared.

—⚬—

Oracle returned his eyes to the orchard he had been contemplating before the dread discourse with the coral had taken place, setting his face beyond the pecan trees to that which could only be seen with the eyes of the heart.

"I must put my paw forward again. The shadow cat, who has become a recluse in the Valley, must be summoned out of hiding. He must join the animal kingdom even in its fallen state, for I perceive that neither the ocelot nor the bobcat is complete in his stewardship until the jaguarundi abides with the two of them. Perhaps the mystery that seems to accompany this tribe will complement the strategy and strength of the other two.

"And with the Cats of the Three Tribes established again, a Court of the Animals can sit, a court I must convene before Man's Three Choices come upon me again. If his choices do not prevent me from my quest, there may yet be a final spring for the animal kingdom before the last sun sets on all seasons.

> *I'll go to the river*
> *I'll go to the sea*
> *I'll bound on their bound'ries*
> *Though Man follow me*
>
> *Three choices await me*
> *Three choices abide*
> *Ere Man overtakes me*
> *I'll run in the tide*

A thud and a snap of an earthbound branch pulled Oracle's attention swiftly to the left. There, beneath a tree still trembling from the weight of the one who had just dropped from it, was a cat the size of a lion, a cat whose hip had betrayed him, sending him south from his mountainous home in search of slower domestic prey. He hissed at the jaguar.

Oracle tensed his body and lowered his head, eyes fixed on the feline. *This is no shadow cat, no jaguarundi in exile. But this is a cougar who tracks the ghosts of man: a ghost cat.*

The lord of the Valley jumped off the porch to the level ground between him and the cougar.

"You are far from home, and so am I," Oracle said. "I have no quarrel with you. We are fellow travelers. We are both on the same road. Therefore, how can one pilgrim be the enemy of another? Behold, I have come down from the superior place from which I could have pounced on you, the steps of this manplace. See, I meet you eye to eye and friend to friend."

The cougar's long growl showed no sign he had comprehended the jaguar's reasoning, no sign of ears to hear. Instead, he threw back those ears, lowered his head, and set one deliberate paw down after the other, ever closer to the jaguar, each paw bristling the claws of ready combat. The air moving in and out of his jealous lungs infused him with an ever-increasing heat, and Oracle's words, like cool water from a spring, turned into a disappearing steam upon their touching him.

A shriek filled the cougar and tore through the darkness, a cry splitting the air and declaring open war. A group of sleeping sparrows darted away and gave their place to a great, empty dread.

The cougar now quite close, Oracle saw that his eyes, like the dusty surface of the antique lamp above him, were clouded over. And behind the fog burned an unnatural glow both cold and alive.

Oracle breathed upon him. The Breath of Remembrance formed a fragrant cloud that christened the cougar's head and embraced the whole cat like arms intent to comfort.

For a moment, Oracle saw behind the cougar's veiled eyes a flash of recognition and surprise. That moment—as short as the shaking of a flower of the field when struck with a single drop of rain—was filled with possibility, as when the sun shines upon a mountain peak belated to the spring, its ice on the glistening verge of melting into streams. And yet that same warm sun that melts the ice hardens the clod of stubborn clay.

The cougar chose the clay. The mystery of possibility ended. The flash of surprise turned to fuming, the recognition to resolution. He called out, and Oracle heard words rebounding within a barren enclosure: the place that had been the ghost cat's heart before it had become home to another spirit, one that would have no remembrance abide with it, no owner of the home other than itself. A spirit refusing all stories but the one the cougar grasped with self-seeking paw:

I *will*. I *win*.
I *leave*. No *kin*.

No *mother*. No *father*.
No *other*. No *farther*.

I *own*. I *vow*.
I *rule*. Fight *now*.

And with this unearthly echo asserting itself within the call, the cougar rose on his pain-racked hindquarters, lifted his paws above his snarling visage, and threw himself down upon the jaguar.

A mingling of forces burst upon the bodies of each cat, a rush of strength and fierceness throwing both combatants off

249

the cliff edge of Eden, a long plunge from paradise into the abyss, a ruinous terror beyond the skill of mind or eye to track as each dread champion flung himself into the death grip of the other.

The rolling of their claw-clenched bodies on the forest floor released such a sound from each cat that the cries awakened hounds of far-off farms and the dogs of distant ranches to bark in alarm that peace had been taken up from the earth, and that nature, red in tooth and claw, clamored for the right to have the final say over all within the realm of Man.

The blood-soaked ferns flattened beneath the warring beasts, and as they did, they took in a rumor that all the pain Oracle had ever endured up to that moment—from the long odyssey in search of the Lonely Tree to his combat with the catfish—had been mere preparation for the pain he felt in the fight with the mountain lion.

Oracle raised his deadly paw as he rolled under his foe, but a claw snagged on a thick, fallen branch, exposing his side. The cougar came down with a vengeance and sank the full force of his fangs into the jaguar's upper thigh. Only the length of the ghost cat's teeth prevented the cougar from tearing any deeper into the body of the lord of the Valley.

The pain worked with such reactive power that the flinch it sent through Oracle flipped the cougar on his back and freed the jaguar's claw. Both fell away from the other, stunned and gasping in suspended seconds.

In that space of time—the jaguar gathering his senses above a drowning flood of shock, the cougar rising on bruised, unsteady limbs slowed by the limp of an unfaithful hip—the moment arrived for the cougar to strike the blow that would return the jaguar to the dust, far from the Yucatán, far from the Valley, far from the friends.

The cougar allied fang and feet for the final blow, approaching the Cat Who Remembers in stern resolve as he gnashed his teeth.

"Why do you torment me? Why do you remind me I am a restless wanderer?"

Oracle mustered his strength to speak, though his eyes had lost their focus as they rolled half-closed from waves of pain. "But you are not cut off to the uttermost. You are still alive, and to live means all things are possible…even a new day."

"I dare not hope again," he hissed as he dragged his frame closer. "I will abide in the name I give myself, the one thing that is *mine*."

Oracle drew in a gasping breath. "But it is 'yours' in the same way a sheet of ice is yours in the spring thaw. Ask our alpine cousins caught on melting lakes. Yes, they do captain that ice broken from its glacial home and can claim it as their own, but it is only a matter of time before the warm waters of this fallen world dissolve it, betraying autonomy, betraying life."

The cougar said nothing. His eyes burned with pain-racked hate. He drew near, his foe of blood-stained rosette spots more a symbol to him of what he despised than a life that truly lived.

Oracle lay exhausted and immobilized, preparing to meet the end with head raised, looking into the face of his final moment.

A shaft of manmade light cut through the night, falling upon the cougar. A broadhead-bearing arrow traveled that sudden corridor. It pierced the cougar beneath his uplifted foreleg, running through rib, lung, and heart; lodging with determination in the life of the cat; swiftly releasing both the cougar himself and the spirit that had taken up residence within him. The one who had found a ready house to dwell in comprising all the painful memories of loss the cougar had carried.

He fell with a cry, no struggle as he expired, his final breath both a wheeze of remorse and a sigh of relief. The forest, which had come alive with anxious watchfulness of the battle, now held its breath in even greater anticipation.

Oracle lay on his side. The manmade light now fell on him. He heard the steps of a Man on the forest floor. His smell reached him, then the Man himself. Brazos Ben carried a compound bow, a quiver strapped to his back, an LED torch clipped to the brim of his oil-stained cap. He knelt beside the jaguar, Bowie blade drawn, to examine him.

"Boy, you sure put up a fight, big fella. I don't think there's any fight left in you to harm me. With all that blood gushing out of your thigh, you're about to meet your Maker just like your opponent if I don't do something. But I think it's worth doing. Never seen the likes of you before in these parts! Let's see if we can't nurse you back to health."

Brazos Ben pressed his bow against the head of the jaguar, pinning it to the ground while he muzzled him with a cord. Then he bound his paws. Oracle was aware, but blood loss had left him in a near faint. He surrendered.

"Sorry, neighbor," said Brazos Ben, "but I'm just makin' sure. Now let me see about this wound of yours. Oh man, that don't look good. Don't look good at all. Golly Moses."

The Man bound up the thigh wound with bandannas and departed.

In the silence, Oracle waited. The dry leaves beneath him tasted his oozing blood. The forest above him faded, his plan of his paw too, along with the vision of reaching the Valley. His friends, the animal kingdom, and everything that could have been became a vapor hard to trace. All was dull under the drowsy ache that covered the cat.

After a time, during which Oracle heard the bleating of goats, Ben returned on an ATV. With the help of a winch and a canvas tarp, he lifted Oracle onto the cargo-carrying portion of the vehicle. He brought him to the barn, where the '66 Mustang and all of Ben's other projects slept. He backed up the ATV to the row of stalls.

"Let's put you in the one where the hay's the freshest," the Man said. "Something tells me my goats won't have nothin' to worry about in the pen outside now that you and the cougar's out of commission. They'll be fine there for a season. Meanwhile, this stall will keep you comfortable, and I venture to say it's cleaner than the Sugar Moon Motel on Highway 6. We're gonna need all the help we can muster to keep you from getting infected. Let's just hope that cougar didn't pass on any bad bugs through that nasty bite."

Brazos Ben departed again. Oracle heard the faint sound of pots and crockery in the tree house galley kitchen interspersed with silence. Then he heard footsteps on the stairs. The Man returned carrying a box and a water bottle. He knelt.

"First thing is to pour a few drops of cold water between these teeth of yours…There ya go…That will boost your morale for a spell. Pardon me while I get rid of these bandannas. They did their job, all right. No more use for these…Oh my, sorry for all the pain this unwrapping is causin'. Easy now, easy… Okay, with those out of the way, let's kill all them critters threatening to infect your wounds."

From the box, Brazos Ben set out three jars, two sacks, a bowl, and wooden utensils.

"This charcoal does it every time. Let's put a heaping load of that in. He's our running back for the play, you see"—he poured the charcoal from a jar into the bowl—"and a good thing I've got dried plantains. They'll help with the infection too, kinda like the linebacker blocking for the running back. Not the same as fresh plantains, but they'll have to do. This jar's been at the back of the pantry since April, and now I see why…There, let's break 'em up and mix 'em in with the charcoal…"

He turned and opened a sack. "And look here: prickly pear! No need to keep a store of these! I just went out back and picked 'em. Never a shortage of cactus here, not even in this drought…Takin' off the spines, you'd think this was a Granny Smith apple…I'll mash 'em into the plantains and charcoal. It will act like a towel to mop up some of the mess in that flesh."

He presented the other sack. "And the final ingredient: two fistfuls of mullein leaves from County Road 301. Let's crush 'em and blend 'em into the compound through and through…All right. Steady now, friend, I gotta open up that meat of yours and drop it in as deep as it will go…Trust me… There we go…There we go, all set…I know it's gonna burn somethin' awful to pack these gashes with this poultice, but that's where we gotta get to. If we don't care for the wound, we won't have a tomorrow."

Oracle received the poultice. He closed his eyes as he felt the work of the plants and the charcoal in his torn flesh. He breathed deeply, adding air to the healing. The pain burned like scattered, smoldering brush fires across the field of his fur wherever his body had borne the wrath of the cougar. But the poultice made the pain in his thigh burn like a campfire, centering him even as it hurt. Oracle sighed and remained perfectly still.

"You sure are calm," said Brazos Ben. "If I didn't know better, I'd say you think you're a house cat. Now, I'm gonna take a risk here, fella…Let's see…"

With head still but eyes turned, Oracle watched as the Man washed out the bowl and poured water mixed with willow-bark powder from the third jar. Bowie knife at the ready, Brazos Ben took off the muzzle and offered him the bowl.

The Man grinned. "Happy holidays, partner. I did my darndest to go solo this time around, but you're a welcome guest on Christmas Eve, I must say. A nick-o'-time guest, I reckon, both for you and for me. Here now, drink this brew. It will take the edge off just like my eggnog...Cheers."

Oracle lifted his head and meekly lapped the tonic for a moment. Brazos Ben rose and departed, leaving Oracle to rest the long slumber of those who have nothing left in them but the hope that waiting would become healing.

ABOUT THE AUTHOR

Kurt helps entrepreneurs discover courage for their calling. With twenty years' experience in forty nations, Kurt draws from a wealth of firsthand accounts to inspire and instruct through his Courage for Your Calling® framework.

Kurt is a sought-after speaker on five continents and a well-respected international life coach, serving in places as challenging as Cuba, Persia, and North Korea. He has written hundreds of articles and published multiple books, including award-winning poetic literature.

Kurt and his wife, Karen, have been married since 1993 and raised their family in Taliban-controlled Afghanistan, where they founded a community development agency. They live in the emirate of Sharjah, near Dubai.

Kurt's roots include the Texas Gulf Coast, the Rio Grande Valley, the Heart of Texas, and New England.

Kurt writes in the prophetic and poetic traditions, inspired by the wonder of creation and the cultures of the nations. Guiding sources for his works include the Hebrew prophets, the Desert Fathers, Dante, Milton, George MacDonald, C. S. Lewis, and Tolkien.

Why? Because thought leaders go back to the beginning to find the way forward. The key to the future always begins with a memory, and our calling comes from the original self the Creator had in mind when He made us.

His website kurtmahler.com features his writings and a subscription to his personal newsletter with free offers.

www.ingramcontent.com/pod-product-compliance
Lightning Source LLC
Chambersburg PA
CBHW031940010726
47493CB00007B/2008